The Tomato Jam Murder

by

Meg Benjamin

Luscious Delights

The Tomato Jam Murder

Cover Art by *Tina Lynn Stout*

The Wild Rose Press, Inc.
PO Box 708
Adams Basin, NY 14410-0708
Visit us at www.thewildrosepress.com

Publishing History
First Edition, 2025
Trade Paperback Print ISBN 978-1-5092-6353-0
Digital ISBN 978-1-5092-6354-7

Luscious Delights
Published in the United States of America

Dedication

To all the burro racers in Colorado and the West, both human and equine. Long may you run.

Chapter 1

"Peggy Sue, don't you dare!"

Peggy Sue turned soulful brown eyes on my friend Laurel Beacham, who was a few feet behind her. She looked like she really, *really* wanted to go through the gate leading to Laurel's front yard.

"Peggy Sue, you listen to me."

Peggy Sue took another tentative step forward. Clearly, she was weighing just how much trouble she'd be in if she kept going. The gate to the front yard of Laurel's cabin was slightly ajar and Peggy Sue would likely be able to step through it in just a moment or two. On the other hand, based on her tone of voice, Laurel clearly meant business.

"Peggy Sue, I will lock you in the barn, so help me."

Peggy Sue gave her another of those tragic looks that conveyed, *How can you be considering something so cruel? So inhumane? All I want is some grass. And it's just sitting there.*

Laurel picked up her pace, but she was still a little far away from the gate. I, on the other hand, was right there. I quickly stepped forward just as Peggy Sue started to push the gate open. I gave it a quick shove so that the latch caught, and the gate snapped closed.

Peggy Sue stared up at me, eyes narrowing. I had no idea if donkeys bit people who annoyed them, and I didn't want to find out. I stepped back. "Sorry, Peggy

Sue, but I think you were about to get into a space where you aren't allowed."

Laurel moved forward and grabbed the burro's halter. "Oh, she was definitely heading for a space where she isn't allowed. And she knows it full well." She pulled Peggy Sue away from the fence. Shaking her head, the burro gave my friend a look that should have broken the strongest heart. She had some of the longest eyelashes I'd ever seen, along with those great big brown eyes. Puppy eyes are nothing compared to burro eyes.

"Enough." Laurel fastened a lead rope to Peggy Sue's halter and towed her to the pasture where the goat herd was having a great time playing goat tag. The kids in particular were leaping over each other and occasionally landing on one another. Laurel's other two burros, Buttermilk and Spats, were staying well away from them, which was probably a good idea.

"She's feeling like she deserves a treat because we trained this morning. And she's right. But I'm damned if I'll let her use my buffalo grass for an amuse-bouche." Laurel pulled off the donkey's halter and opened the gate, so that Peggy Sue could enter the pasture. She paused, giving Laurel one more long look from under those impossibly long eyelashes.

"Oh for Pete's sake, here." Laurel reached her hand toward her donkey, a chunk of carrot resting on her palm.

Peggy Sue picked up the carrot in her teeth and crunched it. Then she sauntered across the field, ignoring both the goats and the other donkeys.

"Diva," Laurel muttered.

"What race are you training for?" I asked.

"We're doing one in Feldspar in a couple of weeks. Probably. All depends on whether I can get someone to take over my booth at the market that weekend. It'll be a good warmup for the other races later this summer."

Laurel didn't gaze in my direction since both of us knew I had more than enough to do with my own farmers market booth every Saturday. My business, Luscious Delights Jams, gets around half of its sales from the summer farmers market in Shavano, and I am there every Saturday like clockwork, cases of jam stacked at my back.

"Maybe somebody in your office?" I suggested. Along with producing goat cheese, Laurel was the part-time Director of Tourism for the town of Coalton, Colorado, which sounds a lot more impressive than it is in reality. Coalton is a small, sort of grubby former mining town a few miles up the road from Shavano, but Laurel was doing her level best to transform it into a summer tourist destination.

She shrugged. "I might be able to get one of the secretaries for the council. Lord knows they don't get paid much for doing the lion's share of the work around that building." Coalton is run on the mayor/city council model, and Laurel wasn't a big fan. Given the quality of the people on the council, I was inclined to agree with her.

"Come on," she said. "I'll get you Nate's cheese."

Laurel's main business is goat cheese made from milk produced by her own goat herd, and her stuff is terrific. I'm not a huge goat cheese fan normally, but Laurel has made a believer out of me. It's rich and creamy with that slight tang you get from goat milk. Nate Robicheaux, part-owner and manager of Robicheaux Catering, is a devotee of Laurel's cheese, although it's priced above the more mass produced kind. But Nate swears that Laurel's goat cheese is so tasty people are willing to pay a premium to have it on their charcuterie trays. I know this because besides being the part-owner and proprietor of the catering business, Nate is also my main squeeze. We share a cabin on the farm I own with my uncle outside Shavano.

Laurel and I first met through the Shavano farmers market, where she set up her booth for the first time this year. The market is big on produce, once the harvests start coming in, along with prepared foods like jam that the tourists can take home with them. Laurel's was the first cheese stand I could remember at the Shavano market, but lines began forming as soon as people tasted her product. I'd helped her find a teenaged assistant when it became clear that she needed help with the crowds. Even so, she still had lines that were longer than mine and almost as long as Bianca Jordan's bake shop, which was still the most popular booth in the market. Laurel sold out regularly, which was another reason the lines were long—people in the know got there early so they could score some cheese before Laurel took off for the day.

Nate put in his orders early in the week so that he never had to worry about Laurel running out of cheese before he could get what he needed. That week I had a free afternoon, so I'd volunteered to come to Laurel's place and pick up his order. I'd arrived just as Laurel and Peggy Sue were heading up the drive, which was how I happened to be in place to keep Peggy Sue from going for Laurel's buffalo grass.

Now, I followed her into the retail part of her cheese building. The cheese factory part was strictly off limits to anyone who wasn't gloved and capped and clothed from neck to foot in overalls. Laurel didn't fool around when it came to potential contamination.

She opened a cooler at the side of the room and lifted out a couple of rounds of cheese. "Did he want any of the flavored stuff this time or just the plain?"

"Just the plain, I think. What flavors do you have?"

"This week we've got cracked pepper and chive. I'll do some with chili before the market on Saturday, but I haven't had time to get to it yet."

My mouth automatically began watering. Goat cheese rolled in cracked pepper sounded delectable, and so did the chopped chive. "I think I'll take one of the cracked-pepper rolls just for me, if you've got any to spare." That was always a question since Laurel usually had lots of orders to fill.

She grinned at me as she dug a smaller roll of cheese out of the cooler. "Oh, I can spare one for you. You helped head Peggy Sue off from my front yard, after all."

"She's adorable," I said, surprising myself. I hadn't thought much about it as I was walking up the drive beside Laurel and Peggy Sue. But despite the fact she was the size of a Shetland pony, Peggy Sue really was adorable. I think it was the big brown eyes mostly, although the eyelashes didn't hurt.

Laurel chuckled. "She's a con artist, don't kid yourself. But, yeah, she's also a sweetheart. All three of the burros are. But Peggy's the boss—the other two let her rule the roost pretty much."

I gathered up my packages. "Do you race all three of them?"

"Sometimes." Laurel shrugged. "Peggy Sue enjoys racing the most, and she's more sociable than Buttermilk or Spats so she keeps up with the herd."

"The burro races are so much fun to watch," I said as I started toward the door. "Maybe less fun to do?"

"They're lots of fun if you're in shape. We train a lot. You should come up with us sometime."

I paused with my hand on the doorknob. "Really? I'd love to see how you train for it."

"Okay, come over next Sunday if you're free. We usually start around ten. Takes a couple of hours."

"Great. I'll look forward to it." And I would. I tucked the package of goat cheese under my arm and headed for my truck.

I should probably explain about burro racing, and the first thing I should explain is that burros and donkeys are the same animal—one is the Spanish word and the other is the English. When you hear the phrase *burro racing,* most people probably picture a little round track with the burros being ridden by tiny jockeys, but that's not even close. In fact, burro racing is a Colorado Heritage Sport because it's supposedly based on the old days when a couple of prospectors might have to race each other to town when they'd both struck a rich vein and needed to record the claim. The guy who arrived there first got the rights, and he'd most likely have his burro thundering along beside him since that was how prospectors carried their gear into the back country.

The modern version of this hypothetical history uses teams of one person and one burro. The burro is loaded up with a pack saddle, pick, shovel, and gold pan, all of which is supposed to weigh at least thirty-three pounds. The racecourses are usually set up to go over mountain trails, and sometimes to go over passes that are well above timberline. The people who are part of the team hang on to their burros with fifteen-foot ropes, and from what I've seen, the burros are the ones who decide how fast the team goes and what route they follow. Theoretically, the burro and its partner have to stay on the trail, and they can be disqualified if they stray too far off it, but a burro's going to do what a burro's going to do. The person half of the team will try to convince the burro to stick to the program, but the burro may or may not decide they'll oblige.

Sometimes the more tender-hearted animal lovers may argue that the burros are being mistreated by being forced to race, but in most cases the animals seem to be enjoying themselves. And anyway there are very strict rules about what can and can't be done to recalcitrant animals. No whips are allowed, no sticks, no prods of any kind. Occasionally, you'll see someone use the lead rope to encourage the donkey forward, but it's against the rules to hit the burro any harder than you'd hit yourself with that rope. Plus a lot of the burros are like Peggy Sue, with close relationships to their human teammates. When they're not racing, they serve as guard donkeys for goat or sheep herds, and they often end up like family pets, given their friendly natures.

And, as I say, the burros enjoy running, particularly when they're running along with a bunch of other burros. Maybe it calls up primordial memories of their days in the wild when they were part of roaming herds. And for some of them, it's not all that primordial—a lot of burros around here are rescues from the Bureau of Land Management roundups of wild burros that happen every once in a while.

I've been to several burro races around the Shavano area. In fact, we're smack in the middle of a prime burro racing region, close to the so called Triple Crown: the races held every summer in the towns of Fairplay, Leadville, and Buena Vista. One of my uncle Mike's friends, Silas Goodman, is a longtime burro racer, with a squad of donkeys in a range of sizes.

I've always been partial to donkeys myself, although my dad and my uncle were adamant about not having them around the farm. Given that most of our acreage is taken up with vegetable and fruit crops, I could see why they didn't want a potentially hungry donkey wandering around the premises. Plus, of course, there was nothing for a burro to do on our farm—no animals that needed guarding and no back country hikers to assist.

Still, whenever I spent time around donkeys, I found myself wishing I could have one of my own. And race training with Laurel and Peggy Sue sounded like a lot of fun.

I swung by the catering kitchen on my way home to drop off Nate's goat cheese order. He and his assistant, Dex, were elbows deep in appetizers for the event they were catering that evening. I held up the round of goat cheese. "Fresh from Laurel's goats by way of her cooler. Where do you want it?"

Nate extended a hand. "Right here. I'm ready to start making the cheese ball. Thanks for picking it up—otherwise I'd have been stuck with whatever they had in at City Market."

"No problem." I stood around watching Nate and Dex create platters full of tasty snacks, although I should have headed home to my own work. But those labors would be centered around a current sore point: my summer special.

When I got my online ordering set up, a marketing

specialist had suggested I try doing a monthly special on my web site. It had been a big hit, although it was also sort of a pain to do. By now, a couple of years in, I'd backed off on the *monthly* part in favor of more seasonal specials. They could run for a couple of months, or even three if there was a lot of interest. That was less work in terms of coming up with new flavors, but it meant I needed to put more thought into deciding what the specials were going to be, and I wasn't in a thinking mood at the moment.

The problem was the embarrassment of riches that is summer in the Rockies. I could do wild stuff like chokecherry jam. I could do some of my special mixes, like blueberry chipotle. I could even put one of my perennials up as a special, like pepper peach, particularly if I got a special on peaches. But none of it got my creative juices going.

I realize the presence or absence of creative juice shouldn't have made much difference. I was running a jam business not an artist's studio. But still, if I came up with something good, I might end up making a lot of jars of whatever I decided would be my special. And I'd be happier and more productive if cooking up those jars weren't totally a chore.

When I got home, I contemplated the flats of fruit I'd picked up earlier in the day at one of the farms down the road from us. We live in prime mountain agricultural country, and there's a lot to choose from in season. I'd found blueberries, blackberries, and a few early cherries. If I added those berries to the strawberries we grew ourselves, I could try a kind of mixed berry jam that might work. Even if it didn't work for the summer special, I could sell it at the farmers market where just about any kind of berry jam flew off the shelves. I'd done mixed berries before, and I knew they'd work. I also knew they weren't exactly creative.

I was still rinsing blueberries when Bridget, my assistant who does all the mail order work, drove up. Bridget waits tables part-time at High Country restaurant in downtown Shavano, but I'd like to find a way to hire her on full-time at some point. Once that happened, I could turn all the mail order stuff over to Bridget, maybe even relying on her to suggest specials since she was in tune with what our customers wanted.

The only fly in the ointment was that I also needed another helper to augment Bridget. While Bridget is terrific at keeping all the orders straight for the website, she isn't into cooking jam, and right then I was desperately trying to find a part-time kitchen assistant, too. For the last couple of years, Dolce McCray had helped out in my kitchen after school and during summer vacation. Dolce's dad is Uncle Mike's foreman, and her mom, Carmen, produced the honey that I used in some of my jam, so we had a close family connection. But Dolce had graduated from high school in May, and she was getting ready to head to Ft. Collins for college. That would be several hundred miles and an entire mountain range away. She still helped out when she could, but she'd cut back on her hours, and I had to face the grim fact that she wouldn't be around after mid-August.

I needed kitchen help, and I needed it sooner rather than later. I'd sent the word out on the kitchen grapevine, telling everybody I knew in the various restaurants around Shavano. But the truth was I wasn't sure I could compete with what the food service people were making in the restaurants around town. I figured my best hope was that someone working part-time at one of the restaurants would be willing to take on a few more hours in my jam kitchen. That wasn't ideal, particularly in summer when we did our biggest production, but it was definitely better than the idea of me producing all my jam with my own two hands.

Been there, done that, didn't really want to do it again, thank you very much. Particularly not now when my business had expanded so much.

Bridget breezed in the front door, tossing her purse in the general vicinity of her desk. "Traffic is a bitch downtown. People are already showing up for the big weekend, I guess."

We were heading into Memorial Day, which was the unofficial opening of tourist season. Which meant I needed to get my ass in gear and produce a lot more jam for the farmers market. The Memorial Day market was traditionally a hot sales day.

Bridget surveyed my flats of berries with a critical eye. "You're doing mixed berry?"

"Yeah," I said. "It should sell well this weekend."

She nodded. "You'll sell out of everything you've got here. Is that going to be the special this month?"

"Maybe." I scowled down at the berries, although it wasn't their fault that I was in a funk.

Per usual, Bridget wanted me to get off my duff and get a summer special up there on the website. "People like mixed berry. It'll be popular."

"Yeah, I know. Probably. Probably that's going to be it." And it probably would be. Just because it didn't make my heart go pitter-pat didn't mean it wasn't a perfectly good monthly special.

Honestly, it didn't.

Chapter 2

Since Nate was working an event that night, I was having dinner at the main house with Uncle Mike and Madge. Ever since my uncle married Nate's mom, we'd been having meals together a few times a month. This was a lot healthier than pretending we didn't all live on the same farm, but it still felt a little weird occasionally. Back in the old days, pre-Madge, Uncle Mike ate dinner with me most nights and breakfast two or three times a week. Now I only saw him a few times a month, and it was different having a step-aunt who was also my boyfriend's mom.

Madge, of course, carried on as if there were no problem at all, which was pretty much the attitude I'd like to achieve for myself. Madge is a terrific person and I'm crazy about her, but she has powers of positive thinking that far exceed my own.

This time I brought along a jar of the mixed berry jam that I'd been working on that afternoon, along with a baguette I'd picked up from my friend Bianca Jordan's bakery. And the roll of cracked-pepper-encrusted goat cheese from Laurel, which would probably be the star of the evening.

"Oh, my," Madge said when I passed her the cheese. "That looks incredible. Maybe I should slice up some of this bread and make crostini."

"That would be good," I said carefully, "but you

could probably just serve the bread as is. It's pretty crusty." Given half a chance, Madge would always go the extra mile, without worrying that it made extra work for herself.

"I've got to try this." Madge cut off a sliver of the cheese, then licked it off her knife. "Oh, this is stupendous," she murmured.

I put the baguette on the cutting board and cut off a few slices. "I love Laurel's stuff, and this is a new flavor. Can't wait to try it."

Madge lifted down a few Talavera pottery plates. She'd definitely upgraded Uncle Mike's kitchenware when she'd moved in. "Let me find my spreader."

No surprise that Madge had a spreader. When she and Uncle Mike came down to the cabin for dinner, I always felt a little depressed by my lack of correct implements. "Here." She handed me a small knife with a pottery handle that matched the plates.

I decided not to be intimidated. I'd brought the cheese, after all. I spread a healthy schmear of cheese and cracked pepper across a baguette slice and took a bite. Madge was right. "Wow."

"I know, right? That girl has such a gift."

"Also the right goats," Uncle Mike said. He picked up a slice of bread and applied a bit of cheese using the spreader. "I don't know what she feeds those animals, but her cheese tastes better than anyone else's, including that chichi place in Antero."

"Is she selling anywhere besides the farmers market?" Madge asked. "What does she do for sales in the winter?"

"She's got a deal with Sylvano's in Geary," I said. "Ted Sylvano buys about half of what she puts out, which is why the restaurant guys have to get their orders in early."

Ted Sylvano owned a very upscale grocery in Geary, a fairly upscale town not far from Shavano. He also sold my jam, and I had a feeling he was interested in more than just Laurel's cheese. But I wasn't about to pass on that gossip based only on a couple of soulful looks I'd seen him cast Laurel's way. Particularly since I hadn't noticed her casting any soulful looks in his direction.

"Good," Madge said. "If she's set up with Sylvano's, she's got a solid toehold in the area. Plus, I'll be able to find her cheese whenever I want instead of relying on you and Nate to keep me supplied."

Dinner was smothered pork chops and rice, a Robicheaux's Café special. Madge did the chops herself, but she'd brought the gravy from the café, and my guess was that she'd brought the rice with her as well. No problem. Robicheaux's Café food was terrific. I'd been eating it ever since I'd hooked up with Nate and never passed up a chance to have a Robicheaux's meal.

"How's Marigold doing?" I asked after we'd all had enough time to appreciate Bobby Robicheaux's gravy artistry.

"She's fine. Bobby's making sure she doesn't overdo, which I think drives her a little crazy. I keep Astrid out with me while the lunch rush is on. She's a great conversation starter."

Astrid was Madge's first grandchild, daughter of her older son, Bobby, and his wife, Marigold. Both of them cooked at the café, but so far Marigold was only doing lunch while Bobby did breakfast, too. I was guessing they'd soon be hiring on a part-time cook to pick up some of the hours since doing breakfast on his own was getting to be sort of daunting, even for Bobby. He'd done it for a lot of years, but those were years when he hadn't had a wife and daughter at home. It was hard to believe that he was actually mellowing, but he seemed to want to spend more time with his family than working the flattop. At least sometimes.

Since Astrid was still a babe in arms, Madge kept her next to her hostess station, hoisting her up onto her shoulder when she needed to move around. The majority of the patrons at the café were long timers, and they took the baby in stride. Plus, of course, she was a center of attention for all the other grannies who came by for breakfast or lunch or just a piece of pie.

Coco, Madge's daughter, was the source of that pie as the café's dessert and salad maker, and she looked after Astrid, now and then. The baby had proven to be a champ at sleeping through chaos. I figured she'd be clearing tables and putting out silverware by the time she was six, just like the other Robicheaux kids had done.

"How's Laurel doing with her tourist office?" Madge asked.

"So far as I know, she's doing okay. It's kind of an uphill battle against the old guard on the Coalton City Council."

Uncle Mike shook his head. "Don't know what the hell's wrong with those Coalton bozos. It's not like they're ever going to be a bigtime mining town again. The coal mine's closed down for good, and they're not likely to start another one these days. That girl's trying to help them get out of their slump."

"Change is scary." Madge reached for another spoonful of gravy. "I think some of the old timers in

Coalton hope the coal industry will pick up again someday. They know how to run a mining town, but they don't know how to run a tourist town."

"It's not like there isn't a lot of experience in running tourist towns around here," Uncle Mike grumped. "They could just ask. That's what Laurel's doing."

Uncle Mike has farmed in the valley for a long time, starting way before Shavano and Geary became the booming tourist towns that they are now. He and the other farmers often complain about property values going through the roof and taking property taxes with them, but on the whole, he appreciates the revenue the tourists have brought to the area. To say nothing of the amount of money they spend at the farmers market in the summer. Uncle Mike sells a lot of arugula and strawberries there.

"If they started asking around, it would mean they accepted the change," Madge said. "Once they make the move to tourism, they're committed. And I think a lot of them are just not ready to do that yet."

"At least they hired Laurel to make some moves in that direction," I said. "Although I don't think they're paying her much of anything, and they don't always accept her ideas for new programs."

Madge passed around the remainder of the goat cheese. "What has she proposed?"

"She wants them to consider doing a Coalton farmers market. They've got several local producers besides Laurel, and she figured they could do it on a weekday afternoon so they wouldn't compete with Shavano's market. The city council thought it was too expensive and too hard to run. Laurel's still pushing it, though."

Uncle Mike frowned. "They may be right about that for once. Farmers markets are hard to get going, particularly when so many of us are already committed to established ones around the state. She might have more luck setting one up that's biweekly or monthly."

"Weekly's easier to deal with. People can get used to coming every week." I'd been selling at area farmers markets for a while, and I had some sense of how people shopped. Plus I was always interested in startups where I might be able to sell some jam.

"But they won't come if there aren't enough stands to make it worth their while," Uncle Mike said. "You need enough people around to make a real farmers market."

That logic was unassailable. "Well, anyway, Laurel's still trying to get them interested," I said. "Plus, she's working on expanding their Prospecting Days celebration in July."

"Prospecting Days?" Madge's eyes widened. "Good lord, are they still doing that? I haven't heard anything about it for three or four years. And it was never as big as the festivals in Leadville and Buena Vista."

"It kind of fell by the wayside," I admitted. "Laurel's going to revive it, and she's got support from some of the newer folks, particularly the ones who've moved into Coalton over the last couple of years."

Uncle Mike took a hefty forkful of rice. "They're probably the best people to work on something like that. The old fogies on the city council would want to make sure she did everything the way they did it ten years ago."

"What does she want to do different?" Madge asked

with a grimace. "It used to be something like a parade and a talent show. And that's not likely to draw the tourists."

"I don't know what else she's doing," I said, "but she's put in the paperwork for a burro race. They want to use the trail up Preservation Pass. It's around sixteen miles total, which Laurel says is sort of medium length."

Uncle Mike leaned in his chair. "Interesting. They used to have a race up at Preservation. I think Silas won it once. Wonder when they stopped doing it."

"Probably just dropped out the same way everything else has dropped out at Coalton." Madge started gathering dirty plates. "You've got to have people who are enthusiastic about keeping things going. That's the big problem with having a city council that's so focused on one thing: the mining industry."

"Well, Laurel says the council is backing her on this idea," I said. "A lot of burro racers live around Coalton, and they train on the Preservation Trail. Plus they could have a parade with the burros and their owners—that ought to draw the tourists. I'd definitely show up to watch the burros myself."

"It certainly should," Madge agreed. "Everybody likes burros."

Uncle Mike gave her a dry grin. "As long as those burros belong to somebody else, I'm fine with them."

I felt like pouting. "We had everything else around here when I was growing up, from chickens to that Holstein that Donnie had when Dolce was little. I never could understand why we couldn't have had a burro or two. Silas even offered me one of his racing burros that had gotten a little long in the tooth."

"It's one thing to have Donnie's Holstein eating hay

and staying in her own pasture; the chickens are happy eating bugs," Uncle Mike said as he sopped up the last bit of gravy on his plate with a bit of baguette. "But I've seen the way Silas's burros look at my arugula fields. Having one around full-time would just be asking for trouble." He stood to help Madge gather up the last of the dishes. "Besides, Herman's almost as big as a burro."

Herman was the dog I shared with Uncle Mike. He had a lot of Great Dane in his background. "It's not just the size," I said. "Burros have got those big brown eyes and sweet dispositions."

"Herman's eyes are plenty big. And he's a sweetheart, as I'm sure you'll agree."

"Herman is a very sweet dog, but he's no burro." Madge began carrying the plates from the table to the kitchen. "I completely understand the way Roxy feels about them. They're adorable. But they probably don't belong on a farm that specializes in green, leafy vegetables. When did you have chickens?"

Way to change the subject, Madge. I got up and helped her carry things away. "They were Carmen's chickens, and I think she still has some. She's not selling as many eggs as she used to, though. Now that Dolce's going to be in Ft. Collins for over half the year, Carmen's cutting back on a lot of her production."

"Oh, my." Madge shook her head. "It's going to be quite an adjustment for her, not having Dolce around. I remember how it felt when Nathan and Coco went off on their own—like I was missing my right arm."

But then Nate and Coco had both returned to help run the family café after their dad had died. "Carmen and Dennis still have the honey business. And all his crops I think she'll have as much work as she wants and then some getting their stuff to the farmers market."

"True. But it's still a hard thing when your kids go off on their own." Madge smiled. "But then they come back. Who wants a piece of the chocolate pie Coco baked today?"

****

I'd saved a chunk of the goat cheese for Nate because I had correctly assumed there wouldn't be any leftovers from the roll I took to dinner. After he got home from the event, he spread some cheese on an oat cracker to go with the soup he'd warmed up for his dinner.

"How'd the event go?" I asked.

He shrugged. "It went. No disasters. Everything got eaten. Client seemed happy—they gave us a bonus. And I'm beat." He nibbled on the cracker then gave me a tired smile. "Tasty. Laurel's stuff is still the best. I wish we could afford to use her cheese in the small cheese balls, but it's still beyond our price point. Works well in the bigger cheese balls, though." He paused for a jaw-cracking yawn.

"Is everything okay?" I asked.

He gave me a rueful smile. "I'm just tired, like I said. Summer is hell for events. Figured out what you're doing for your summer jam yet?"

Which tossed the ball into my court. I considered yawning back. "No, I'm still weighing options. I did some mixed berries today, and that might work." I brought over the open jar and a spoon so that he could take a taste. Nate's one of my best testers, in part because he's willing to give it to me straight. When something doesn't work, he won't pretend that it does. Now he tasted a spoonful of the jam and considered it, staring off into space.

"What do you think?" I asked, trying to sound disinterested.

"It's…good," he said. "Tasty. Solid. People will enjoy it on their breakfast toast."

I recognized that tone, damning with faint praise. "But?"

"But it's kind of predictable. I mean, there's nothing wrong with it. And I think you could add it to your regulars, assuming you can get enough berries. People will like it. But your specials are usually more unexpected. The kind of thing people see and think, *that's unique.* Mixed berry is tasty, but it's not unique."

Dull, in other words. I'd actually reached that conclusion myself.

I sank into a chair. "You're right. I'm just not coming up with anything unexpected, though. I mean, I've already done everything I can think of with peaches, added booze and herbs and nuts—the works. And we have so few apricots I hate to mess with them. And plums are great, but we won't get many until late in the summer. So I'm sort of stuck with berries, but I don't know what else to do with them."

Nate stretched out his legs in front of him, folding his arms behind his head. "Maybe think outside the box. Does it have to be sweet? Does it have to be jam? I mean you do chutneys and pickles sometimes, right?"

"I do," I said slowly. "But I don't rely on them. And I don't sell that many, to be honest. I mean at the farmers market, you've got Annabelle at Mountain Pickler. Her ferments are better than mine, and I'm not up to competing with her, so pickles aren't a good option. I guess there's chutney. I hadn't thought about it." I'm not crazy about chutney myself, but a lot of people like it.

And it's sort of in my wheelhouse as a jam maker. I sold cranberry chutney during the holiday season.

It didn't exactly make my heart go pitter-pat, though. I know that's not a good reason for ruling something out, but it was the best I could do.

"Hot sauce," Nate went on. "Salsa. Even ketchup."

"Ketchup?" I wrinkled my nose at him. "Everybody thinks they know what ketchup should taste like because they've been eating the same brand forever. And there's no way I could reproduce that taste, even if I wanted to."

"Outside the box," Nate cautioned. "Something savory and unexpected. And I've seen ads for artisan ketchup."

"Yeah, but you haven't seen their profit statements." But my thoughts had begun to tick over now. *Savory. Sweet and sour. Sweet and salty.* "Tomatoes," I said slowly.

Nate narrowed his eyes. "Ketchup does involve tomatoes."

"Not ketchup. Definitely not ketchup. But tomatoes…" My brain was rummaging through all the detritus of jam recipes I'd assembled over the years. "Tomato sauce, tomato confit, tomato paste." Long pause. "Tomato jam."

Nate's expression told me he wasn't exactly buying in. "Really?"

"Really. I've never made it, but there are lots of recipes for it—some with chilies, some with citrus, some with citrus and chilies."

Nate looked even more dubious. "And sugar?"

"Some sugar, not enough to make it sweet. If you're remembering childhood encounters with stewed tomatoes, just cool it."

"But what do you do with it? I mean, nobody's going to put it on their breakfast toast, right?"

"Right. But you could spread it on crostini with a little fresh basil. Or use it in a cheese sandwich. Or put it on top of meatloaf or burgers. I won't know what all I can do with it until I experiment." My creative juices were beginning to flow. "Now all I need are some decent tomatoes."

Nate sighed. "Good luck with that. The local ones won't hit the market for another six weeks or so."

"No, but I might be able to pick up some from greenhouses in a couple of weeks. And for now I could try using some cherry tomatoes—they've got good flavor year-round." I rubbed my hands. "Okay, this is going to be fun. Thanks for getting me going in this direction."

Nate sighed again. "You're welcome. I think."

Chapter 3

I spent the next few days researching tomato jam recipes and tracking down tomatoes. As it turned out, Romas made more sense than the cherry variety. First, because they're better for cooking than for eating out of hand. Second, because you need to simmer tomato jam until it thickens up, and cherry tomatoes have a lot more liquid than Romas do. Yes, you might say, but don't you have to simmer the liquid out with any jam? Yep, but with fruit jams you've got a fair amount of natural sugar helping that thickening along. Tomatoes are sweet, but they don't have as much sugar as fruit. And you want savory, so you don't add as much sweetening.

In some recipes, in fact, you don't use any sweetening at all, relying on the limited natural sweetness of the tomatoes. Later in the summer, when we got local tomatoes, that natural sweetness would be at its peak. Right now, however, I'd have to use the supermarket variety, so I planned on hedging my bets by adding a bit of sugar, just to get things going.

Some recipes I found called for cooking times of one to two hours because they were relying on the tomatoes' natural pectin to thicken things up. Other recipes went in the opposite direction, putting the chopped tomatoes in a sieve to drain all the extra juice out of them before you put them in the jam pot. I figured I'd try both variations before I decided on my approach, but my guess was I'd go with some version of the long, slow cooking option since it would concentrate the tomato flavor. If I needed to, I'd add some powdered pectin to help the jam to gel, but I'd try natural first.

Bridget and Dolce both arrived as I was chopping up my first couple of pounds of Romas. Bridget narrowed her eyes. "Making salsa?"

I shook my head. "Tomato jam. I'm considering it for a monthly special this summer."

Bridget's eyes stayed narrow. "Tomato *jam*? Never heard of it."

"I have." Dolce frowned. "I've never tasted it, though. Is it sweet?"

"Not supposed to be," I said. "I mean, there's some sweetening in it, but it's mainly the sweetness from the tomatoes. And you throw in some savory spices like cumin."

Actually, some of the recipes went with sweet spices like cinnamon and cloves. But we were in Western Colorado, and although we're not New Mexico, we do tend to go for spicy. My tomato jam was going to have both ginger and chilies, along with the cumin.

"Interesting." Dolce studied the colander full of tomatoes I had draining in the sink. "Can I help?"

"Once I get the recipe down and geared up for production, absolutely. For today, though, I need you to stir up some strawberry and some peach, so we're set for the weekend."

"I can do that," Dolce said. "But I want to watch, too, to see how you do a savory spread."

Bridget looked about as dubious as Nate had when I'd first suggested tomato jam as a possibility. You think people will buy in on something like this? When they've never tasted it or maybe even heard of it?"

"What do you think? You're the expert on our customers."

Bridget grinned. "Glad you think so. I don't know exactly how they'll react. We've done okay with the monthly specials in the past, but they've been mostly in the traditional jam categories with maybe a little extra spice or something. I think we'll want to put up some suggestions on the web site for how you could use this."

I nodded. "I'd already thought of that. I'll work up a couple of recipes and maybe a list of things other people do with tomato jam. So far most of the suggestions I've seen go with sandwiches or grilled meat, but it could be a natural to combine with cream cheese in a dip."

"BLT's," Dolce said. "Instead of mayo. Maybe on top of scrambled eggs. Or mixed into mac and cheese."

Bridget held up her hands. "Okay, you've sold me. For now. I'll taste it when you've got something you're happy with."

Getting happy with it was going to be the test, of course. Now that I'd dived this deeply into the idea of tomato jam, I needed to come up with something I liked. I decided to go simple for my first go-round. I put the two pounds of tomatoes into my jam pot, along with some lemon juice, salt, sugar, cumin, grated ginger, and a couple of dried ancho chilies I'd reconstituted with boiling water and then chopped in my processor. After a few vigorous stirs to get everything as mixed as I could, I put it on a back burner of the stove and set the heat to medium so I could get it boiling. After that I reduced it to low and let it simmer away happily, figuring on somewhere between an hour and an hour and a half before it thickened enough and became dark red.

I spent the rest of the morning getting enough of my regular jam done to stock my farmers market booth that weekend. It was still early summer, and the crowds hadn't hit the peak numbers they'd have during July and August. But we were getting more people each weekend. And I'd learned long ago that it was better to have a little jam left over at the end of the day than to have to turn away potential customers because I'd run out of the flavor they wanted.

After an hour and a half, I checked the tomato jam. It was thick and kind of brick red. I had my usual impulse to taste it but given that it was the temperature and consistency of lava, I resisted.

Dolce peered over my shoulder. "Wow. That's an interesting color."

"It is." I fished two half-pint jars out of a pot of hot water, then let them drain on the sideboard.

"You're not going to process them?"

"Just refrigerator jam to begin with. I'll try doing some processing when I've got the recipe down." Refrigerator jam is easy and tasty, but I can't sell it since it needs to be refrigerated. On the other hand, it's fast and doesn't require as much time and equipment as jam that's sealed and boiled in a canning kettle. And it usually doesn't need pectin.

Bridget got up from her computer to see. "It's pretty."

"It's all in the taste, though." I ladled the jam into the jars, using my trusty wide-mouth funnel. It *was* pretty, sort of like diced tomatoes in ketchup. I hoped it didn't taste like that. I wasn't making ketchup, after all. Or anyway, I hoped I wasn't.

I set the jam pot over near the dishwasher to cool

down so I could rinse it. Dolce and Bridget both eyed it a little curiously. There's always a little bit of jam left in the bottom, and it's always cooler than the stuff I'd put into the jars. "Okay," I said. "Okay. We'll try a little of the scrapings but be careful not to burn yourselves."

I handed them a couple of tasting spoons then took one for myself. Carefully, I scraped up a bit of the jam left in the pan. It was warm, but not lava. I tasted carefully, licking a bit off the end of the spoon. Sweet, tart, very tomatoey, not ketchup. Definitely not ketchup. But I wasn't exactly sure what it *was*.

"That's…interesting," Bridget said. I knew how she was feeling. It wasn't awful, but I wasn't sure it was good yet.

"Needs more spice," Dolce said flatly. "I know you put in a couple of chilies, but I don't taste them at all."

"You're right," I said.

"Maybe you need something stronger. Like a couple of fresh jalapenos? Or even a serrano?" Dolce gave me a questioning look.

"Jalapeños might work." I narrowed my eyes. "It's got to cut through a lot of sweet tomato flavor. And it's got to kick ass."

Dolce nodded and Bridget grinned. "This isn't bad, but it isn't there yet. What can you do with it?"

I shrugged. "I'll use it for something; it won't go to waste. Maybe I could glaze a meatloaf with it."

"Be good on hamburgers," Bridget said.

Oh, don't say it. Don't say it.

"Sort of like ketchup," she said.

Well, crap. Maybe I'd made ketchup after all.

****

I hadn't forgotten about doing the training run with

Laurel and Peggy Sue. In fact, I was looking forward to it after a sort of grueling farmers market on Saturday. As the weeks went on, the crowds were building; at the same time, their patience was beginning to wear thin. I had a couple of people almost come to blows over the last jar of mixed berry jam—and it really was the last jar. I had more of my basics, but mixed berry had been a sort of test batch, and I only had a little over a case. Next week I'd definitely need to make more.

Laurel was there, too, dealing with her own long lines for goat cheese. She'd hired one of Dolce's high school friends to help out, but even with two of them, the crowds were intense. We had time to exchange a couple of words, but mostly we both spent our time being vendors.

I wasn't sure what to wear for burro race training. Normally, I'd wear my running shoes for a race, but this course was up a relatively steep mountain trail that involved a lot of rocks I'd need to hop or climb over. I could use my hiking boots, but they were too heavy for speed. I compromised by borrowing Nate's trail running shoes, which were sort of midway between running and hiking. They were a little big, but I figured I could get by with heavy oversize socks to stuff up the empty spaces.

I'd told Laurel I'd meet her at the trail head, since it was between Shavano and Coalton, and I pulled into the parking lot around nine forty-five. I wasn't expecting much in the way of crowds. It was Sunday morning, after all, and I figured those who weren't in church were probably either snoozing or having brunch somewhere. Surprisingly, the parking lot was full.

Laurel had pulled her truck and horse trailer into one of the larger parking spots at the end of the lot, and I walked over to join her. "Are all these people here for race training?"

She shrugged. "A lot of them are. Check out the trailers."

Now that I took the time, I saw a lot more horse trailers scattered around the edges of the lot.

"And that doesn't count the people who walked up from town," she said. "When we do the race, the starting point will be down in front of Taylor's Saloon, so some of the guys are getting their animals used to the distance. I'll do that in another week or so. Today, it was easier to just drive Peggy Sue over."

Peggy Sue stood next to the open trailer, looking bored. Laurel had strapped on the pack, but not with the required pick and shovel and gold pan. She'd probably work up to the full weight later in her training. "You ready for this?" she asked me.

"Sure." I worked on sounding confident, but in reality, I was a little nervous. It had been a while since I'd done any serious hiking, and the trail up to Preservation Pass came across as serious as hell.

Apparently, my imitation of confidence wasn't as effective as I'd hoped. "We'll take it easy. It's our first time out on this trail this season. We don't have to go all the way to the top of the pass." Laurel took hold of the lead rope attached to Peggy Sue's halter, and we headed for the beginning of the trail.

Now that I looked up the mountain side, I could see several burros trotting along the trail. The burros were doing fine. The people with them, on the other hand, were working. The trail to the pass zig-zagged up the mountain in a series of long switchbacks, occasionally disappearing into clumps of pine and aspen but more and more out in the open as it reached the higher elevations. Preservation Pass itself was around ten thousand feet, and we were starting around eight thousand. We had a lot of hard climbing ahead. At least hard for Laurel and me. I was guessing Peggy Sue would take it in stride, so to speak.

Another couple of burros and their human companions, two men in their forties, arrived at the trailhead around the same time we did. "Hey, Laurel," one of them said. "Using Peggy Sue this time?"

"Yep," Laurel said. "Her turn."

She stood aside to let the men and burros go by first, letting them advance up the trail a bit before we started after them. "Competitors?" I asked.

Laurel nodded. "From Leadville. I hope this means they're entering the Preservation race. We need to get the word out and draw as many racers as we can." She stepped away from Peggy Sue so that the burro could take the lead up the trail.

"Where do you want me?" I asked.

"You always stay behind the animals on the climb up the hill. I let Peggy Sue choose her route, within reason. She's supposed to stay on the trail, but we've got some leeway about how she gets over and around the rocks." Laurel gestured up toward the trail above us, where some chunks of granite jutted out of the dirt at the side.

The beginning of the trail was wide and relatively easy. Laurel got Peggy Sue up to a trot and we jogged along behind her. "Stay on the left if you can. Peggy doesn't kick on purpose, but she might get you by accident."

Even an accidental kick didn't strike me as fun. I

shifted to the left of the trail, following Laurel. Peggy Sue seemed to be enjoying herself, trotting along at a good clip and occasionally breaking into a gait that was almost a gallop. The sound of her hooves clicking over the occasional rock was a nice accompaniment to the sound of the breeze in the aspen and a raven's cry ahead of us. I began to enjoy myself.

This enjoyment lasted until we came to the next switchback, and I saw the trail ahead. The grade was a lot steeper than the trail we'd already climbed, and I could see white rocks pushing up through the trail dirt. The wide, well-groomed trail had given way to a narrower, steeper climb.

"Come on, Peggy," Laurel clucked, giving the lead rope a little flip. Peggy started up the slope with a determined air, her gait slowing to a fast walk as she worked her way around the rocks.

I managed to navigate the rocks after Peggy Sue and Laurel had gone on ahead. As anticipated, Peggy Sue continued to treat the trail like no big deal, but it was beginning to become a bigger deal for me. "This is rough," I panted. "Don't they groom the trail before the race?"

"Nobody's in charge of trail grooming around here. I'm afraid if I suggest anything, they'll put me in charge of it, which would mean I'd probably end up doing it myself." Laurel gave me a dry smile. "Most burro race trails get pretty rugged. We're all used to it, and the burros don't care."

I glanced up the trail again. The two guys who'd preceded us were still slightly ahead, urging their burros on when they took their time navigating around rocks. I could hear the sounds of voices farther up the mountainside, and the clicks of more burro hooves as they climbed over obstacles. Everybody was in a relaxed mood. Maybe I was making too much of the steep trail ahead.

Then again, maybe I wasn't. Another switchback brought us to an even steeper section. "How long is this trail?"

"Around eight miles to the summit. Eventually I'd like to map out a long trail and a shorter one, but this time around we're all doing the short."

"Sixteen miles is short?" I was already wondering if I'd even make it to the summit.

"Oh, yeah. The long course at Fairplay is over twenty-nine miles, and it's up in the clouds. Mosquito Pass is over thirteen-thousand feet." She shrugged. "I've taken Spats up to the top of the pass, but not during the race. You can get a little light-headed."

I'd undoubtedly be more than a little light-headed. In fact, I might be puking my guts out. I only hoped I wouldn't do that today.

"How are you hanging in?" Laurel asked.

I decided it was better to be honest than to have a crisis farther up the trail. "I'm hanging. I haven't hiked more than five miles in a while. I don't know if I'll make it to the top of the pass."

Laurel smiled. "Just do what you can. Peg and I are more used to it. We've been training on this trail for a while. And I may not go all the way up myself this time."

We looped around another switchback, this one with a ladder of rocks along the slope. Peggy found her own route, stepping carefully over some of the rocks and dodging around others. I decided to let her guide the way since she had more experience climbing over rough trails

33

than I did. I put my feet carefully in the same spots where Peggy Sue had put hers.

"Peggy Sue seems pretty happy." I tried not to sound envious. It was a little daunting to be bested by a burro.

Laurel grinned. "She's a trooper. I've had burros that were sort of lazy, that didn't like going uphill or running, but Peg has always been terrific. A real climber."

Peggy kept up her fast walk. After a few more minutes, we passed the two guys who'd started out ahead of us, resting their burros at the side of the trail. "Go, Peggy," one of them said, and it only sounded a little sarcastic.

We made it to the top of the next turn, maybe three miles up the trail or so, when Laurel stopped dead in her tracks in front of me. Peggy Sue jerked to a stop beside her, giving her the donkey version of an annoyed look. "Laurel?" I said.

"What's he doing here?" Laurel said flatly.

The man ahead of us was towing a burro around a rocky outcropping. The burro, an unusual shade of dark gold, didn't seem to be enjoying himself. Neither did the guy. At least not at first. When he heard Laurel's voice, though, he paused and turned around. "Well, hey there, sweetcakes," he said, giving her the kind of smile that made me want to smack him.

I realized when I saw that smile that I knew him. And he was definitely an annoying guy. Smacking him didn't seem out of the realm of possibility.

Chapter 4

It took me a minute to recognize Kell Moorhead, Laurel's ex-husband.

He'd always struck me as one of those men who was too handsome for his own good—golden hair, sparkling blue eyes, broad shoulders. And the kind of smile that told you he absolutely wasn't to be trusted under any circumstances. I'd met him a few times when he'd been hanging around Laurel's booth at the market. They'd been separated for a while, and I thought their divorce had come through a couple of months ago.

"Morning, Kell. Mind if we go through?" Laurel sounded calm, but her shoulders looked tense.

Kell concentrated on his burro. "Buster's almost over the rocks. Just give him another minute."

Buster, who I assumed was Kell's donkey, was working his way up the path more slowly than Peggy's gait down below. He seemed a little more hesitant, and not nearly as happy. "His first time up?" I asked.

Kell shrugged, offering that absolutely untrustworthy smile as he moved a few steps uphill to keep up with his burro. "He's a trooper. Just getting his racing legs."

Laurel arched an eyebrow. "Whose is he?"

A flicker of annoyance passed over Kell's bland face. "He's mine. I leased him for the summer."

"You're going to be in the race?"

Kell returned to his insolent grin. "Of course. Wouldn't miss it. I figure it's part of my duties as town manager."

Buster finally made it to the top of the outcropping and started ambling up the trail again a little doggedly. "Well, see you later," Kell said. "Gotta keep up with my burro." Given the way his burro was plodding along, *keeping up* wouldn't be much of a problem.

Laurel narrowed her eyes as she squinted after him. Peggy Sue shook her head impatiently. She was ready to go even if we weren't. Laurel loosened her grip on the lead rope and moved toward the next rock ladder. "Let's do it, Peggy."

I followed them without a word. Laurel's sunny mood had darkened considerably, not that I blamed her. Kell Moorhead was enough to darken anyone's mood. Finally, we reached another natural stopping place, and Laurel pulled her water bottle out from the pack on Peggy Sue's back.

I grabbed my own. "Does Peggy Sue need water?"

"Nope. Donkeys can go quite a while without water. The only animal that can go longer is a camel."

"I didn't know Kell raced." That was a nonjudgmental way to raise the subject we were both avoiding.

"He used to make jokes about me and my donkeys." She grimaced, screwing the cap onto her water bottle with just a bit too much force. "He just wants to be in this race because I planned it."

"For support?" Kell didn't seem supportive, but then, I didn't know him very well.

"To keep me from getting a win," she said. "If the race goes well, he'll find a way to claim it was his idea.

36

If it bombs, he'll say I messed it up. Either way he's going to be up here on the mountain side, gladhanding."

"I forgot he was town manager, to tell you the truth." And I had no idea if the job was all that important or if it was largely grunt work.

Laurel shrugged. "It's not full time, but he's held onto the office for five years or so. And to give him his due, he's probably the one who recommended me for the PR job. That was after we'd separated, but he still told them I was qualified."

"At least the town's finally considering something besides mining as a way to make money." I tried for a positive spin, particularly after what I'd heard from Uncle Mike and Madge.

"Yeah, but they're not considering that hard," Laurel said dryly. "They accept maybe one out of any three proposals I give them."

Okay, so we weren't into positive thinking at the moment. "You got your race, though. Peggy Sue gets a chance to kick ass and take names."

Laurel's grin looked a little forced, but she tucked her water bottle in the pack again. "And Peggy Sue's ready to do some ass kicking, aren't you, sweetheart? Of course, we'll have to deal with the racing tourists."

"You mean people who watch the race? Do they get in the way?"

"Not just watchers. There are some ranchers who rent out burros if people want to try burro racing without the investment. Some of the renters are serious about it— they just don't have any room to keep a burro. They're the ones who lease the burro for several weeks or months, like Kell. But a lot of them are just up here to screw around. Sometimes they lose their burros or get off the trail or just get in everybody else's way." She sighed. "Hazards of a newly popular sport, I guess."

Peggy Sue shook her head again. Of the three of us, she seemed to have the most enthusiasm for the remaining trial which was logical enough. "You ready to do this, Peg?" Laurel rubbed her nose against her donkey's muzzle. "Let's go show 'em how it's done."

I put my water bottle away and got on the trail, prepared to be shown up by an energetic donkey.

****

That night, after I'd taken a long bath to loosen up my sore muscles, I tried out my first version of tomato jam as a meatloaf glaze. It was risky, since Nate and I both had some nasty memories of ketchup glazes in the high school cafeteria. But I figured the tomato jam wasn't really ketchup.

Or so I kept telling myself.

In the interests of full disclosure, I told Nate what I was doing. He'd tasted the jam after it had cooled in the refrigerator, and his conclusion was a lot like mine: okay, but not there yet. Out of curiosity—or maybe perversity—I decided to jazz it up a little bit before I put it on the meatloaf, so I added some chili flakes and a couple of teaspoons of honey.

Nate's first reaction was a series of blinks. "That's got some style," he said finally.

"Good style or bad style?"

He paused. "Jury's still out."

On the whole, I agreed with him. The chili flakes had given the jam some kick, but the honey was kind of a distraction. Fortunately, it blended fairly well with the meatloaf, although if I had a choice, I doubted I'd use it again.

"How was the burro training?" Nate asked.

I shifted a little uncomfortably in my chair. We hadn't done the full sixteen miles, but it had still been a lot more hiking than I'd done recently and my muscles were still complaining. "Interesting, gnarly course. I don't know how anyone could make much speed there, but the burros seemed to enjoy it." I thought of Kell's golden burro who hadn't looked like he was having a lot of fun. "Well, some of them did, anyway."

"Burros? Plural?"

"Oh, yeah. There were a lot of people out there, training on the course with their burros. I didn't realize what a big deal it was until today." I told him about the tourist burro racers Laurel had described.

"That's nuts. People who've never had any experience with burros going into a race with people like Laurel and Silas? Sounds like a great way to end up in the hospital."

"Laurel says the renters have to take a safety course first, so they know how the burros are likely to react. But it's still not much. I mean, Peggy Sue's a sweetheart, but even she's been known to kick if you get in her way." Or so Laurel had told me.

Nate shrugged. "Sort of like the guys who go river rafting when they've never seen a class four rapid, let alone learned how to navigate one."

"'What the hell, it's just like canoeing, right?'" I quoted one of the more clueless would-be rafters who'd had to be talked out of it by the patrons at Robicheaux's.

Nate grinned at the memory, then raised his eyebrows at me. "So I assume you won't be chasing down a burro to race at Coalton."

I rubbed my sore shoulder muscles. "It's a very

tough course, and I'm out of shape, but that doesn't mean I don't wish I could do it. Or get a burro of my own. The ones I saw today were all cutie pies."

Nate shook his head. "Just being cute isn't enough. Herman's cute, and he needs a lot of tending."

"I wouldn't call Herman cute," I mused. "Majestic, maybe."

"Except when it thunders."

Herman didn't like thunder, but then neither did I. "Burros are a lot cheaper than horses. You can adopt one from the BLM wild horse and burro auction for around a hundred bucks. And the upkeep costs are less than with horses, too."

Nate gave me a long look. "But you're not considering a horse, right? What would you do with this burro if you got one? We've got no livestock that needs protecting. You're not interested in racing. We don't go into the back country much, although I wish we could get away a little more than we do, so we don't need a pack burro. And we've got no little kids around who want burro rides."

My face flushed. Although we'd agreed we wanted to get married at a future date, we'd never talked about kids. And I wasn't about to let a conversation about burros morph into something entirely different. "Maybe Astrid would like burro rides when she gets a little older. That field out behind your mom's old house would be perfect for a burro."

Bobby and Marigold had moved into the old Robicheaux family home after Madge had decided to move to the farm when she married Uncle Mike. But I still thought of it as Madge's place.

"We can continue this conversation sometime in the

future," Nate said. "Just swear to me you won't bring home a burro without a lengthy discussion and buy-in from everybody around here."

"I promise," I said. Not that I needed to promise anything since there was absolutely no chance I'd end up with a burro without having cleared it with Nate, Uncle Mike, Madge, Donnie and Carmen, and all the other farmers who were within sound of a burro's bellow.

No chance at all.

****

As it happened, the week after my training run, I was in Coalton again. Enough time had passed for my muscles to return to normal after doing more climbing than I was used to. Laurel had put together her first small, impromptu farmers market on Franklin Avenue, Coalton's main street. I'd agreed to come sell some jam, along with produce from Uncle Mike and Donnie and Carmen. It wasn't a whole lot of produce, mind you, because they'd sold most of it the weekend before at the Shavano farmers market. But we had some arugula and spring onions, along with peppers and tomatoes from Donnie's greenhouse.

The idea was to give Coalton a taste of what they could have from their own regular farmers market. With any luck, Laurel was hoping to overcome the skepticism of the city council, enough to get them to buy in on a small monthly farmers market.

Nate was free for the day, so he volunteered to come help me sell jam. Laurel had set up a potluck dinner for the vendors to be held at her place after the market, and Nate was providing a pot of Asian meatballs, one of the most popular apps at the catering company. Fortunately for all concerned, Laurel had refrigerator space at her place, so we didn't have to worry about food spoilage while we were selling jam.

Coalton is a neat old town, even if it suffers from economic problems. It has spectacular scenery on all sides and still boasts a lot of the nineteenth century architecture that was a feature when the town boasted a few silver barons. That the historic architecture was still in place because nobody had much wanted to develop Coalton was both a blessing and a curse. Franklin Avenue had been blocked at both ends to let us set up free from passing cars. The locals were largely okay with detouring a couple of blocks west since a lot of them were trying to find market parking spots anyway.

Nate helped me set up my booth, surveying the street. "At least it's asphalt. Two blocks up it's still brick."

"That's sort of cool, though. It goes along with the old-timey vibe here."

"Yeah, it's definitely retro. If they could get a few more boutiques and a couple more restaurants, the tourists would love it."

The few tourists who made it to Coalton did love it, judging from the number of pictures posted to social media. But getting more of them to make the short detour off the major highway to see the town was the tough part.

There were maybe a dozen booths in the Coalton farmers market, not nearly as many as you'd find in Shavano or the major markets like Boulder. Some of them were booths in name only—folding tables with produce or honey jars arranged across their width and a vendor sitting on a camp chair at the back.

Still, the crowds were healthy. People strolled along the center aisle, considering the items for sale and occasionally stopping to examine them more closely. I sold out on Donnie's peppers and tomatoes quickly, although I had to caution the customers that they were hothouse rather than garden.

"They'll still taste better than the stuff you get at City Market," one woman said, and I had to admit she was probably right. It was fresh picked even if it hadn't been grown outside.

People all around us were doing a brisk business. The honey stand had a line, and so did the lady selling fresh baked bread and scones. And Laurel had her usual crowd, although she was handling them without the assistant she used at Shavano.

I let Nate do the produce side of things while I sold jam. I hadn't brought much—just the usual peach, strawberry, raspberry, and pepper peach. But the novelty of having someone selling fresh local jam on the main street of Coalton was enough to attract a lot of customers. I sold out of strawberry quickly, which was no surprise since it's everybody's favorite. But the other jams sold well, too. First raspberry disappeared, then peach. Which left me with pepper peach, the most problematic of my standard jams. But the Coalton shoppers were more adventurous than the Shavano shoppers had been when I'd first introduced jam that combined ripe peaches with Pueblo chilies.

By two-thirty, I was sold out and feeling a little embarrassed for having underestimated the number of customers Laurel would draw for her first-ever market. Uncle Mike's arugula was the last thing we had to sell, and the bags of greenery looked a little sad lying there all alone. But we sold them all anyway.

The market was scheduled to run until three thirty,

but at three we closed up shop, folding down my booth to put it into my truck. When I checked up and down the street, I noticed we weren't the only ones who'd shut down. Apparently, we'd all underestimated the enthusiasm of the Coalton shoppers.

I'd be better prepared next month, always assuming we had another market next month. It seemed pretty obvious that there should be, but I never counted on city councils, particularly when they were made up of men like the ones who ran Coalton.

I swung by Laurel's booth to let her know we were done. She still had a line, but she'd crossed off two of the three flavors of cheese she'd been offering.

I stood next to her as she rang up the remaining customers. Since she only had one kind of cheese left, things went quickly. "Wow," she said when she was done. "I figured this would be popular, but I had no idea *how* popular."

"It's a screaming success," I said. "Once the word gets out, you'll probably have to fight off vendors who want to get a piece of the action. I think you're the only weekday farmers market in the region."

Laurel nodded. "We are. I did a lot of checking before we scheduled this one. If we were closer to Denver, we'd have more competition."

"If we were closer to Denver, we'd all have more competition." One of the advantages of being in the mountains.

"So you're done, too?" Laurel asked.

"Yeah. We closed down around three. I underestimated the amount of jam I'd need."

"Just like I underestimated the cheese. Come on to my place. We can have a beer and toast our accomplishments."

I found Nate talking to one of his chef buddies, someone who was also headed to Laurel's with a cooler full of strawberry shortcake. Obviously, a man after my own heart. By the time we got there, the field next to Laurel's house had begun to fill up with SUVs and trucks, the mountain town transportation of choice. I waved at the people I knew, including Ted Sylvano, who was helping Laurel put hamburgers onto her smoker grill. Ted owned the high-end grocery in Geary where Laurel and I both sold our stuff.

Nate retrieved his Asian meatballs from Laurel's refrigerator and put them out with the other appetizers after a quick reheat. Most of the people milling around Laurel's yard were vendors from the farmers market, all of them slightly dazed and more than a little delighted about the day's sales. I saw Lynn Bridger, a farmer and beekeeper who lived down the road from us.

"How'd you do?" I asked.

"Terrific. I had some spinach that wasn't quite ready for Shavano and some cucumbers and carrots and potatoes—just normal stuff, you know? Sold it all. And I sold out of honey within the first hour. Should have brought more, but who knew?"

This was the refrain I was hearing from everybody. We'd all gone conservative on the amount of stuff we'd brought for sale, and we'd all sold out. And we were all swearing we'd bring a lot more next month, assuming Laurel got the city council to authorize another farmers market. Surely they would, everyone kept saying.

As I headed for Nate's meatballs, I saw a knot of older men I hadn't noticed before. I was pretty sure they weren't vendors from the market because I knew most of the farmers and ranchers in the Collegiate Peaks area. One of the men looked vaguely familiar, but it took me a moment to recognize Kell Moorhead again. Laurel's ex was the only one in the group under fifty.

Kell said something and the men all laughed. I saw Laurel glance their way, frowning. Out of curiosity I inched closer.

"You don't think spinach is going to take care of the city budget?" one of the older guys asked with a smirk on his weathered face.

"Oh, hey, we all love spinach, don't we, guys?" Kell grinned. "Make us all into a bunch of Popeyes, am I right?"

More laughter. Either these guys were starved for jokes, or they were laughing at something I didn't get myself.

"Everybody seemed like they were having fun," one of the other guys said a little tentatively.

"Oh, they were having fun," Kell said. "I'll grant you that. But fun doesn't pay the bills now, does it?"

"Maybe not, but it pays a lot of people who live here." Laurel stood with her fists on her hips, regarding her ex-husband with narrowed eyes. "And it brings people who are likely to spend some more money before they leave."

She scanned the other men in the group. "I hope you'll have time to talk to some of the other people here. Most of them were vendors at the market. Ask them how their sales were, and if they'd be interested in returning for another market next month. I'll tell you how much the town cleared from fees at the council meeting next week, but I think you'll be pleasantly surprised." Her smile was a little tight, but she still had one. If my ex had been undercutting something I believed in, I'd probably have had trouble smiling, too.

"Burgers are ready," Ted Sylvano called. "Come get 'em while they're hot."

The older men, who I guessed were members of the Coalton city council, started toward the grill, most of them avoiding Laurel's gaze. Kell stayed where he was; then he turned to Laurel with his own tight smile. "Still want another market?"

"Oh, yeah. We cleared a few hundred on this one. And we'll get more vendors next month."

Kell's smile slid into something closer to a sneer. "A few hundred won't pay the bills. Not even close."

"It won't pay all of them, but it won't hurt. It's a few hundred we didn't have before." Spoiling for a fight, Laurel leaned close to Kell. "If you're going to eat, feel free to grab some food. Otherwise, feel free to hit the road."

They stared at each other for a moment, unsmiling. Then Kell grabbed a paper plate. "Wouldn't miss it."

Laurel watched him head for the food tables, then blew out a long breath. "Asshole. He couldn't stand to see one of my projects work out. Even if it made some money for the town." She reached for a plate of her own. "Grab a plate, Roxy. Don't let my problems keep you from eating all this good food people brought."

I picked up a plate, but my appetite was a little off. Trust Kell Moorhead to transform a triumph into a backstabbing opportunity. And trust the Coalton city council to go along with the backstabbing guy rather than the hard-working woman.

Still, I hoped they'd okay another market next month. Surely they wouldn't be dumb enough not to,

Chapter 5

After we got home, I told Nate about Kell's attempts to undermine Laurel with the Coalton city council.

He shook his head. "Stupid. They won't make a ton of money on a farmers market, but they'll still make some. And they'll lay the foundation for future markets that could make them a lot more money."

"I don't understand what Kell's up to," I said. "Is it possible he's got a project of his own he wants the city council to back?"

"Possible, I guess. But I don't know why he wouldn't back Laurel's, too. I mean, it's not like her farmers market is going to undercut something he's planning. Unless it's another farmers market."

"Could he have found another mining company who'd come into Coalton? That might kill off any efforts to make the town tourist friendly." Mining activities had a tendency to dampen the enthusiasm of hikers and campers, plus cutting down on the land available for them to explore.

"Maybe. It's not likely, though. Coal mining's not exactly a growth industry around here right now. More likely he just wants to keep control of the council."

That was probably true. But I couldn't get over my feeling that Kell was up to something, although that something might well have been just undercutting his ex-wife.

****

The next week I returned to my tomato jam quandary. I wanted something savory and spicy but with a hint of the tomatoes' natural sweetness. I tried jalapeños, but they hadn't done much to spice up the jam. You could tell they were there, but only if you knew it in advance. My new idea was to greatly increase the number of jalapeños I used and add a little smoked paprika to give the jam some more punch.

If the jalapeños still didn't work, I could try Hatch or Pueblo chilies or maybe even Serranos if I wanted to go for a real punch.

Locally grown tomatoes were beginning to pop up now, but they were still expensive. And they tended to be cherry tomatoes when I needed some Romas. I'd just returned home with another couple of pounds of Romas from City Market when Dolce and Bridget arrived.

Bridget narrowed her eyes. "Still going for the tomato jam?"

"Still trying to. But today we'll work on the stuff for this weekend. I ran out of mixed berry last Saturday, so I'm thinking we'll do two or three cases this week."

Dolce smiled. "I'll get to work cleaning the berries."

She prepared enough strawberries for the mixed berry jam, then went on to prepare enough for the kettle of strawberry jam she usually did early in the week. I felt a pang as I watched her stir the berries and the sugar together in her jam pot. We'd been working together for so long that she'd headed right into her strawberry jam prep, without even asking me if she should. I wondered, not for the first time, what I was going to do without her.

A few minutes later Dolce paused as her jam pot began to simmer. "So are you still after an assistant for when I leave?"

Not only was she a talented jam maker, she was also apparently psychic. "I haven't started yet, but yes, I know I need someone. Probably within the next month so you can help them learn the procedures around here, such as they are."

Dolce gave the jam a quick stir, then paused. "I think I know somebody who'd be interested. If you're ready to interview people, that is."

Dolce had recommended her friend Beck to be my assistant at the farmers market, and Beck had become a great help. I trusted Dolce's judgment. "I'm ready. Who is it?"

Dolce appeared to take a deep breath. "Jarrod Perrone."

There was a sort of blank silence after that as Bridget and I both stared at her. "A guy?" I said. "A guy wants to make jam?" This was an entirely sexist reaction, but I'd never run into any guy who was interested in jam. Other than chefs, of course, who tend to be interested in anything food related.

"He was in my family and consumer science class at school," Dolce said quickly. "He's really into cooking. I think he wants to be a chef. And he's a great cook."

"This isn't exactly the chef kind of cooking," I said slowly. "If he wants to get into professional stuff, he'd be better off working for somebody like Madge."

"He's watched me make jam. He's interested in how it works." Dolce gave her jam another brisk stir. "And he wants to get a start in the food business. Maybe you could try him out and see."

"Is that Walt Perrone's kid?" Bridget asked.

Dolce turned toward her. "I think so. He lives with

his dad anyway."

Bridget nodded. "That's Walt. Haven't seen him in years."

"His dad works in Geary. He commutes to town. They live over by the highway." Dolce gave her jam pot another stir.

I didn't know any of the names they'd mentioned, and I was still adjusting toward having a male assistant. "Have you talked to him about this? Is he interested?"

"I didn't want to get his hopes up until I talked to you. If you'd be willing to consider him, I'll ask him if he might be interested."

"I'd be willing. If he's interested, have him give me a call. We can get together and talk about it."

Dolce gave me a brilliant smile. "Okay, great. I'll call him."

Across the room, Bridget looked thoughtful but didn't say anything more. I had a feeling she'd be talking as soon as Dolce left for the day, though.

Dolce took off around three since she had some errands to run for Carmen before dinner. After she closed the door behind her, I turned to Bridget. "Okay, spill it."

Bridget shrugged. "I went to high school with that kid's mom, Camilla Perrone. Only she was Camilla Garcetti then. She was a holy terror. Everybody was shocked when she married Walt Perrone, who's always been a decent guy. And then see what happened. She ran off and left him with a little boy to raise on his own."

"You think the boy might be some kind of problem?" I wasn't going to buy in to any kind of *sins of the mother* idea. My own mother had left my dad and me when I was a baby.

"Nope. Like I said, Walt Perrone is as decent as they

come. But I'm guessing he and the boy haven't had it easy. Last I heard Walt was working two jobs, one in Geary and one in Shavano."

"So maybe Jarrod needs a job to keep the family afloat." And maybe making jam wouldn't provide enough money.

"Maybe." Bridget looked at me. "He could be a great hire."

"Mostly I need someone who'll show up when he's supposed to and do what I need him to do." And if he liked jam, that could be a plus.

"My guess is, he'll be fine." Bridget turned to her computer, and I made another stir of my tomato jam.

That night I had dinner with Uncle Mike and Madge. Nate was off serving chicken alfredo to a bunch of insurance agents, so it was just the three of us. Since Madge knew everything about everybody, I'd already decided I'd bring up Jarrod Perrone. "Dolce thinks she may have found someone who'd like to take over her job when she leaves for Ft. Collins." I kept a bland smile in place.

"Really? Who?" Madge passed me some sauce to go with the Swedish meatballs she'd brought home from the café.

"His name's Jerrod Perrone," I said. "He's a friend of Dolce's."

"Good for her," Madge said flatly. "Jarrod Perrone is a great kid as I understand it."

Uncle Mike raised his eyebrows. "I know Walt, but I don't know Jarrod. When did you meet him?"

"I haven't met him," Madge said. "But I know people who have. He sweeps up for Tal Nguyen at the Jade Garden. Tal's got nothing but great things to say about him."

"That's good," I said. "Tal would be a good reference."

Madge gave me a long look. "Do you know about Camilla?"

"Bridget gave me the outlines. It must have been tough on Jarrod to have his mom take off. Particularly if the other kids knew about it." And the other kids *would* know about it. That was the kind of information that would spread around Shavano. And nobody can be as cruel as kids who sense a weakness in someone else.

"It probably was," Madge conceded. "But so far as I know, he's never been in trouble. And the people who have mentioned him to me have all had positive things to say."

"Glad to hear it. I told Dolce to have him call me if he's interested. I'll find out how he feels about jam making."

Uncle Mike frowned. "Don't usually think of boys making jam. Seems more like a female kind of thing."

Madge and I both gave him long, cool stares, although technically I'd thought the same thing that afternoon. However, I'd had time to adjust my thinking, and I was now firmly on the side of having a male assistant.

Uncle Mike raised his hands. "Okay, okay. I get the point. People can do whatever they want to do, long as they've got the time and the skills. I'm probably influenced by my granny, who was a world-champion jam maker and possibly the source of Roxy's innate ability." He gave me a quick grin. "You could probably teach anybody to make jam, kiddo. Let's just hope the boy knows how to turn on a stove."

****

I wasn't sure how long it would take me to hear from Jarrod—the adolescent sense of time tends to be different from the adult sense of time. But I got a call the next morning as I was making myself some coffee.

"Ms. Constantine?" an adolescent voice said.

"Yes."

"This is Jarrod Perrone. Dolce McCray said she'd talked to you about me?"

I could almost hear the strain in his voice, trying so hard to make a good impression over the phone lines. "Yes, Jarrod. She said you might be interested in a job with my jam business."

"Yes, ma'am, absolutely. That is, if you have a job and you need someone, I'd like to apply or whatever." He sounded so earnest it almost made my teeth ache.

"Could you come to my place to talk about it? Say today or tomorrow?"

"Oh, yes, ma'am, I can do that. I've got time today. What time do you want me there?"

"Say around eleven? Would that work for you?"

"Absolutely. Yes."

"Do you know where I am?" I asked. Because not everyone did, although I tended to think of Shavano as one big, small town.

"Yes, ma'am. You're right down the road from Dolce."

I was used to thinking of Dolce as being right down the road from me, but that was a matter of perspective. "That's right. So I'll see you at eleven?"

"Yes, ma'am. Eleven. I'll be there."

I had a feeling he'd be sitting outside my door by ten-thirty, but that was okay. I'd rather have someone like Jarrod show up early. Early beat late.

Jarrod knocked on my door promptly at ten fifty-five. I wasn't sure what I was expecting—maybe a tall skinny kid with a prominent Adam's apple and acne. But what I saw was totally different. Jarrod Perrone was around five feet three or so and small boned. He looked like a natural target for bullies, and I hoped he had some self-defense moves of his own. He had dark hair that he continually pushed back over his forehead in a nervous gesture and dark eyes when I could see them. Like a lot of teenagers, he tended to stare down at his feet around older people.

At the back of my mind, I'd thought Jarrod was maybe Dolce's boyfriend. I'd never known much about her social life, but it stood to reason she had one. But Jarrod was a good three inches shorter than Dolce. As a Very Tall Person, I'd dated my share of men who were smaller than I. But the size difference here was extreme. Plus, now that I'd seen Jarrod in person, I was guessing he was a couple of years younger than Dolce.

"Come in, Jarrod," I said, sounding a lot more formal than I meant to sound. "Would you like something to drink? I've got coffee and iced tea." He'd probably have preferred a soda, but I was fresh out.

"No, no, ma'am, that's okay. I'm okay." His face flushed, he looked around the room quickly, as if he was trying to find a place to hide.

"Have a seat."

I gestured toward the couch, and he dropped down on it, grasping his hands in front of him, as if he wasn't sure what to do with them exactly.

"So I guess Dolce explained what she does here. It's mostly prepping the fruit for my jam, and then some jam making on your own after you get acquainted with the process." I figured I'd have Jarrod do the cleaning and chopping at first and let him watch Dolce and me do the actual jam making. That was how Dolce had started.

Jarrod nodded hard. "Yes, ma'am. I understand. Dolce talks about what she does a lot, and I've tasted some of her jam. It's really good."

"It is," I said. "She's learned quite a bit over the past couple of years." I felt another pang. Dolce was a natural in the kitchen. I had no guarantee that anybody who took over her job would do it as well as she did.

Jarrod nodded again. "I've done a little jam making. We tried it out at school."

"How did it go?"

For the first time he seemed to relax a little. "It had its good points and its bad points. We used frozen peaches, so it was a little watery. Dolce explained that to me, so I drained mine more than the other people in class, and it wasn't too bad. And I was careful with the sugar. A lot of the other people put in a bunch because they thought the peaches tasted weak. But I figured when I boiled the fruit it would concentrate the flavor more, so I held off on the sugar. It turned out to be just the right amount of sweetness."

"That was smart," I said and meant it. Overly sweet jam is one of my pet peeves.

Jarrod flushed again, this time in pleasure. "Thank you."

"Well, let me tell you what the job involves," I said, wanting to sound professional. "I'll need you here between eight and ten hours a week. Dolce usually shows up after she's through with school and stays until supper time. But she lives within walking distance. I don't know how hard it will be for you to get here. Are you driving yet?"

He shrugged. "Sort of. I ride my scooter just about everywhere. I can get here."

He could get here now, but we might need to reassess when the snow started falling. The drifts out here can get substantial. "I'd also like a couple of references if you can provide them. Dolce's already given you a good one." I'd decided I'd ask for references just to see what happened. If I was hiring an adult, I'd ask for them, and it didn't seem unreasonable for a kid.

Jarrod straightened. "Yes, ma'am. My home and consumer science teacher will give me one. And Mr. Nguyen."

"I heard you were working for Tal. Do you want to work two jobs?"

He shook his head. "I'd rather work for you if I can. I was hoping I might get to do some cooking for Mr. Nguyen, but all his cooks are part of the family. It's a great place, but I'd rather cook than sweep."

I was absolutely with him on that one. "Okay, I'll give you my email address. Have your teacher and Tal email me. And if you can come by tomorrow around eleven, Dolce can show you the kind of things she does for me."

Jarrod's smile lit up his whole face. "Yes, ma'am, I can absolutely do that. Thank you for giving me a chance."

"My pleasure, Jarrod," I said. And I really hoped that would be true.

Chapter 6

I made a quick trip to Laurel's place the next day to pick up more goat cheese. I could probably have gotten some at Ted Sylvano's market, but if I went directly to her house, I got to see the burros. Win/win.

Laurel was working in her cheese room with her assistant, Teri. The two of them wore white coveralls and head coverings that looked sort of like the shower caps you get at mid-level motels. Making cheese requires a lot of attention to hygiene because contamination can ruin a whole vat of cheese. Not all cheese makers were as tough as Laurel, but her cheese was terrific, so I wasn't about to argue with her methods.

I called her on my cell to let her know I was outside at the counter. It took her a moment to remove her food gloves and come out to join me. "Hey, Roxy," she said. "What do you need?"

"Nate wants a pound and a half of plain, and I want more of that cracked-pepper roll, if you've got it."

"I think I do. Hang on while I check."

A few moments later she returned with a box for Nate and a roll for me. "Here you go."

I dug out the money, then pocketed the receipt so Nate could reimburse me since the plain cheese was for the catering company.

"You want to go training with me and Peggy Sue again?" Laurel asked.

"Sure. When?" My sore muscles had recovered enough over the past couple of weeks to make me want to try getting up that mountain again.

"How about tomorrow afternoon around two? That way I can get some cheese made before I run myself into a collapse."

I frowned. "A collapse? Are you sure you want to do this?"

"Oh, I'm just being dramatic." Laurel waved a hand. "I need to get out and run. I've been working here or at city hall all week, and I'm brain dead."

Considering the guys she dealt with on the city council, that was an understatement. "Okay, I'll meet you at the trailhead tomorrow at two."

****

I got to the cabin a little before eleven, only to find Jarrod waiting patiently on the front steps. I hoped he'd settle down after he'd worked with me for a while. Dolce showed up as I was unlocking the door, and Bridget was there a few minutes later.

"Hi, you must be Jarrod," she said, extending a hand. "I'm Bridget Sullivan, but you can call me Bridget. Do you live over near Cheyenne Elementary?"

Jarrod looked a little overwhelmed. "Yes, ma'am. A block to the south."

"I thought I'd seen you around. I live over there, too. If you decide to take this job, we might be able to carpool."

Jarrod turned bright pink, and I figured he was either pleased at being recognized or embarrassed about not having a car to carpool with. On the other hand, if Bridget could give him a lift, that could take care of days when the weather was too threatening for his scooter.

"Bridget's in charge of the mail order business," I explained. "She keeps all the orders straight."

"And makes sure the FedEx guy doesn't forget to stop by and get the boxes," Bridget said darkly. "Amazing how forgetful those guys can be."

"Dolce can show you what she's doing now. It sort of varies by season, but this is our busiest time of year." We were busy enough, in fact, that I could afford to hire Jarrod along with Dolce to help.

I had several boxes of strawberries from the farm, along with a flat of blueberries and another of blackberries that I'd picked up over the weekend. The mixed berry jam was selling nicely, and so was Dolce's strawberry.

I felt another twinge: Dolce wouldn't be here to make the strawberry jam in a couple of months. If Jarrod stuck around, I hoped he'd learn how to do what she was doing now.

Dolce set Jarrod up hulling the strawberries and then chopping them into half-inch chunks. He had some good knife skills, which was useful. Trying to teach someone how to handle a knife from the ground up is time-consuming, not to mention risky. We didn't have time to run anybody to the emergency clinic because of a chopped finger.

I did a couple of batches of pepper peach and regular peach. We weren't quite in the fresh peach season yet, so I was working with the last of the frozen peaches I'd put up last year. Jarrod paused in his strawberry work to watch me empty the bags of still-frozen peaches into my jam pot and set the heat to low. I gave him a quick smile.

"You defrost the peaches on the stove?" he asked.

"You can let them defrost overnight in the

refrigerator, but I'd rather start with frozen peaches, so we don't lose too much juice."

After the peaches were mostly defrosted, I grabbed my potato masher and got to work reducing them to irregular chunks. I had a feeling Jarrod was still watching, but he was also chopping up strawberries, which was what I wanted him to do.

"Are you going to try the tomato today?" Dolce asked after a few minutes.

"I'll see how much time I have. I'd like to."

Jarrod looked a little confused, but he was too polite to ask what I was talking about. "I'm working on a tomato jam," I said. "It's for a seasonal special."

"Oh." He nodded, his brow furrowing as he took it all in.

"It's a savory jam," Dolce explained. "Sort of like ketchup."

I managed not to sigh.

I did get another version of the tomato jam onto the stove an hour or so later. I knew from experience that the fumes from the jalapeños could be fierce if the peppers were on the spicy side, so I put the pot on the back burner and warned everybody to stay clear if possible.

By three the tomato jam was done, and Dolce was ready to head off. "I need to help Mom with the honey this afternoon." She explained. "I'll clean up, though."

"I can do that," Jarrod said, then glanced at me. "If that's okay."

"That's fine," I said. "Go for it."

Dolce grinned her thanks then headed out the door. Jarrod finished a half hour or so later, sponging the last of the jam slick off the counter.

I figured he'd done enough for his first day and dug

into my purse for some cash to pay him. "Here you go."

He stared down at the money in his hand, then at me a little nervously. "Should I come tomorrow?"

"Absolutely." I paused. "If you want to, that is. Do you feel like this is something you want to do?"

"I want to." He gave me a shy grin. "It was fun. I learned a lot."

"Glad to hear it. See you tomorrow then."

Bridget and I watched him mount his scooter and putt-putt up the drive. The scooter was the kind I associate with Rome and *La Dolce Vita.* Very cool and all, but maybe a little lightweight for the Rockies.

Bridget turned to me. "Nice kid."

"Seems like it." I hadn't supervised Jarrod that closely, but every time I'd checked on him, he was doing a good job. And I figured Dolce would have set him straight if he hadn't done the strawberries to her specifications.

"He's riding a scooter from his house? That's a few miles from here."

"I know, but I figure it's okay for now. We'll see what happens in a couple of months. Assuming he's still interested in the job." Jarrod hadn't yet seen the craziness that erupted around getting the cases ready for the farmers market, after all.

Bridget picked up her purse. "I'll figure out a way to give him a ride part of the time. Maybe he can pay some on gas."

"That would be good. Thanks, Bridget."

I put the new version of the tomato jam into a couple of half pint jars and put them in the refrigerator without tasting them. I decided we'd rushed things the first time, tasting the jam before it was ready to go, and was determined to be more careful this time. Plus, I felt a little superstitious about it. If I didn't taste it right away, maybe it would taste the way I wanted it to.

****

Jarrod and Dolce finished all the berry jam by lunchtime the next day. I shooed them both on their way, then got ready to go off on the trail with Laurel and Peggy Sue. The parking lot at the trailhead was a lot emptier this time around. It was a weekday, after all, and that probably made it a little tougher for most people to take time off for training. Like me, Laurel could set her own hours.

She was parked at the side again. When I got there, she was leading Peggy Sue down the ramp from the trailer. The burro seemed a little impatient, as if she were annoyed she'd had to wait for these slow humans to get a move on.

"This time we'll probably go all the way to the top," Laurel explained. "But don't feel you have to keep up with us. Sixteen miles may feel kind of long for a day hike."

Sixteen miles felt long for any kind of hike, but then I was a well-established wimp. "I'll see how far I can go. But yeah, I probably won't make it all the way to the top."

Laurel fastened the pack saddle around Peggy Sue's middle, then attached a pick and shovel. "She's usually okay with all of this, but she needs to remember what it feels like to have a pick and shovel on her pack." She stroked the burro's neck. "How's it going there, Peggy?"

Peggy shook her head and took a couple of steps toward the trail, clearly anxious to be underway. Laurel chuckled. "Just a few minutes more, girl. We humans have to gear up." Five minutes later, loaded with water bottles and jackets that might be needed farther up the mountain, we hit the trail again.

After the last time, I'd decided to go with my own running shoes for burro training. Nate's trail runners were just a little too big, and I worried about blisters. And I wasn't about to deal with my heavy hiking boots on a trail where we wanted to make some time.

Laurel got Peggy Sue up to a trot without much urging. I had the feeling the donkey would probably have enjoyed an even faster pace, but Laurel and I were trying to save some energy for the higher track. We made it through the first couple of turns without losing much speed. At the first bunch of rocks, we slowed, and I heard someone call my name. I glanced up and saw Silas Goodman with one of his burros, pausing at a point farther up the trail ahead of us.

Silas is one of Uncle Mike's cronies, and he's about my uncle's age, too. He's also one of the Grand Old Men of burro racing, having been in on the beginnings of the sport in the eighties. He has a rotating herd of burros, some of which he owns and some of which are boarders, owned by burro racers who don't have the space to keep an animal at home. He also leases some of the burros out to tourists who want to either try burro racing or use pack animals for long hikes.

"Hey, Silas," I called. "Are you doing Laurel's race?"

Silas got a sort of foxy grandpa look. "Oh, I'm thinking about it. It's a tough trail, though, and sixteen miles round trip. That's a lot for an old guy like me."

That whine was, of course, crap. Silas was in his sixties, but he did the Fairplay long course regularly. I figured he was already playing some pre-race mind games. He was a pro, after all.

Laurel gave him a dry grin. "Don't worry, Silas. If you falter, Peggy Sue and I will make sure you get to the bottom okay."

"Thanks, sweetheart, I appreciate it." Silas returned the grin. "That's a pretty lady you've got there. Didn't you use her on the Georgetown race last year?"

Laurel nodded. "She did Leadville with me, too. She's a tough competitor. Are you still racing Stanley?"

Silas's grin faded. "Wish I were. This is Stanley's son Oliver. The old guy's gone out to pasture."

I didn't know if Oliver recognized his name or not, but he reached over and gave Silas a firm shove with his nose. Silas patted him on the neck. "Guess he's anxious to get on up the trail. See you ladies at the top." He grabbed hold of Oliver's lead rope and began a quick trot along the trail above us.

Laurel narrowed her eyes. "Old guy like him, my ass. He'll be pushing us all out of the way before you know it. And grinning while he does it."

We worked our way up the trail, moving a little more swiftly than we had the last time we'd run the course. At least Laurel and Peggy Sue moved more swiftly. I was still adjusting to the higher altitude. I knew racers who came in from the Midwest and gave themselves a few weeks to get used to running on less oxygen. Since I lived up here, you'd think it would be easier for me. But an extra thousand feet or so can really make a difference in your respiration. Plus I was out of shape.

I didn't want to hold Laurel back, but I also knew I couldn't go much faster than I was already going.

Finally, I waved a hand and dropped down on a smooth rock. "Go on, go for it. I'm going to catch my breath and then work my way down."

"Okay, if you're sure. We can always go a little slower." Saying that was mainly courtesy on her part. Of course, they could go slower, but neither of them wanted to, judging from Peggy Sue's impatient head toss.

Laurel didn't look all that sorry to take off without me, and I couldn't blame her. If she stayed at my pace, every burro on the mountain would be passing her on race day.

I watched the two of them trot up the next slope toward another rocky switchback. *Better them than me.* I wondered if Silas had already reached the summit and was headed down. The last time I'd been up with Laurel, the trip down had been a lot faster than the trip up. Laurel had kept ahead of Peggy Sue, since otherwise the burro would probably have dragged her down the mountain, and the two of them maintained a good pace all the way down.

Ah, well, this time I was on my own, so I'd have to take care of my own descent. I tied the sleeves of my jacket more securely around my waist and started down the mountain a lot more slowly than I had before. If I dawdled enough, somebody might catch up with me for company on the way down.

On the way up, I'd been mainly paying attention to my footing, trying to anticipate where the trail was going to get nasty. Now that I wasn't hurrying, I could take a little more time taking in the scenery. It was spectacular. We live in a gorgeous part of the Rockies.

The trail shifted from stands of pine to aspen groves, with the beginnings of alpine wildflowers dotting the green hillsides. An occasional breeze rattled through the aspen leaves as clouds passed overhead, shadows providing moments of cool in the midst of the intense mountain sunshine.

I'd just begun to wonder about the likelihood of an afternoon thunderstorm—always a possibility when you hike the high country—when from somewhere ahead of me, I heard a donkey's bray. Probably more burro racers training on the trail, but this burro didn't sound happy about it. I hoped I wouldn't run into someone who was mistreating his animal. That would need to be reported, but I wasn't sure to whom.

I rounded another curve and came out of the trees to see a small golden-brown burro standing by itself on the trail. As I watched, he threw back his head and brayed again, shaking the lead rope attached to his halter. He was wearing a pack saddle, but no gear was attached.

"What the hell?" I muttered, moving forward carefully. I didn't want to startle him, but at the same time I wanted to see where his handler was. It wasn't unheard of for burros to run away from their handlers, particularly if those handlers were beginners who didn't know what to expect. It also wasn't unheard of for those handlers to be injured when they parted company from their burros.

"Hey, there, boy. Where's your human?" I kept my voice gentle. If the burro had run away and was upset, he might not feel particularly friendly toward strangers.

He shook his head and pawed at the ground, both indications that he wasn't happy. I wasn't sure what to do, based on my limited burro experience. I reached out and stroked his nose carefully. "You're a pretty boy, aren't you? Did you run away?"

The burro pushed his golden nose against my hand, and I rubbed a little harder. Whatever had upset him didn't include me. "That's a good boy," I said softly.

He looked familiar in a way I couldn't quite define, and I didn't know why. He obviously wasn't one of Laurel's burros, and they were the only ones I'd spent any time with. Still, his coloring was distinctive, and I was sure I'd seen him before.

"Let's see if we can find your human." I picked up the burro's lead rope and started down the trail slowly. He seemed happy to follow along, his hooves clicking on the rocks as we descended.

I studied the brush and trees on either side of the road for signs of a struggle. I was guessing whoever had brought the burro up on the mountain hadn't let go without a limited fight. I was also searching for any other people on the trail who could help me, but we had everything to ourselves at the moment.

Below the next switchback, the burro came to a sudden halt, shaking his head again. "What's the problem, boy?" I peered around his shoulder trying to see into the dense stand of evergreens on the uphill side of the trail. A flash of color caught my eye under one of the trees. "Hello?" I called. "Anyone there?"

The burro jerked against its lead rope as I spoke. "It's okay." I reached out to rub his nose again, but he pulled away from me. I looked around for someplace I could tie the lead rope so that he wouldn't wander off while I checked out whatever was underneath the pine tree. The brush wasn't that sturdy, and putting the rope under a rock would probably lead to a missing burro.

"Hello?" I called again.

"Hello yourself," a male voice called. I put a hand

to my hammering heart then stepped back and peered up the trail. Silas and his burro were on the switchback above us. "What's going on?" he asked.

"I don't know. I found this little guy wandering around, and I'm trying to find his handler. I think there might be somebody in this clump of trees." I watched Silas climb down the trail above us. Oliver, his burro, wasn't all that excited about slowing down his descent.

"Okay," Silas said when he was level with me. "Give me the lead rope. I'll hold onto him while you see if his owner is around."

I handed over the rope gratefully enough and stepped into the evergreen grove. The dense thatch of branches blotted out a lot of the light, but the trees were a little farther apart as I walked away from the trail.

A man was lying face down in the center of the grove. On the trail, I'd seen the bright red of the bandanna he had knotted around his neck. "Um…hi?" I said, tentatively. When he didn't move, or give any sign that he'd heard me, I stepped closer. "Mister? Are you okay?"

Something about the stillness of that body made my throat tighten. I'd seen a few dead bodies in my time, but most of them had been clearly and thoroughly dead. This guy was just lying there. Very quiet.

You've got to check. You know that. I did know it, but I didn't like it. I leaned forward and put my hand on his shoulder. I felt the cool dead flesh through his thin cotton shirt. Yanking my hand away, I stumbled to the trail where Silas waited.

"Call 911," I gasped. "There's a dead guy in there."

Chapter 7

To his credit, Silas took me at my word and punched in the number on his cell. The Coalton cops didn't pay much attention, though. I guess they thought it was some kind of prank because they kept switching Silas's call from phone to phone.

Finally, he got someone whose name he recognized. "Brendan Kennedy, you listen to me," he snapped. "This is Silas Goodman. I'm up here on the Preservation Pass Trail and we've got a dead body. We're about a third of the way up and he's lying underneath a pine tree about ten feet off the trail. I'm holding onto his burro. You send some men up here, pronto. You understand me?"

Whatever Brendan Kennedy said was apparently better than what Silas had been hearing up until then because his voice moderated a bit. "That's right. I'm up here with Roxanne Constantine. She's the one who found the burro, and then she found him, too." He paused, rolling his eyes. "No, I don't know what happened. You need to get up here and figure it out."

A moment later he disconnected, grimacing. "That's what you get when you choose your cops based on whose nephew they are or how much money they contributed to the last city council campaign. At least he's on his way up here. Now whether he'll know what to do when he gets here—that's another question."

I took another in a series of deep breaths. This

wasn't how I'd expected to spend my day, that was for sure. The little burro turned to me, large brown eyes looking tragic. I reached out and rubbed his nose. "You knew that guy was here, didn't you, boy. You brought me right to him."

Silas rolled his eyes again. "Much as we'd all like to believe burros have superpowers, I doubt he led you to this guy. On the other hand, he may have smelled something he didn't like, which could explain why he stopped."

"What's going to happen to him?" I asked.

Silas looked confused. "You mean the dead guy?"

"No, the burro." The dead guy was undoubtedly important, but the burro was my immediate concern.

"Once we find out who the dead guy is, we can find out who owns the burro. If he belongs to the dead guy, we'll have to find somebody to take care of him. We'll take him down with us once the cops get their asses in gear." Silas handed me the burro's lead rope. "Here, you hold onto him while I tend to Oliver."

In truth, Oliver seemed sort of put out that Silas was paying so much attention to another burro. Silas rubbed a hand along the donkey's neck, murmuring something soothing, then dug into the pack on Oliver's back and pulled out a couple of carrots. "Here. Give this one to the little guy and remember to hold your hand flat." He stepped to Oliver and held out the other carrot.

I did as I was told. The little golden burro nibbled delicately at first, then snarfed up the carrot in no time. I rubbed his neck like I'd seen Silas rub Oliver's, and he seemed to like that, too.

Just then, I heard footsteps from above us and saw Laurel and Peggy Sue trotting down the trail. Laurel pulled up sharply a few feet away. "What's going on?"

Oh, Lord, where to begin? "We've got a sort of situation here," I stammered.

"What are you doing with Buster?" Laurel broke in, staring at the burro.

"You know this burro?" Silas asked.

Laurel nodded. "It's Kell's. Or anyway, it's the one he's using for the race."

My heart promptly dropped to my shoes. That was why I'd recognized the burro. It was Kell Moorhead's burro, Buster. And if this was Buster, the guy under the pine tree was most likely... *Oh, shit.*

"What's the situation?" Laurel asked, frowning.

"Roxy found a dead guy in there." Silas pointed at the pine grove. "We're waiting for the cops."

Laurel's eyes widened as she stepped toward the pine grove. "A dead guy?"

Silas was faster than me, catching her by the arm and pulling her back. "Don't go in there, sweetheart. Not until the cops have had a chance to check things out. Not that they're likely to find much as long as Brendan Kennedy's in charge." Silas sighed. "Have to bring in CBI on this one."

Laurel stood very still for a moment, then turned to me. "You saw him. Is it Kell?"

"I don't know. He's lying on his stomach, and I didn't see his face." *Thank God for that.*

"And you're sure he's dead." Her voice trembled a little, and I got the feeling she was working very hard on not losing control.

"I touched him, and he felt cold." I took another deep breath and managed not to shudder. "Yeah, I'm pretty sure he's dead."

At that very opportune moment, I heard voices below us and the sound of several pairs of boots hitting the trail. The voices didn't sound particularly happy to be there, but why should they be? None of us was happy either.

The first man to round the curve was around fifty and big, six feet three or so. He was also beefy, with a flushed face and thinning red hair combed across his scalp. He wore a khaki uniform that had seen better days. Brendan Kennedy, I was willing to bet.

He was followed by two younger guys, both glancing around as if they expected to see Jack the Ripper leap out of the underbrush. Based on their clothes, they were also cops. Based on their behavior, they hadn't been on the job long.

"Hey, Goodman," Kennedy grunted. "This where you've got your body?"

Silas showed admirable restraint in my opinion, in that he didn't do much more than harrumph. "It's not *my* body, Kennedy. We just found him. Far as I'm concerned, he's all yours." He gestured toward the pine grove. "He's in there. This is probably his burro here."

Kennedy stared at Buster for a moment then turned to Silas. "Who is he?"

"I don't know." He gestured in my direction. "I didn't go in there, Roxy did."

Kennedy turned my way and blinked, which is not an unusual reaction when someone encounters a six-footer like me. At least he was taller than I am, so we didn't have to play the game where he tried to assert his authority while staring up at me. He gave me a faintly suspicious look. "Who are you?"

"Roxanne Constantine," I said. "I'm from

Shavano."

If anything, Kennedy appeared even more suspicious. "What are you doing over here?"

"I was doing some training with Laurel and Peggy Sue, but I came down ahead of them." I wasn't sure why Kennedy was interrogating me instead of finding out who the dead guy under the pine tree was.

"Laurel?" Kennedy raised an eyebrow.

"Me," Laurel said, raising a hand. "And my burro, Peggy Sue. Roxy did the first three or four miles with us."

Kennedy checked back and forth between us, narrowing his eyes. He still looked suspicious, and he still hadn't bothered to check out the dead guy.

"Well?" Silas said. "Aren't you going to do some investigating?"

Kennedy checked back and forth again then glanced at the two baby cops still standing on the trail. "Watch 'em," he said, then stalked toward the pine grove.

The baby cops stared at us in confusion, maybe trying to figure out what we were likely to do that they needed to watch. Laurel stared at the pine trees as if she could see through them and identify the man lying inside. Silas rolled his eyes.

A moment later Kennedy stepped out of the trees, his face maybe a little less florid. He yanked his phone out of his pocket and punched in a number. "Hey, Myron, this is Kennedy," he said. "You need to get up on Preservation Pass Trail with a unit. There's a dead guy up here, and I need him down the mountain ASAP."

After he disconnected, Laurel stepped toward him. "Is it Kell? Is Kell dead?"

Kennedy narrowed his eyes again. "Why would you

think it's Kell Moorhead? Did you see him up here?"

Laurel gestured toward Buster. "I haven't seen him this week. But that's his burro. Roxy found it on the trail. Is it him, or did somebody else have that burro up here?"

"I can't comment on the identity of the deceased." Kennedy drew himself up as if he'd suddenly remembered he was chief of police, then surveyed the three of us like he was searching for clues. It occurred to me I'd never seen him when he wasn't looking suspicious. Maybe that was just his usual expression. Or maybe he figured we'd conspired to murder the dead guy for reasons yet to be determined.

"It's Kell, isn't it?" Laurel's shoulders slumped. "What happened?"

"That's what I want to know," Kennedy snapped. "What happened on this trail today? Why were you three all up here? What went down? How did you all end up next to a corpse?"

Laurel flinched when he said *corpse*, which I think was what Kennedy had in mind when he said it. I was beginning to think Brendan Kennedy was a both a jerk and a moron. My only close experience with cops up to now had been the smooth competence of Ethan Fowler and his Shavano guys. In fact, most of the cops I'd known in my life had been decent people trying to do a tough job with varying degrees of success. I'd never run into a cop I disliked on sight.

Until now.

Kennedy gave me his standard suspicious-cop look. "Let's start with you. What happened?"

"I came over here around two to train with Laurel. I parked in the parking lot next to her truck and trailer; then, she and I and Peggy Sue climbed up the trail. We didn't see anybody except Silas, and he was ahead of us."

"Peggy Sue?" Kennedy checked around the trail as if he expected to find someone hiding in the bushes.

"My burro," Laurel said, gesturing toward Peggy Sue. She looked like she was gritting her teeth. So did Peggy Sue.

Kennedy seemed to be examining that statement for hidden sarcasm. Peggy Sue herself shook her head impatiently. Clearly, she couldn't figure out why she had to stand around instead of heading down the mountain.

Kennedy turned his suspicious gaze on me again. "When did you find the burro?"

"I got tired and came down instead of going all the way to the top," I said. "I found Buster when I came to this part of the trail." I paused. "Well, actually it was a little above this spot. Buster led me down to this grove of pines."

"The burro led you here?" Kennedy's suspicion had morphed into sarcasm. I was pretty sure he didn't believe me, and I wondered if I needed to care.

"I was searching for his owner," I explained. "Buster has a pack saddle and lead rope. I figured someone had brought him up here, and maybe he'd run away from them."

Kennedy was vastly unimpressed. "So you just wandered down the trail trying to find some stray burro racer?"

"Pretty much." I gave him my most bland expression. "Buster led me down the trail and stopped here."

"And you went into the grove and found the guy?" Kennedy narrowed his eyes again.

"Well, not right away," I said. "I thought I saw

something in the pine grove as I was following Buster, so I called out to see if anybody was around, and Silas was coming down the trail just then. He called to me."

Kennedy glanced at Silas, who nodded. "I heard her calling *Hello* as I came around the bend with Oliver. I held the lead rope on the little guy while she went into the grove to see if someone was there."

"When did you get here?" Kennedy asked Laurel.

"After they called you," Laurel said. "I recognized Buster, and Silas told me about the dead man in the pine grove. I thought it might be Kell."

Her voice quavered, and I decided Brendan Kennedy was not only a jerkface moron, he was also cruel. He must know Kell Moorhead. They both worked for the city of Coalton. I couldn't see any reason for him not to tell Laurel whether the dead man was her ex-husband. She was clearly suffering, and he was clearly acting like an asshole.

Just then another group of men arrived, this time the medics from mountain rescue. I wasn't sure why Kennedy hadn't called the usual emergency crew from the fire station, but maybe he figured this qualified as some kind of rescue operation since it was up on a hillside. The guys were carrying a stretcher, and Kennedy set about directing them how to place the body on the stretcher and head down the mountain.

I was pretty sure this wasn't the way he should be doing any of this. In Shavano, Ethan Fowler would have waited until the medical examiner had signed off and his small forensics crew had finished collecting evidence before anyone would have touched the body. But Kennedy was clearly in charge, and nobody was interested in telling him how to do his job. Maybe he figured the dead guy in the pine grove had died a natural death.

I thought that was unlikely, but I didn't have anything much to go on except instinct. It just seemed improbable that someone would have staggered into the pine grove to have a heart attack. And I didn't see anything in there that could have caused a fatal accident. Unless the dead guy had been amazingly unlucky or amazingly clumsy, there was nothing for him to have stumbled over and fallen to his death.

"Hey, Brendan," Silas called, as Kennedy paused in his directions to the mountain rescue guys. "Can we go now? The burros need to get down the hill."

Kennedy scowled, as if he was trying to figure out whether Silas was dissing him at some level. Just then Silas's burro brayed lustily and kicked his heels in the general direction of one of the baby cops who'd come a little too close.

"All right, all right," Kennedy grumbled. "Go ahead. I've got your contact information."

That was the one thing the baby cops had managed to do, and for once I was thankful. Now we could leave before they brought out the body. That felt like a good idea to me, but not to everybody. Laurel stood at the edge of the grove, peering in. She looked miserable and confused. Not entirely sure what she should be doing.

Silas stepped beside her, putting his arm around her shoulders. "Come on, sweetheart, you don't need to be here."

She took a deep breath, then went to the trail, pulling Peggy Sue's rope gently. "I guess not. Come on, girl, let's get down the hill."

Silas followed with Oliver, which left me with

Buster. I guessed in the broadest sense, Buster was evidence, but I wasn't about to leave him on the trail where Kennedy might or might not have him taken to the bottom again. I figured he'd be far better off with Laurel or Silas than anyone Kennedy could supply.

We did the rest of the trail in silence. The burros followed each other placidly enough after Laurel had let Silas and Oliver go first. Oliver was a fierce competitor, or maybe he just didn't like seeing the back end of another burro. Laurel seemed numb, but she was concentrating on navigating the trail down and making sure Peggy Sue kept out of the rocks. I had no idea if I was doing the right thing with Buster, but fortunately he seemed to be fine with being led and with being at the end of the line.

We pulled into the parking lot a half hour later, and Laurel and Silas both began removing gear from their burros. I cleared my throat. "Any idea what we should do with Buster?"

They both looked up, frowning. In the confusion surrounding Kennedy and his "investigation" they must have forgotten all about Buster and what was going to become of him. Laurel turned to Silas, but he shook his head. "I'm full up right now with my own burros and the boarders. Plus Oliver doesn't work and play well with others."

Laurel bit her lip. "I can't take him either. Buttermilk's the same way, and a couple of my nans are about to have kids. All three of my burros are likely to be territorial."

They looked at me again, and I took a deep breath. "I can keep him if it's temporary. But I can't do it for very long. I don't have a good place for him." As it was,

Uncle Mike and Nate would both hit the ceiling, but they'd be more likely to accept the situation if they knew someone was going to come get Buster soon.

"I'm sure it will be. Give me a day or so to find out who owns Buster and leased him to Kell." Laurel paused, and I had a feeling she was pulling herself together again. "We'll find somebody to take him, Roxy. I promise. And I'll get him over to your place as soon as I take Peggy Sue to the farm."

That was also a relief since I had no trailer of my own and no way to transport a burro, no matter how docile. I waited in the parking lot, wondering if I'd still be there when Kennedy and his men brought the body down. I wasn't sure if that would be a good thing or a bad thing. If somebody in the group could take Buster, I'd be out from under the responsibility of taking care of him. But on the other hand, Buster and I had sort of bonded through all of this crap. He stood beside me now, rubbing his nose against my arm. I reached out and scratched his ears as his big brown eyes watched me dolefully.

I wondered if he'd been fond of Kell. I wondered if he'd miss him. I was still wondering things along those lines when Laurel pulled up again with her trailer. "Let's see about getting him into the trailer. Then we can head to Shavano."

I paused as Laurel began removing Buster's pack saddle. "That raises a point."

"What does?" Laurel squinted at me.

"The trailer. Where's the trailer that brought Buster here?"

Laurel glanced around the parking lot, frowning. "There's nobody here. But they could have hiked up from town. A lot of people training for the race have been doing that so their burros can get used to the distance."

"Would Kell have done that?"

Laurel gave me a stricken look that made me feel like a jerk. But we both knew the odds were that the guy up on the hillside was Kell. "Maybe. I think he was serious about the race."

"Did he have space to keep Buster at his place?" I had no idea where Kell lived, now that he didn't live with Laurel.

"Probably," Laurel said slowly. "He had a big yard. The house was a rental, but I don't think the owners would have minded if he kept a burro there."

"He said he leased Buster."

Laurel shrugged. "A lot of people do that, lease a burro for the season. That way they don't have to worry about year-round pasture and taking care of them in the winter."

I wasn't sure where to take the conversation next. What did I need to find out about burros anyway?

"I'll follow you," Laurel said. "You know where you're going to put Buster."

I do? Actually, I didn't. I headed for my truck, knowing the next couple of hours weren't going to be fun, either for me or the burro.

Chapter 8

I'd sort of been hoping that no one would be home at the farm when I got there. I needed time to get Buster situated without having to explain about him until I'd figured things out. But I was out of luck. Nate's SUV was parked next to the cabin—he had a rare afternoon off.

I pulled into my usual parking spot, and Laurel pulled up beside me. I got out and walked over to her truck as she opened the trailer. "Where shall I put him?" she asked.

Good question. I took a quick survey of the unfenced yard next to the cabin and rejected it. It wasn't like Buster was a dog you could chain up outside. In fact, I didn't hold with chaining up dogs either. "We might be able to use the dog run," I said.

Uncle Mike had put in a fenced area next to the main house where he could keep Herman when he didn't want him wandering around loose. Of course, putting Buster there would mean Herman would have to be kept elsewhere since dogs and burros don't get along all that well.

Laurel studied the yard, checking for other optimum sites. "He probably won't like being somewhere that smells like a dog. It could make him anxious. How about back there?" She gestured toward my vegetable garden, which was indeed fenced and currently not sporting any vegetables since I hadn't gotten around to planting a crop yet.

"I guess so," I said hesitantly. "Maybe he'll help dig the soil up, so I don't have to rototill."

"At the very least he'll provide you with some first-rate fertilizer." Laurel grinned, leading Buster toward the gate.

At that not particularly opportune moment, Nate stepped from the cabin. He paused, staring at Laurel and Buster, then turned to me. "Roxanne," he muttered, "what have you done?"

"It's just temporary," I said quickly. "His owner was killed on the mountain, and he needs a place to stay until we figure out who can take him."

Nate blinked. "What?"

I took a deep breath and gave him an abbreviated account of my afternoon on the mountain. He looked a little dazed by the end. "And no one else can take him?"

"Laurel's going to find out who Kell was leasing him from. They'll probably take him back, particularly if it's a burro ranch. Maybe they can rent him out again for the rest of the summer."

Nate stared at Buster as Laurel led him to through the open garden gate. "Do you think it was Kell up there?" he said more quietly.

I bit my lip. "I'm afraid it was. I didn't see his face, but whoever was lying in that grove was a young guy. And Kell claimed to be leasing Buster."

Nate sighed. "Shit."

"Shit is right."

Laurel stepped beside me. "Hi, Nate. Do you want me to close the gate, Roxy, or do you want to feed him now?"

"Feed him?" I stared at her. Until that moment I actually hadn't thought about feeding Buster. Did the feed store have burro kibble?

"Hay's best," Laurel said helpfully. "You can give him a handful of oats now and then. Carrots are good treats, and so are apple slices."

"Donnie probably has some hay he could let you have. I'll go ask him." Nate jogged off across the yard toward the McCrays' house.

I gave Laurel a look that was probably as helpless as I felt. "I've never done anything like this before. I hope I don't hurt him."

"He'll be fine." Laurel patted my shoulder. "Burros are very low key. Hay and water will work. And Buster seems gentle. After you have him for a couple of days, you may want to hang onto him."

"Roxanne," Uncle Mike shouted from the parking area, "what have you done?"

Or not.

Laurel left as I was explaining the situation to Uncle Mike. Nate and Donnie showed up a few minutes later, pushing a wheelbarrow with a hay bale. "You can't keep him," Uncle Mike said. "You know that, right?"

"I do know that. I'm just helping out in the middle of a bad situation."

Uncle Mike softened. He likes Laurel, and he's a sucker for a damsel in distress. He patted my shoulder. "It'll all work out, I guess. But we don't need a burro of our own."

By then we were surrounded by family and friends. Carmen and Dolce had come down to see Buster. Madge had come out the front door of the main house to see what all the commotion was about. Buster himself was regarding all of us with a troubled air, maybe trying to figure out if any of these people were likely to bring the hay bale a little closer to his enclosure.

"Nice animal," Donnie said. "Always did like burros." He reached out and rubbed Buster's ears.

"Useless," Carmen grumbled. "Just like horses."

"I like him." Dolce grinned at me. "How long can you keep him?"

"Until they find his owner or figure out who he should go to," I said. "He's such a pretty little thing and so gentle. I can't imagine there'll be any trouble."

Uncle Mike rapped his knuckles on the wooden fence post. "Knock on wood. Don't make statements that are likely to tempt your luck."

Madge gazed at Buster's big brown eyes, smiling. "Isn't he a sweetie. Maybe I'll go get him a carrot."

Uncle Mike rolled his eyes, but he wasn't about to say anything negative to Madge.

Just then Herman came galumphing out of the main house, probably muttering to himself about the annoyance of having his humans take off without refilling his food bowl. Buster moved away from the gate, pawing at the ground as Herman came closer. Herm was clearly curious about the new animal in his back yard.

"Better keep him back," Donnie cautioned. "Burros don't like dogs."

Uncle Mike grabbed Herman's collar, while Dolce frowned. "Why not?"

"Reminds them of coyotes and wolves," Carmen explained. "Burros are good at protecting sheep and goats. I'll give them that."

Dolce looked dubious. "How could a burro protect

anything from a wolf"

"They can raise a racket, and they do. If you ever hear a donkey hee-hawing its head off, better go find out what's up." Carmen narrowed her eyes at Buster. "Which isn't to say I want to hear much out of this one."

Buster made a sort of anxious sound, as he watched Uncle Mike drag Herman away. Buster and Herman were actually close to the same size, but I figured Buster would be using his hooves in self-defense if Herman came any closer.

"Come on, dog," Uncle Mike said. "Time for you to have some dinner."

"We'll keep him in the dog run," Madge said reassuringly.

Buster wasn't convinced that was far enough, but he seemed to relax a little as Herman retreated toward the main house with Uncle Mike and Madge. Donnie pushed the wheelbarrow with the hay bale a little closer to the garden. "You can bring the barrow when you get a chance."

I felt another of those jolts of panic I'd been feeling ever since I'd brought Buster to the farm. "Should I just give him the whole bale of hay? How do I do that?"

Donnie shook his head. "No, you don't want him to overeat, or to spoil the hay. Tell you what, I've got a hay bag from when we had Cottontail. I'll bring it over for you. Just pitchfork some hay in there and hang it from the fencepost. He'll graze from it."

"And water?" I asked. I figured I might as well get all my ignorance out front.

"You got any of those galvanized water tanks you grow flowers in?" Donnie asked. "Those would work fine."

Fortunately, I did have an empty water tank that wasn't in bad shape. It wasn't currently full of geraniums, which was also a good thing.

Nate raked hay into the hay bag, which resembled an oversized string shopping tote, then hung it from one of the fenceposts. I put the water tank into the garden and filled it from the garden hose. Buster watched us placidly enough, then ambled over to pull some hay from one of the openings in the hay bag.

We stood watching him for a moment, making sure this was all going to work. "Food and water," Nate said. "He's good for the night, assuming it doesn't rain."

I closed my eyes. I hadn't even considered shelter for the burro. I hoped I wouldn't need to.

"Come on," Nate said. "You've had a day. Let me feed you."

That sounded like a super idea, although it sort of put me on a level with Buster. I followed him inside and started looking for a bottle of wine while he finished up on the spaghetti and meat sauce he'd been making when I drove up with Laurel.

After dinner we sat out on the front porch, watching the sunlight disappear from the sky. Nate put his arm around my shoulders, pulling me close. "How freaked out are you by all the stuff with Kell?"

"I'm still sort of…shaken," I said. "One minute it was a nice afternoon on the mountain, and the next I'm finding a dead body in a pine grove. Not a normal day."

"No." He leaned his forehead against my hair, and I pressed closer, huddling in the warmth of his body as the evening air cooled. "You really think it was Kell?"

I blew out a breath. "Yeah. I do. I think he was murdered when Laurel and Silas and I were all up a little farther on the trail."

"Not an accident?"

"Unlikely."

Nate paused. "But you didn't see the burro on the way up."

"Buster?" I frowned, thinking of the scene on the trail. "I think I would have if he'd been there. I mean, I suppose it's possible he could have wandered off the trail and then wandered back after we'd passed, but I don't think he'd have been that easy to hide. If nothing else, I think Peggy Sue or Oliver would have known he was there and kicked up a fuss about it."

"So he and Kell must have come up after you did."

"I think so," I said. "Although Kell's truck and trailer weren't in the parking lot when we came down. Laurel thought he might have walked over from Coalton. That's the route the race will take."

"Do you have to go back tomorrow?"

I frowned. "Not so far as I know. The Coalton cops know who I am and where I am. If they need to find me, they can. Meanwhile, I've got jam to make for the farmers market. And Sylvano's. Ted emailed that they're running low."

Nate nuzzled my earlobe. "You free on Saturday night?"

"Probably. For what?" I envisioned several delectable possibilities.

"Helping me out with a private party. Dex has a family thing."

"Oh." I managed not to sigh. At least we'd be together on Saturday night, which was no small thing these days. At moments like this one I realized how much I needed to be with Nate now and again.

"Besides, you'll like this party." Nate returned to nuzzling my ear again, and I encouraged him.

"Why will I like this one?"

"Because it's the Blavatskys," he said triumphantly. "You remember them. Meatloaf and frozen peas?"

"Oh, Lord yes," I said. "They were so sweet." They'd hired Nate for a surprise anniversary family dinner featuring Mr. Blavatsky's favorite foods: meatloaf, mashed potatoes, and frozen peas. Not exactly your usual catered dinner, but Nate had done himself proud. They were a remarkably amiable family, and Mr. Blavatsky had been so pleased with the surprise dinner his wife had arranged that he'd given us all a big bonus. It was a very pleasant memory, even though Nate had been involved in a hit-and-run accident later that evening.

"It's Mrs. Blavatsky's birthday, and he wants a special dinner for her."

It had been fun, and Nate had done a superb job. But I wasn't up for doing it again. "Not meatloaf again."

He shook his head. "It's her favorite food this time. Roast chicken." He gave me a very satisfied smile, for good reason. Roast chicken is the test of a good chef, and Nate's a great chef. He loves doing it, and I knew he'd do a superlative job. Mrs. Blavatsky would have a very happy birthday.

"How about the rest of the dinner?" I asked. At the last dinner, we'd had to come up with retro apps and side dishes to complement the sort of retro meatloaf.

"Mr. Blavatsky wasn't specific beyond the chicken, so I'm thinking roast potatoes and steamed asparagus. Maybe hollandaise. Green salad to begin. Not sure about apps, but Dex has been working on crudités."

"How about a cheese plate? I could pick some up from Laurel, and if I take some jam to Sylvano's, he'll have some cheese, too."

"Perfect." He moved from my ear to my neck, and I was having a little trouble concentrating.

"Dessert?" I asked.

"Birthday cake. Coco's got a friend who's going into the custom cake business." He seemed to be losing his concentration, too.

Just as well. We had much more pleasant things to concentrate on. Which we proceeded to do. Every once in a while, it was good to remind myself just how lucky I was to have Nate in my life.

****

The next morning I went to check on Buster. The garden had one shaded corner, but the burro was standing out in the sun, yanking some hay from the hay bag. He seemed to have made it through the night without mishap. I pulled out the carrot I'd tucked into my pocket and offered it to him then I rubbed his neck.

"How's it going, Buster?" I murmured. "Any bad memories?" It stood to reason that Buster had been around when Kell had been killed, but maybe he hadn't realized what was going on.

I wondered if I could find out if the victim had been positively identified yet. I could probably have phoned Laurel, but that felt a little insensitive. Kell might have been a loose cannon with questionable ethics, but he was still her ex-husband.

I wondered if Fowler would know or could find out.

No. Don't even go there. I hadn't had any dealings with the Shavano Chief of Police since Uncle Mike and Madge had gotten married on New Year's Eve. I'd seen him around, but we hadn't even had a conversation. And I figured it was best to leave it at that.

Fowler and I had a complicated relationship, more friendly than not, but not always friendly. And Fowler and Nate didn't always get along.

"Wow. Is that a burro?"

The voice had me twisting to see who was behind me. Jarrod stood there with his scooter. I'd been cogitating too hard to hear him putt-putt down the drive. "Yeah," I said. "I'm burro-sitting for a while. This is Buster."

Jarrod approached cautiously, although his huge grin wasn't cautious at all. "Wow," he repeated. "I've never seen a gold-colored one before."

"He's pretty unusual," I agreed. I knew not all burros were gray, but Buster's gold was unique.

"Can I pet him?"

"Sure. He likes having his neck rubbed."

I kept my hand on Buster's nose, just in case he wasn't happy with having a stranger come so close. But he seemed to be okay with Jarrod, leaning into his neck rubs like a cat trying for scratches.

"Do you want to take him around for a walk so he gets some exercise?" The idea had occurred to me when I realized Buster didn't have a lot of room to walk around inside the garden fence.

"Sure." Jarrod gave me a huge grin, as if I'd awarded him an awesome prize. "I love animals. We've got a couple of dogs at home and a guinea pig. When I was a kid, I really wanted to live on a farm."

I managed not to roll my eyes. When I'd been a kid, I *had* lived on a farm. It wasn't all that magical. I found the halter Donnie had taken off Buster yesterday and put it on again, attaching the lead rope. "Maybe just walk him around the farm. But don't get too close to the dog run—he's not a dog fan. And Herman might get jealous."

"Got it." Jarrod took the lead rope then carefully guided Buster through the gate. I watched them head down to the drive and then across to the open field that lay at the front of the property. Buster could eat a little grass and a few wildflowers if they were to his taste. With Jarrod holding the lead rope, he couldn't veer off into the arugula.

Dolce arrived a few minutes later, smiling when she saw Jarrod and Buster. The two of us got the jam pots going with strawberries and the mixed berry mélange. We were coming to the end of the berry season, so I was getting some decent prices on bruised and unlovely fruit. That wouldn't affect the jam quality, and I'd probably put the mixed berry on special at the market that weekend.

The tomato jam I'd made with extra jalapeños had had enough spiciness, although it still wasn't entirely right. I decided I'd spend a little more time experimenting that afternoon to see if I could come up with the right formula.

After Jarrod brought Buster to the garden, he thoroughly washed his hands and started working on the berries. Bridget arrived a half hour later, "Is that the burro I've been hearing about?" she asked me as she tucked her lunch into the refrigerator. "The one that you found when you found Kell Moorhead?"

I was a little taken aback that the news about Kell and the burro had traveled so fast, but I shouldn't have been. Bridget worked at one of the more popular restaurants in town, and she could have heard about

Buster and me from any number of people. "I found him yesterday, but I don't think it's been confirmed about Kell." Not that I'd heard, anyway.

"Oh, yeah, it has. That big oaf Brendan Kennedy was spreading it all over Coalton, so of course it spread to Shavano."

That fit with my assessment of Brendan Kennedy, although it was probably not the way to instill respect for authority among our younger employees. "Did he at least tell Laurel before he spread it around town?"

Bridget shrugged. "He should have, obviously. But that doesn't mean he did."

No, of course it didn't. I was pretty sure Laurel had concluded the victim was Kell, but she hadn't had confirmation. I grabbed my cell phone and stepped out onto the porch. Laurel answered after a couple of rings. "Hi, Rox. I'm on the track of somebody to take Buster, but I haven't nailed him down yet."

"That's okay, we're fine. Are you okay?" Which was as close as I could come to asking her outright if she knew her ex-husband was dead.

There was a pause on her end. "Yeah," she said finally. "I'm okay. I was pretty sure it was Kell, so it wasn't a shock to find out. They had me identify him."

Oh good grief. Kennedy wouldn't think about how unfeeling it was to keep Laurel in the dark at first and then make her identify the body. "Do you want to come over here?" I would have offered to come over to her place, but I was up to my hips in chopped berries, and I didn't want to leave.

"No, I've got cheese to make. I'm doing all right. But thanks anyway, Roxy. I appreciate it."

"That's okay. I guess I'll see you Saturday at the

market."

"I'll be there. Does Nate need anything?"

"Oh, yes, thanks. I almost forgot." I rattled off Nate's standard order, hoping it would match what he wanted on the cheese plate for the Blavatskys. Even if it didn't, I figured the cheese would be used up one way or another. Laurel's cheese never went uneaten.

"Okay, I'll bring it on Saturday. Bye, Rox. Thanks again."

I hung up, feeling a little useless. I had wanted to make sure Laurel was okay, but I wasn't sure I had. She *sounded* fine, but was that enough? I made a quick check on Buster. He was standing inside the garden fence, looking doleful. But I didn't know him well enough to know if that was something new or his normal expression.

Get to work, Roxanne. You've got tomato jam to perfect. Do not *waste time worrying about a donkey's mood.*

Good advice. I needed to work on taking it.

Chapter 9

The rest of the week flashed by in a blur of jam making and burro raising. Jarrod took charge of Buster's morning walk, and I walked him around a little at the end of the day. I felt a little guilty about his cramped quarters in my garden plot, but there was no alternative.

A couple of days later, Laurel called. "Okay, I found the guy who actually owns Buster. I guess Kell was just leasing him for a couple of months, which makes more sense than him leasing the burro for the entire summer. The owner is named Dusty Vance, and he has a burro ranch outside town. Should I have him come pick Buster up? Is there a time when somebody will be around to show him where Buster is?"

"Sure, have him come. I'm usually around during the morning, and if I'm not, Uncle Mike will probably be here. Actually, Buster's not that hard to find since he's still in my garden. But I've got his pack saddle in the barn where Uncle Mike has his office."

"Okay, good enough. I'll give Vance a call."

I felt a bit of a pang after Laurel hung up. I'd gotten used to Buster, with his soulful brown eyes and docile demeanor. We'd done a little communing over his morning carrot. I'd miss him, and so would Jarrod. In fact, Jarrod would probably miss him more than I would.

I told him the news when he came in from walking Buster. "Laurel Beacham found Buster's owner. He's supposed to come pick him up some morning this week."

Predictably, Jarrod's expression became somber. "Oh. I guess that'll be good for him. Going where there's more space and all."

"I'd say so. He'll have more room. And he'll be with other burros again." I was making all of that up. I had no idea whether Dusty Vance had more room for Buster, and I was just working on the assumption that he had other burros. Since he was in the burro rental business, that seemed likely.

We returned to work, although I took a few minutes mid-day to make sure Buster had enough water and that his hay bag was still relatively full. When Jarrod went out to say goodbye before he putted off down the road on his scooter, I was very careful not to be around. I already felt guilty for not offering the burro a permanent home. Of course, since both Nate and Uncle Mike were firmly opposed to the idea of another animal, and since Buster belonged to somebody else, that decision had been pretty easy.

Around three, after everyone else had gone home for the day, a battered pickup truck with a horse trailer came jouncing down the drive toward my cabin. It had to be Vance, although he was significantly later than I'd thought he'd be. Fortunately, I was around, loading cases of jam for the trip to the farmers market tomorrow.

The truck rolled to a stop about midway between my cabin and the main house. The man who climbed out was less than impressive—maybe five-feet-six or so, lank hair the color of corn silk, faded jeans and plaid shirt with a tear along the pocket. He stopped about six feet away from me. "You Roxanne Constantine?"

I nodded. "That's me. Are you Mr. Vance?"

He nodded back. "Come to get my donkey."

"I'll show you where he is." We climbed the short slope up to the garden plot.

Buster saw me coming and ambled over to the gate. I dug into my pocket and pulled out the piece of carrot I'd taken to carrying around. Buster extended his neck over the garden gate and delicately picked the carrot up off my hand.

Vance stood behind me, radiating impatience.

"He likes carrots," I said, watching Buster chew it down.

Vance didn't seem particularly impressed. "Most of 'em do."

I sighed inwardly. It was probably too much to hope that Buster's real owner would share my affection for the little guy. "I'll get his stuff."

A few minutes later Vance had Buster in his halter and had put the pack saddle into his truck. A man who'd obviously done this hundreds of times before, he got the donkey into the trailer with a minimum of struggle. I wondered if I'd look like a complete goof if I went up to the trailer and said goodbye.

Probably.

I stood watching as Vance closed the trailer.

He paused for a long moment, maybe wondering what I expected him to say. In fact, I hadn't a clue. "I owe you anything?" he asked, finally.

"Owe me?"

"For the burro. He cost you anything?"

"Not really," I said. The hay and water had been free, and I didn't begrudge him a few carrots. I suppose I could have charged him for Jarrod's time, but that seemed stupid.

"Okay, then, I guess we're square." He turned on his heel and headed for the truck.

A thank you would have been nice. I watched him head up the drive again, wishing I didn't feel like I should have done something more. Just because this Vance person wasn't talkative or especially polite didn't mean he'd be mean to Buster. He'd handled the donkey with brisk efficiency, the way most farmers handled their livestock. But most farmers treated their livestock decently since those farmers knew just how much those animals were worth.

"You'll be fine," I muttered. I wasn't sure whether I was talking to Buster or myself.

****

I got to the market early the next morning, with plenty of time to set up. I was just arranging the jam jars into something approaching a pyramid when Laurel walked up. "I've got Nate's cheese. Do you have somewhere you can keep it?"

"Sure, I've got my cooler." It currently held my lunch, but I figured I could fit the cheese in around my sandwich and fruit.

"Did Vance show up?" Laurel asked as she handed me the cheese.

"Yesterday afternoon. He seemed sort of…terse."

"He's not exactly loquacious." Laurel shrugged. "He's got a ranch on the road to Geary, raises burros mostly. He's also got a boarding stable. He's one of the ones who rents out burros to the tourists."

"So he treats them okay?"

Laurel gave me a narrow-eyed look. "Don't tell me you lost your heart to Buster."

"Not really. Even if I had, Nate and Uncle Mike

would take him right back to Vance themselves if I tried to keep him."

"Those big brown eyes will do it every time." Laurel grinned as she shook her head. "If you get lonely, come around and talk to Peggy Sue. She's always up for a little companionship."

If I got lonely, I already had Nate, who was much more fun to cuddle than Buster. But I appreciated the offer.

My assistant, Beck, and I sold a lot of jam, although I'd become better at estimating how much we'd need each week, so we didn't sell out of our perennials. It was just too bad Beck wasn't interested in cooking, given that Jarrod wouldn't be around full time after the school year started.

And I already missed Dolce. Jarrod was a nice kid, and he did a good job chopping fruit, but he wasn't what I was used to. Not that that was his fault.

I broke my booth down when the market closed at two, then drove over to Robicheaux's Café where Nate was working in the catering kitchen. "I've got the goat cheese from Laurel."

"Great. I've got some cheddar and a chunk of sausage from Marcus, along with Bianca's baguettes. You have time to make me some crostini?"

"Sure." It had been a while since I'd done any work in the catering kitchen. I was glad Nate had hired Dex as his assistant and that Dex could work full time when he wasn't substitute teaching. But sometimes I missed the camaraderie of getting the special meals ready for Robicheaux Catering. Back in the early days of the business we worked together, figuring out the menus and then preparing the food. I wasn't sad that the business had grown so much, but I did have some nostalgia for the *before* times.

I sliced one of the baguettes into thin pieces then drizzled them with olive oil and a little salt and put them in the oven to crisp up. They'd be terrific spread with goat cheese and maybe topped with a slice of Marcus Jordan's garlic salami.

"Everything else ready?" I asked. The kitchen was full of divine smells, which told me the roast chicken was pretty much done and pretty much perfect. Nate had done some extra breasts and legs, just to make sure there'd be enough meat, and he was roasting them all at the various times required to make them sublime.

He gave me an absent smile. "We're good. You want to go home and change? I've got my stuff here."

I was wearing a decent pair of jeans and a Luscious Delights T-shirt, which had been great for the farmers market. But they were a little on the casual side for a catering gig. "Okay. Should I come back and meet you?"

He shook his head. "I'll swing by and pick you up. The Blavatskys' place is on the other side of the farm."

****

I still had my black chef's coat and beanie from my very brief career as a line cook when I was fresh out of culinary school. I wore them sometimes when I worked formal gigs. But the Blavatskys were having their party at their house, and I didn't want to get too fancy. Having a couple of chefs in coats and toques in your kitchen for a birthday party would probably count as over the top. Instead, I found a pair of khakis I wore when I wanted to look good but not that good, along with a button-down shirt with rolled-up sleeves. When I got to the Blavatskys' place, I'd put on my Robicheaux Catering apron and possibly the matching ballcap, depending on how conscientious I was supposed to be about keeping my shoulder-length curls out of sight.

Nate pulled up in the catering truck at four-thirty. This was a new addition to the fleet of vehicles we now commanded—a panel truck outfitted with built-in containers that would keep the food warm or cool depending on what we wanted. Madge had bought it from another caterer a few towns over who was leaving the business. It wasn't luxurious by any means, but it did the job. It was also equipped for the mountains where we lived: all-wheel drive and sturdy tires that could climb over the nastiest ruts. We didn't get many situations where we had to drive through crap to get to a catering job, but now we were ready for them if they arose.

We were supposed to be at the Blavatskys' house at five so that we could get the apps set up and the rest of the dinner warmed and ready to go. The chicken was almost roasted, but Nate would crisp the skin in a hot oven, along with the roasted fingerling potatoes. By that point in the summer, I was usually sick of asparagus. But Nate was going to whip up some hollandaise that would make the difference between everyday asparagus and elevated asparagus.

"Who's our server?" I asked as we unloaded the food from the catering truck into the Blavatskys' kitchen.

"Donnell," Nate said, naming one of our veterans. Most of the servers for the catering company also worked for the café. Since the café didn't serve dinner, many of them had free time in the evening and were perfectly happy to pick up some extra cash serving private parties.

Mr. Blavatsky helped us get everything inside. I

wasn't sure what he did, but he seemed to be successful at whatever it was, judging from the size of the house and the furnishings, to say nothing of the kitchen with its shiny appliances. On the other hand, it didn't occur to him to let the hired help carry the pots and pans into the house. He gave me a blissful smile after we'd gotten everything inside. "Sure smells good," he said.

"It'll taste wonderful," I assured him. "Nate loves to do roast chicken."

"Great." He grinned again. "My daughters came by and set the table this afternoon. Looks terrific. Well, I'll get out of your hair."

"What time should we plan on serving?" Nate asked before he could duck out the door.

Mr. Blavatsky paused, blinking. Apparently, he hadn't thought everything through. "Seven? Would that work for you?"

Nate nodded. "That'll be fine. We'll have it ready to go."

I got to work setting up the cheese and sausage with crostini. Last time we'd been at the Blavatskys' it had been Mrs. Blavatsky who'd been in charge, and everything ran like clockwork. Mr. Blavatsky seemed a little more vague about what he needed to have done and when, but we could work with him. By now, Nate had worked for everyone from high society to a barbecue joint.

"What else goes out with the apps?" I asked him.

"Crudités. There's a bowl of dip in the cooler. And Dex threw together some pinwheels with ham and cheese just so we'd have everything covered."

"More than covered, I'd say." I took out the platters we'd brought for the apps and started arranging pinwheels in roughly symmetrical patterns.

We had the first serving of apps arranged on tables in the living room before Donnell arrived. She grinned at Nate as she stepped into the kitchen. "I remember this place. Meatloaf, right?"

"Right. Tonight it's chicken. I'll carry it out and let everybody see how pretty it looks, then bring it back in here for carving. You and Roxy can bring out the sides. And there's a salad to go out on the table in a little while."

"Got it." Donnell draped her jacket over one of the kitchen chairs. "How about apps?"

"First round's already out in the living room. But you can check to see what needs refills. I don't how many people are out there now."

"Bartender?"

"Customer's taking care of it." Mr. Blavatsky did the pouring himself.

The next forty-five minutes were spent getting everything ready to be served, whenever we finally got it on the table. At the anniversary dinner, Mrs. Blavatsky had been like a general organizing a campaign: she had a schedule, and everybody stuck to it. For this dinner, Mr. Blavatsky was more like an indulgent granny making sure everybody was having a good time. He'd said seven, but the closer we got to the hour, the less likely it was that the people in the living room would be moving to the dining room table any time soon.

Nate's jaw was getting tighter as he checked the clock. The chicken would be perfect at seven. That's what he'd planned on. It would still be very good at seven-fifteen, although not perfection. By seven-thirty, things would begin to trend downhill. I could almost see his blood pressure rise as I watched.

"Let me take the last crudité refills up. I'll make sure Donnell put the salads out on the dining room table, and that everyone knows they're there. Maybe when Mr. Blavatsky sees food on the table, he'll remember he's supposed to herd the guests into the dining room." I grabbed the container with the remaining crudités and headed out to the living room.

I found Donnell and made sure the salads were in place. Meanwhile I put out the veggies and gathered up the empty pinwheel platter, trying unsuccessfully to catch Mr. Blavatsky's eye.

"Yeah, I don't know what they're going to do now that Moorhead's dead," someone nearby said.

I paused. I didn't normally listen to conversations when I was working, but the mention of Kell's name made me glance quickly to the side to see who was speaking. Two men, neither of whom I recognized.

"He was the point man," the other man said. "Pristine Refuse was talking to him. I don't know if the whole deal falls apart now."

I slowed down my refresh of the crudité tray, hoping they'd go into a little more detail, but as I straightened, someone put a hand on my shoulder. I turned around to see Mrs. Blavatsky, wearing a terrific red dress and some spectacular diamond earrings. "Hi, there," she said, grinning. "I bet Art has forgotten when he said dinner was going to start. Am I right?"

"Well, he said seven. I'm still hoping we'll make that." Although I had to admit everybody looked very settled in the living room.

"We'll be there," Mrs. Blavatsky said firmly. "Tell Nate to get ready." She had her general-in-charge expression in place. Even though she hadn't planned this party, she was about to exercise a bloodless coup.

Back in the kitchen Nate's jaw was still rigid. "Any movement?"

"There will be. Mrs. Blavatsky is assuming command. She told me to tell you to get ready." I stacked the empty platters on the counter. Donnell would finish clearing once the guests had shifted to the dining table.

"Is she coming down here? Do we need to hide the birthday cake?" Nate's gaze darted around the kitchen.

"Relax. I don't think she's coming, but if she does, I've already put the cake cover over it." Mr. Blavatsky had supplied us with a terrific cake plate with a matching cover, and we'd transferred the birthday cake from its box to the plate when we'd been setting up.

"You're a jewel among women." Nate gave me a quick kiss, then went to deal with the chicken.

Five minutes later, Donnell breezed in carrying the empty tray that had held the salad plates. "Everybody's at the table. I'm guessing fifteen minutes on the salad."

"Sounds about right."

I held the platter as Nate transferred the chicken from the roaster. It was a spectacular shade of golden brown, like something a food stylist had been slaving over for a couple of hours. Nate arranged branches of rosemary at the sides of the platter, then stuffed the cavity with fresh herbs so that they completed the greenery effect. He inserted some orange quarters here and there. The whole effect was gorgeous

He raised an eyebrow at me. "Potatoes and asparagus?"

I gestured at the crispy roasted potatoes piled in their bowl and the asparagus laid out like a stack of logs on a matching platter. "Is the hollandaise ready?"

"In the silver sauce bowl. All it needs is a serving spoon."

I found the serving spoon and placed it next to the bowl. We were ready to go as soon as Mrs. Blavatsky gave us the high sign. Or Mr. Blavatsky. Or anybody, really.

Finally, Nate decided to go for it. I placed the chicken platter in his arms, and he headed out toward the table. "Tonight's entrée is roast chicken," he said diffidently.

There were the expected oohs and aahs. Mrs. Blavatsky looked ecstatic. Mr. Blavatsky looked terrified. "Can you take away the decorations so I can carve it?"

Nate smiled. "We'll take care of the carving." He headed toward the kitchen where I had the carving set and cutting board all set up.

"Sounds like it was a hit," I said.

"Or something." Nate lifted the bird onto the cutting board and got to work. When you know what you're doing, carving a chicken takes no time at all: drumsticks, wings, sliced breast and thigh meat, and lots of tasty tidbits. Nate added the extra breasts and legs to the platter, and the result was bountiful. He shouldered the tray again, and Donnell and I followed him out with sides. At the last minute I grabbed the basket with some of Bianca's delectable dinner rolls.

It was a hit, judging by the emptiness of the platters after an hour or so. We still had birthday cake and ice cream to come, but the evening had relaxed into a series of raucous toasts. We figured Mr. Blavatsky or one of his family members would let us know when they wanted us again, so we settled down with the tail end of Laurel's cheese and the crostini.

"I heard something strange out there when I was doing the apps," I said as I spread some goat cheese.

Nate narrowed his eyes. "Regarding the food?"

I shook my head. "Regarding Kell Moorhead. And his death. Somebody said he was doing some kind of deal with something called Pristine Refuse. Ever heard of them?"

"Nope. Sounds like a contradiction in terms. Or like a fancy name for a trash collector."

"Yeah, it does. Maybe I'll look them up if I remember."

Just then the door swung open, and Donnell came in with an empty bottle of wine. She'd been doing refills during dinner. "They're almost done," she said. "Do we have to get the candles on that cake?"

I shook my head. "He went with the tactful version." I picked up the single flower- draped-candle. There was even a flower-draped holder to go in the cake.

"Nice." Donnell grinned. "Probably need to get it out there."

Nate sighed, pushing himself to his feet. "Showtime."

Chapter 10

I promptly forgot about Pristine Refuse for the rest of the evening. We were too busy cutting cake and dishing ice cream and pouring champagne for the last toast of the night. Mrs. Blavatsky was tearful, and Mr. Blavatsky looked suspiciously bright eyed while their friends and relations all cheered lustily. The cake, made by Coco's friend, was a big hit, which was a relief to Nate since he'd recommended her.

Mr. Blavatsky gave us a bonus, which we split with Donnell who grinned as she tucked the money into her purse. "I've always liked working for these folks."

We loaded all the pots and pans into the truck, but this time we decided to go straight home rather than stopping to unload everything at the catering kitchen. Tres, the café's janitor/dishwasher, didn't work on Sundays, so we'd need to load them in the dishwasher ourselves.

And that was a job that could wait until tomorrow afternoon.

Back at the cabin, I dug out some sausage from Marcus Jordan's shop along with a jar of brown mustard and the end of a loaf of sour dough. Not exactly a banquet, but enough for a late- night reconnoiter. Nate pulled a couple of bottles of beer out of the refrigerator and sank down beside me at the kitchen table. "Another one taken care of."

"It was fun. I love that couple."

He nodded. "Good people. Here's hoping they keep having parties they want us to cater." He reached over to rub my shoulder. "Thanks for helping out. You're a lifesaver, along with being a great sous chef."

"I enjoyed it." And would go on enjoying it as long as it was only an occasional thing. Still, I always liked working with Nate.

He sawed off a chunk of sausage. "I noticed the burro has departed."

"The guy who owned him came with a trailer yesterday afternoon."

"He's probably happier where there's a field he can roam around in."

"Probably." I still felt a little blue about Buster's exit, but I wasn't about to admit it.

Nate paused. "We could always get another dog. Herman would probably enjoy the company."

I sighed. "I'm okay. I don't need a dog to cheer me up now that my donkey's gone." Of course, he wasn't my donkey, really. He'd just felt like mine for a couple of days.

"Any news about Kell? Any suspects?"

I shook my head. "Not that I've heard. Unless they find a witness, it may be hard to solve. So far as I know, they've got nobody."

As it turned out, however, that wasn't exactly true.

****

Laurel called me mid-morning on Monday. "Hey, Roxy. Could you do me a favor?"

Her voice sounded sort of tight, not the normal easy breezy Laurel. "Sure, if I can. What's up?"

"I'm at the police station, and I may be here a while.

109

My cheese-making assistant can take care of the goats, but I need somebody to feed and water the burros. I hate to ask, but could you…"

"Of course," I said. "Are you likely to be there long?" I wanted to ask her what was going on, but if she was at the police station she might not be free to talk.

"I don't know exactly. I just want to make sure the burros are okay." Now she sounded more than uptight. In fact, her voice was trembling.

"Laurel, do you need me to come to the station? Are they accusing you of something? I can tell them I was with you. I know you had nothing to do with what happened to Kell." The whole thing sounded ludicrous, but Brendan Kennedy hadn't struck me as a logical thinker.

"I…" Laurel paused. "Actually, if you could recommend a good lawyer, I think that might be more helpful right now."

"Hang on," I said. "I'll call Madge. She'll know somebody. I'll text you the information." My aunt by marriage knew everybody, including every decent lawyer within hailing distance.

Fortunately for both of us, it was after the noon rush at the café, so Madge was available to talk. "Hi, Roxy," she trilled. "What do you need, sweetheart?"

I explained what I'd heard—and hadn't heard—from Laurel and asked for recommendations. I kept my own indignation under control, but it was probably obvious to Madge.

"That's horrible!" she said. "That's…idiotic. Laurel Beacham wouldn't have had anything to do with that murder. You give me her number. I'll get someone over there right away."

I figured Madge would be much more effective than I would in rescuing Laurel. When that woman was pissed, she was a force of nature, and she sounded well and truly pissed. But that left me with burros to take care of.

Jarrod was chopping strawberries for Dolce when I came into the kitchen. "How far along are we on the strawberry jam?" I asked.

Dolce gave me a quick smile. "Far enough. We can probably shift over to peaches now."

"Actually, I've got something else for Jarrod to do, if he's free."

Jarrod frowned as he turned to me. "I'm as free as I ever am, I guess. What do you need me to do?"

"Take care of some burros," I said.

Jarrod's face lit up. Clearly, taking care of burros beat chopping strawberries.

I explained as much as I could on the drive over to Laurel's place. Jarrod had been feeding and watering Buster during his brief stay with us, so he had a rudimentary idea of what the burros needed. I figured I could leave him at Laurel's place to look after Peggy Sue and her buddies while I went into town to find out what was happening with Laurel. Given his devotion to Buster, Jarrod would probably enjoy it.

Meanwhile, I was going to remind Brendan Kennedy that Laurel had a witness who could vouch for her whereabouts while somebody else was killing Kell.

I helped Jarrod find the food and water for the burros at Laurel's place and then introduced him to Peggy Sue. I figured if Peggy Sue vouched for him, Buttermilk and Spats would go along with it. After that, I drove on toward Coalton. I'd never been to their police station, but given the town's small size, I figured it couldn't be that hard to find.

It wasn't. The small concrete block building with a sloping red roof squatted on the corner across from the courthouse. *Coalton Police* was printed on a sign outside. I parked in the city lot and grabbed my purse, ready to storm the ramparts to learn who was holding Laurel and why. As it turned out, *storming* wasn't necessary. Brendan Kennedy stood next to the counter and gave me a jaundiced glance. "Help you?"

"I'm here for Laurel Beacham. Is she still back there?" I gestured toward the hall that seemed to lead to more rooms.

Kennedy raised an eyebrow. "You a lawyer?"

"No." I was pretty sure I knew what was coming.

"Then you got no reason to see her." He started to move away.

"You remember I told you I was with Laurel until I turned around halfway up the mountain," I said flatly. "We didn't see Buster. He wasn't there. Which means Kell Moorhead wasn't there either. Which means Laurel had nothing to do with what happened to him."

"Who the hell is Buster?" Kennedy asked.

"He's the burro. Kell's burro."

Kennedy shrugged. "Probably wandered off the trail so you didn't see him."

"That wouldn't make any difference," I said. "I met Laurel in the parking lot. The two of us started up the mountain together with Laurel's donkey. She didn't have time to do anything."

"You two got to the trailhead at exactly the same moment?" Kennedy's tone of voice indicated he didn't believe that possibility.

"No, but…"

"She got there after you did?"

I took a breath to keep from snarling. "No. She was there before me, but she was unloading her burro when I got there."

"Doesn't mean she'd just shown up there, does it?"

I was beginning to see the outlines of Kennedy's hypothesis, but it still didn't make sense. "She wouldn't go off somewhere and leave her burro in the trailer. It was sitting in full sunshine." Plus why on earth would she bring Peggy Sue if she was planning to kill Kell?

Kennedy's response was a snort, probably meant to convey his skepticism toward Laurel's worrying about Peggy Sue.

I took another breath, searching for something I could use to challenge Kennedy's firm conclusion that Laurel had killed Kell before I got there.

"Chief Kennedy?"

The firm voice from the doorway had us all turning. A small, roundish woman dressed in a bright blue suit stared fixedly at the top of Kennedy's head. He pulled himself up a little straighter. "I'm Kennedy."

The woman nodded briskly and strode forward, briefcase in hand. "I'm Magdalena Ramos. I represent Ms. Beacham. I need to talk to her. Immediately."

Madge had obviously gotten to work in record time. I'd never met Magdalena Ramos, but I'd heard a lot about her over the years. As lawyers went, she was one of the best in the Collegiate Peaks area. Her name was likely to inspire both annoyance and dread in the average chief of police.

Kennedy, however, was no average chief of police. "Beacham didn't say anything about you being her lawyer."

"I suggest you ask Ms. Beacham if she's retained me. And I suggest you do it in my presence." Ramos gave Kennedy a long look—the kind she'd been using for a lot of years on a lot of police officials who were a lot more impressive than Brendan Kennedy.

He decided not to push it. "Come with me," he said, starting up the hall.

I took a couple of steps after them. "Ms. Ramos?"

She glanced at me, frowning. "Yes?"

"I'm Roxanne Constantine. Would you tell Ms. Beacham we'll take care of her animals as long as she needs us to?"

Ramos's frown relaxed. "Yes, of course. But Ms. Beacham should be coming home soon. Quite soon." Those last words were directed toward Kennedy, who scowled at her.

Nevertheless, my money was on Ramos.

I thought about waiting at the station to see how quickly Ramos could get Laurel out of Kennedy's clutches but decided to head to her place instead. After all, Laurel might want to talk to her lawyer for a while before she came home. And I'd left Jarrod on his own.

He was still in the pasture with the donkeys when I got there. The goat herd was beginning to migrate his way, but he didn't seem too upset about it. Given the blissful behavior of the three donkeys as he rubbed their necks, I figured any goats who got too inquisitive would be moved off by donkey nips before they could become nuisances.

I pulled into a space next to Laurel's house as Teri, her cheese assistant, stepped onto the porch. "Have you talked to Laurel?" she asked.

"Just a little over the phone. But she's got a good lawyer now, and she should be home soon." I didn't even cross my fingers as I said it—I was that confident Magdalena Ramos could do her thing.

Teri frowned, rubbing a hand through her spiked hair. "I can't go on working here if she's involved in a murder. My parents will freak out."

"She's not *involved* in a murder. She happened to be there the day it happened. So was I."

Teri's chin went up. "That's not what Chief Kennedy says. And it was her ex-husband."

"Chief Kennedy is an idiot," I shot back, without pausing to think about it. "I was there. He wasn't."

"You're not from around here," Teri said, eyes narrowing.

"No, I'm from Shavano. Where we have a first-rate chief of police. Trust me, I know the difference between good and bad cops."

Teri still didn't appear to believe me, but she started toward her car. "I gotta get home."

"Did you feed the goats?" I called after her.

She glanced over her shoulder, but she kept on walking. "Yeah, I fed the goats. Don't know if I can come back tomorrow, though. My folks may not let me. If Laurel's in jail, she'll need to get someone else to help her. I'm not working for somebody who killed her ex-husband."

I gritted my teeth. She was young. She was from Coalton. Maybe she just didn't know the difference between right and wrong, to say nothing of differences between smart and dumb. "She won't be in jail. She's probably on her way home now."

Teri shrugged and walked toward the car, clearly

unimpressed by a Shavano resident with insufficient respect for the Coalton chief of police. I only hoped Laurel wasn't relying on her too much.

I'd just decided to get Jarrod and head home when Laurel's truck turned into the drive and pulled up in her parking space. She climbed out, and I got my first good look at her. She was about as frazzled as I expected, and that was as frazzled as I would have looked in her place.

"Roxy," she called. "I'm glad you're still here. Thank you for getting Ms. Ramos on my case and for taking care of the animals. I've been a nervous wreck worrying about everything."

"Madge was the one who got Ms. Ramos involved," I explained. "She's a regular at the café. I figured Madge would know a good lawyer, and she knows the best." Thank the Lord for Bobby's pot roast, which I'd heard was Magdalena Ramos's favorite.

Laurel nodded. "Certainly seems that way. Was Teri still around when you got here?"

"She was here. Briefly." I weighed whether I should tell her Teri might not show up tomorrow, but in her place, I'd want to know. "She made some noises about not coming back, said her parents might not let her. She sounds like a Kennedy fan."

Laurel closed her eyes. "I may end up as a pariah around this town. People liked Kell. And a lot of them think Kennedy's a good cop."

Possibly because they had nobody to compare him to. I wondered if it would be possible for me to talk to Fowler, the chief of Shavano's police, about all of this. Probably not

"It's crazy," I said flatly. "The whole thing is crazy. I've told Kennedy more than once that you and I were together when we climbed the trail and Kell wasn't there. No matter what he says, Buster couldn't have wandered off where we couldn't see him. There wasn't that much cover up there."

"And Peggy Sue would have let us know if another burro was nearby. She gets skittish around unfamiliar animals. I guess Kennedy's bound and determined to find me guilty. I don't know what would have happened if Ms. Ramos hadn't shown up. He kept asking me the same bunch of questions over and over, even though I kept giving him the same answers."

"Does he think you killed Kell before I got there?"

Laurel sighed. "I guess. I don't even know how Kell was killed. Or when." Her voice trembled a little at the end, and I held her hands. They were icy cold.

"It'll be okay, Laurel," I said. "You didn't kill anybody. Sooner or later Kennedy will have to admit that. He's just settling on you because you're handy, and he's not much of a cop."

She gave me a shaky smile. "Here's hoping you're right. Ms. Ramos did seem to shake him up some. But now I've got to find someone to fill in for Teri. I don't have time to get a new assistant with everything else that's going on."

I glanced over at the field where Jarrod was leaning against the fence watching Peggy Sue and her cohorts. A goat was nibbling at his shoe, but he pushed it away easily. He looked like he was experiencing that ideal farm life he'd wanted as a kid.

"If you need some temporary help, I could loan you Jarrod. If he's okay with it, that is." I figured he'd be happy doing something that involved animals and cooking. As long as he wasn't cooking the animals.

Laurel frowned. "It's great that he's good with the animals, but I'd need him to help me in the cheese room, too."

"He's been my apprentice jam maker for the past couple of weeks, and he's done a good job. And he used to work for Tal Nguyen. Dolce vouched for him, based on a cooking class they did together."

"Does he have a car? With everything else that's going on, I don't have time to pick him up."

"He's got a motor scooter. One of those little Italian things. Like something out of *La Dolce Vita*." I'd worry about Jarrod driving that thing on the highway, but there were lots of back roads between Coalton and Shavano.

Laurel's smile was more solid. "Okay, let's ask him."

Jarrod seemed a little confused at first, and then a little concerned, maybe because he thought I was firing him. I straightened him out on that. "Laurel's assistant just quit on her, and she's in a real bind. I'll still have Dolce to help me out for a few more weeks, and we thought maybe you could work with Laurel until she's through this rough patch." I didn't bother telling him the *rough patch* included possible murder charges.

"Oh, well, sure then," Jarrod said. "Cheese-making sounds cool. I'd like to learn more about it."

Laurel breathed a sigh of relief. "Good. Why don't you plan on being here tomorrow around eight-thirty or so. You can help me with the milking."

Jarrod's eyes widened, and I wondered if that would be a deal breaker. "You need me to milk the goats? Cool!"

"See you tomorrow then. I'll have you fill out some paperwork. I'll pay you what I was paying Teri." She mentioned an amount that was a lot higher than what I paid Jarrod. It was, in fact, a lot higher than what I paid Dolce.

"Cool," Jarrod repeated. "I'll be here."

I gave Laurel a hug and told her once again not to worry, then walked to the car with Jarrod at my heels. He was bubbling with excitement. "Goats," he said. "And burros. This is going to be so great."

Apparently, Laurel had just gotten an enthusiastic assistant. Maybe more enthusiastic than he'd been about chopping strawberries. Then again, I could see his point. After all, I had no burros to offer.

Chapter 11

I brought Jarrod to my place so he could pick up his scooter. I'd have to explain to Dolce tomorrow why he wasn't going to be working with us for a while. As I started for the cabin, I saw Madge striding purposefully down from the main house.

"Did Magdalena get there in time to get that child out of jail?" she asked as I unlocked the cabin door.

"Magdalena Ramos arrived like the Seventh Cavalry," I said. "I don't think Brendan Kennedy knew what hit him. Laurel's home now."

"Good." Madge followed me inside. "That man should never have been hired in the first place. If he bungles this investigation, maybe the town will finally understand just how incompetent he is."

"How did he get the job?" I took it for granted that Madge knew. Coalton was only a few miles down the road, and she seemed to keep up with the gossip for at least fifty miles around.

"Oh, he was a policeman in some other mountain town, but his wife was Coalton born and bred. When their old police chief retired, he was first in line for the job. And since everybody knew her, they figured he must be all right. Not that they probably had all that many candidates besides Kennedy." Madge grimaced. "And now see what he's done. The idea that Laurel Beacham could be involved in a murder is just ludicrous. Even if it was her ex-husband."

"I agree. But Kennedy's in charge." I paused, wondering again if I could talk to Fowler about any of this. But what could he do? It wasn't in his jurisdiction by even the farthest stretch. And he probably wouldn't talk to me about a fellow police chief. Maybe it went against their code or something.

Madge shook her head again. "Keep me posted. And you should spread the word to her other friends here in town. I know Marcus Jordan buys her cheese, and that means Bianca probably knows her, too. It wouldn't hurt to have a show of support from the people around here. Just to remind Coalton they're not operating in secret."

I wasn't sure what good a show of support from Shavano foodies would do. But Madge was right that Laurel had friends in town. And those friends included one very important one—my own bestie, Susa Sondergaard.

****

Susa's company ran Laurel's web site, as they did for most of the commercial sites in the area. And Susa and I had joined forces in other investigations that had turned out all right. And, last but absolutely not least, Susa and Ethan Fowler had a sort of relationship. I was never sure if they were on or off, but these days they were more often on.

If Fowler could provide any advice, Susa would be a means to ask him.

She picked up on the second ring. "Hey, Rox, what's up. And before you ask, Kip fixed the problem with the drop-down after Bridget phoned it in."

I had no idea we'd had a problem with a drop-down. I wasn't even sure what a drop-down was. But I didn't

121

want to admit that to Susa. "Okay, good, I'll tell her. But I actually wanted to talk to you about something else. Have you heard about Laurel?"

"Laurel Beacham? No, what's happened? Besides her ex-husband getting killed, that is. I did hear about that."

"This is related, but different." I summed up the day's events as succinctly as I could, but I'm not known for my brevity.

"Wait, hold on," Susa said. "That idiot Kennedy is trying to arrest Laurel for murdering Kell when she was with you at the time? Really?"

"Really," I said. "I called Madge, and she sent Magdalena Ramos over, so Laurel's home. But I doubt Kennedy will give up on his assumptions just because of that."

"No. If anything, he's liable to be even more determined to push those assumptions to the limit just to show everybody he was right. The man's a numbskull."

"He is," I agreed. "Which is why Laurel needs help. He's not going to listen to reason."

"No, he's not. Kennedy doesn't know what reason is. What do you want me to do?"

"The usual. Check out other things Kell was involved in that might have made someone want to kill him."

"Jealous husbands would be my first guess," Susa mused. "With jealous ex-boyfriends my second."

"Actually, I've got something a little more interesting." I explained about the weirdly named Pristine Refuse which Kell may or may not have had a hand in.

"Pristine? Sounds sketchy." I could picture Susa's

skeptical look. "Have you checked them out?"

"Not yet. I got caught up in some stuff." Mainly burros, but I had meant to do some research on the company, assuming that's what it was.

"Okay, that's something I can do. I'll let you know what I find out. Do we need to talk to Ethan?"

That question came out of left field. I'd wanted to work the conversation around to possibly getting help from Fowler, but I hadn't expected Susa to drop it right out there. "Do you think he'd talk to us? It's not his case, and it's way out of his jurisdiction."

"If it was his case, he'd never talk to us. That's a given. The fact that it's not his case probably makes it a little easier for him to answer questions, although he definitely won't track down any information for us. At least I don't think he will. It probably depends on how much he dislikes Kennedy. And since everybody competent hates Kennedy, I don't think that will be a problem"

"Okay, then yeah, I'd like to talk to Fowler about what's going on. Maybe he can give us some suggestions about ways we can help Laurel."

"Maybe." Susa sounded less certain about that possibility, and I could see her point. Still, if nothing else, maybe he could help us understand the procedures Kennedy was likely to follow. Although I had a feeling it would be foolish to count on Kennedy doing anything the way a competent cop would do it. After all, I'd seen his preliminary investigation when we found Kell's body—I hadn't been impressed.

Susa promised to ask Fowler if he'd talk to us about the case, which was probably better than me ambushing him at Dirty Pete's over margaritas and chips. And I set about fixing dinner, which gave me a chance to work off some of the adrenaline still coursing through my system as a result of my run-in with Kennedy.

I had leftover rice and some spicy sausage, which were perfect fried rice ingredients. Nate walked in as I did an experimental toss of the aromatics. Fortunately, they all returned to the wok from whence they'd come.

He grinned. "Going for the open kitchen special?"

"Why not?" I said. "Maybe Tal Nguyen needs somebody at Jade Garden." Tal wasn't quite in the Japanese steak house category, but his chefs did get a lot of mileage out of General Tso's chicken.

Nate set to work whipping up a stir-fry sauce to add once I got all my ingredients blended together, which cut my prep considerably. I added the sauce and did a couple more careful tosses, then brought the wok to the table.

"Did Mom help Laurel?" Nate asked as he served himself a couple of heaping spoonfuls.

"She did. She sent Magdalena Ramos over to get her out of Kennedy's clutches. Unfortunately, I think that's only temporary. Kennedy has decided Laurel's his killer, and nobody's going to talk him out of it."

Nate grimaced. "That's stupid. Even if you weren't able to supply her with an alibi, it would still be stupid. But given the fact that you can vouch for her, it's beyond stupid."

"I don't know when Kell was killed," I cautioned. "Kennedy thinks Laurel did it before we started up the hill. But that's also stupid because if Kell's body was already in that grove when we started up the hill, we would have found Buster on the trail."

"Kennedy didn't buy that?"

"Nope. He thinks Buster wandered off somewhere

after Kell was murdered and then wandered back before I got down the mountain. But there aren't that many places for a burro to hide on that trail. It's steep and there's not a lot of greenery around. That grove where they found Kell's body is pretty much it. I don't know if Kennedy thinks Buster was in that grove. I'm pretty sure he wasn't because I don't think he'd stay around when someone had been killed, and because Laurel's burro would probably have reacted if Buster was close by. And she didn't."

Nate sighed. "Kennedy doesn't strike me as someone who's willing to admit he's wrong. Even when he very clearly is. If he actually charges Laurel, she'll need Magdalena more than ever. And Magdalena doesn't come cheap."

"What are you thinking?"

"We could put together a fundraiser if she needs it. For legal expenses. We could get every foodie in the Collegiate Peaks area to kick in—they all know Laurel, and most of them use her cheese when they can get it."

"That sounds great, but right now it's premature. We don't know if Kennedy's going to push this to trial, or if the county attorney will let him. And you'd need to ask Laurel before you launched anything." I didn't think Laurel would reject the idea, but I didn't want to jump into anything without her approval. And right now, we didn't even know if she'd need it.

"Right. And we'll have to wait to see how things shake out over the next week or so. But if that jerk decides to charge her, I think the restaurant community needs to swing into action."

"Yeah, show Kennedy and maybe Coalton that Laurel isn't without resources. You should talk to your mom, too. She'll probably have some ideas of her own about how to help."

"Knowing Mom, she'll come up with her own fundraiser, one that'll put my ideas in the shade."

"She probably will. It's right up her alley." The idea of all the foodies in the region coming together to help one of their own made me feel a lot better. Personally, I was looking forward to thumbing my nose at Kennedy. But maybe I needed to talk to Fowler first.

****

Susa called me the next day to invite me to lunch with Fowler at Dirty Pete's, our favorite restaurant in Shavano. I should probably have told Nate what I was going to do, but I didn't. He and Fowler had a kind of touchy relationship in the past, and I didn't want to go into the meeting feeling uncertain. I'd tell him after the meeting had taken place. But I'd also emphasize that Susa had been there, too.

Unfortunately, she wasn't there yet when I strolled up to Dirty Pete's. Fowler was sitting at the side of the dining room, drumming his fingers on the table. I took a quick breath and walked over. "Hi. Is Susa on her way?"

He looked up at me, frowning slightly. "Yeah, far as I know. Are you joining us?"

Well, damn. I'd thought Susa would have let him know what this was about. On the other hand, if she had, he might not have come. "I am, is that okay?"

"Fine by me." He scooted over so I could pull out a chair. "You two have something going?"

I shrugged. *Might as well get into it.* "We've got some questions we need to ask you about a friend of ours, Laurel Beacham." I checked Fowler's expression, but he didn't seem to recognize Laurel's name.

"What kind of trouble is she in?" he asked. Of course, he assumed she was in trouble, and, of course, he was right.

"She's being harassed by an officer of the law." Susa dropped into a chair beside him, then grinned at me. "Hi, Rox. Sorry I'm late."

Fowler frowned. "You mean one of my guys is harassing her?"

Susa shook her head. "Nope. Another town. We need some information."

"So this is a set-up?"

"Sort of." Susa gave him a bright smile and waved at the waitress while Fowler narrowed his eyes.

After we'd all ordered lunch, Susa turned to him again. "Okay, so we have a friend who's having trouble, and we need your input."

Fowler frowned. "Wait. Is this that thing in Coalton?"

"Our friend Laurel lives in Coalton," I said. "She's their director of tourism, or something like that. Her ex-husband was murdered a few days ago, and now she's under suspicion when she shouldn't be."

Fowler folded his arms across his chest. "Just because she's your friend doesn't mean she couldn't have killed someone."

I squared my shoulders. "She shouldn't be under suspicion because I was with her when her ex-husband was killed. She couldn't have done it, but Chief Kennedy won't let go of her as a suspect. And he doesn't appear to be investigating anybody else."

Fowler gave me a long look, then sighed. "Okay, tell me the story."

I did. By now I'd told it enough times that I could

do it fairly quickly. Fowler sat listening to me, more inscrutable than usual. "You're certain the guy was killed after you went up the mountain," he said finally.

"I didn't see his body on the way up, and I also didn't see the burro, which was definitely there when I climbed down. Kennedy thinks the burro had wandered off and then wandered back again. I think that's unlikely. There aren't many places he could wander around unseen except down the hill, and I doubt he'd climb up again once he got down."

"You don't have a time of death?"

I shook my head.

"And you think your friend had just gotten there when you drove up?"

"I'm pretty sure she had. She was working on getting her burro out of the trailer. Peggy Sue can be temperamental."

Fowler frowned. "Thought her name was Laurel."

"Peggy Sue's the burro," Susa cut in. "She's a sweetheart."

"Anyway," I said. "Laurel was guiding Peggy Sue out of the trailer. She'd pretty clearly just gotten there."

"Did you touch the truck? Was the engine still warm?"

I blinked. "No."

"Why would she?" Susa said.

"Just checking. What was her demeanor like?"

I felt like asking him if he meant Laurel or Peggy Sue, but that would just be annoying. "Laurel was fine. Smiling. Calm. Talking to Peggy Sue. Like I said, the donkey's kind of temperamental, so Laurel had to let her know she was loved."

"Any delays getting up the trail?"

"Not that I recall. She had to get Peggy Sue geared up so she could start getting used to the pack saddle and the pick and shovel."

Fowler stared at me. "What the hell?"

"It's for the burro race," I explained. "The burros have to carry a pack saddle with a pick and shovel and gold pan, just like they did back in the day. It has to weigh at least thirty pounds. Laurel was getting Peggy Sue in shape for the burro race season."

"There's a burro race season?" Fowler looked like he wasn't altogether sure we weren't making this up as we went along.

"It's a big deal around here," Susa said. "And it's the state heritage sport. People come from all over the country to do it. And we've got champions right here in the Shavano Valley. Silas Goodman has won the Triple Crown."

Fowler still looked suspicious. "The Triple Crown."

"Leadville, Fairplay, and Buena Vista. Those are the towns with the three biggest races. The course at Fairplay is over twenty-five miles."

"That's marathon distance," Fowler said. "They do this all in one day?"

I nodded. "A lot of the serious racers came to burros from endurance racing. They say most burro races are endurance races under another name."

"There are 'non-serious' racers?" Fowler asked.

"Tourists." Susa sniffed. "They come in and rent a burro for a day. Then they get in the way of the real racers. At least the places that rent them the burros usually make sure the tourists have had a couple of hours or so of training before they actually hit the trail. I think they're required to have an hour-long safety course."

Fowler checked back and forth between us, forehead furrowed. "I had no idea."

"It's a sort of specialized sport," Susa said cheerfully. "It doesn't get covered in the newspapers usually. Not everybody knows about it, even up here. I mean, Shavano doesn't have a burro race of its own. But now that you know, you can go watch the Coalton race, or the start of it, and understand what's going on."

"About Laurel," I said. I figured we still needed to get some information about what was likely to happen with Laurel and Kennedy.

Fowler had his inscrutable look again. "Okay, she got the burro out, everything was fine. You went up the mountain and didn't see anybody?"

"Well, Silas. Silas Goodman. He's the guy Susa was talking about, the Triple Crown winner. He's a friend of Uncle Mike's."

"And he was up on the trail, too?"

I nodded. "He was training his own burro. He was ahead of us, though. I mean we said hello to each other and then he took off up the trail. He was going a lot faster than we were."

"Foxy grandpa." Susa gave me a dry grin. "He's got to be in his sixties, right?"

"At least."

"Wait." Fowler held up his hand. "Another guy was on the trail at the same time you were? Did Kennedy question him?"

I paused. "I don't know. Silas was there when I came down, too. After I found Buster and started searching for his handler, Silas came down the trail above us. He held Buster while I went into the pine grove to check on the guy I'd seen lying there. It was Kell, and he was dead."

"Could this Silas have been waiting for you to come down? Could he have been beside the trail somewhere?"

"I don't think so. I mean I think I would have seen him if he was around. He had a tough burro, too. I don't think he could have hidden Oliver. Not without Oliver objecting loudly."

All of a sudden, I felt uncomfortable. I hadn't thought about Silas as a suspect, and obviously neither had Kennedy. But he'd been up there with us. And I supposed he might have a reason to kill Kell, particularly if Kell was involved in something nefarious with Pristine Refuse, whoever they might be.

"And you don't know if Kennedy eliminated this guy as a possible suspect before he zeroed in on your friend," Fowler said carefully.

"I don't know. The thing is, Silas has been around forever. He has a ranch over toward Coalton. Everybody in town probably knows him. I think he was even on the town council a while ago."

"And you think that would make a difference?" Fowler's expression hadn't changed, but his tone of voice sounded dubious.

"In Coalton? Absolutely. Laurel's only lived there a few years. She's got her goat cheese business, and she works part time for the city, working on some projects that might get tourists to come to town. But she's not what they'd call popular. Particularly not after she divorced Kell. He was the city manager."

Fowler muttered something under his breath that was probably profane. "Did he question you?"

"Yeah. I was the one who found Kell's body after I found Buster. Although Silas was there by the time I actually went into the grove where Kell's body was. Kennedy asked me how I'd found him, and then he wanted to know about Laurel. He didn't talk to me very long, though."

"Were you the one who called 911?"

I paused. "No. Actually, that was Silas. I was sort of freaked out after I found the body."

Fowler rubbed his eyes. "This sounds like a first-class fuck-up. But you realize I can't do anything about it. It's way outside my jurisdiction."

"Could the Colorado Bureau of Investigation come in and take this over? I mean, if Kennedy is botching the case, could CBI just sort of relieve him of command?" I was beginning to think that would be the only way to get the investigation on track again.

Fowler shook his head. "CBI only moves in if the local police request it. Most of us do request help on something like this—we need CBI's forensics resources at the very least. But if Kennedy decides to hold onto this for himself, nobody can tell him not to." He paused. "I take that back. The county attorney can call in CBI if he thinks the case that's being made isn't enough to bring to trial. But that can't happen unless Kennedy decides to charge your friend, and the county attorney doesn't like the case."

I blew out a breath. "Even if Kennedy doesn't charge Laurel, he's probably made most people in town think she's the one who killed Kell. She'll have that hanging over her until he charges somebody else. Assuming he ever does that."

Fowler grimaced as if he was tasting something sour. "Like I said, a fuck-up. But nobody can do much about it."

"Could you find out if they have any other suspects?" Susa asked. "Just, you know, sort of informally?"

Fowler appeared less than thrilled with that possibility. "I can ask around. But don't expect much. Kennedy's not going to share information with me. We're not close."

"It's just...this isn't right," I said slowly. "Laurel didn't do this. She's got a solid alibi. I don't know why Kennedy's so bound and determined to prove she's guilty, but he's screwing around with her life."

Fowler shrugged. "It happens."

Susa made a sound that was a lot like a teakettle blowing out steam. "Which doesn't make it right."

"It doesn't," he agreed. "But it still happens."

Which didn't make any of us feel any better.

Chapter 12

By the time I finished work in the early evening, I was thoroughly depressed. Because I hadn't been around as much as I should have, Dolce and I struggled to get all the jams ready for the coming week's farmers market. Jarrod continued to work for Laurel, who thanked me profusely and assured me she wouldn't have been able to function without him. That was great but it meant we didn't have a fallback helper. Dolce was a gifted jam maker in her own right, but she couldn't carry the whole load by herself.

Trying to finish a monster run of peach jam, I continued to work after Dolce left for the day. We were okay on strawberry and raspberry, both of which were relatively easy to make. But with it being the beginning of peach season, I needed to have lots of peach and pepper peach for the people who'd come to the stand drooling for that special flavor.

I was still using frozen peaches to make the jam, and that meant the mixture required careful tending to get rid of the extra liquid. I was tired, frustrated, and still very worried about Laurel and what Brendan Kennedy was doing to her.

As I was putting another load of filled jars into the processing kettle, Bridget stepped into the kitchen doorway. "I've finished up all the pending orders we had from email. What's the decision on the tomato jam? Is it our special? If it is, I need to get it up on the web site so people can start getting their orders in, and you'll know how much to make."

"Oh, Lord," I moaned. "I haven't even thought about that for the past week. Too much has been going on."

The latest version of the tomato jam had been considerably pepped up by using extra Serranoes, along with a healthy dose of jalapeños, but it still wasn't what I wanted. I hate putting out anything that isn't just right. On the other hand, I didn't have time to come up with an alternative.

I sighed. "Yeah, let's run it. I haven't got anything else to put up. I'll try to get time tomorrow to start a run, so we'll have a dozen jars or so on hand. I've got a couple of jars you can use to take pictures."

"What about recipes? Tomato jam's unusual, and people are going to want to know what they can do with it."

I closed my eyes, trying to think. Too many things were going on, and my brain was too scattered between Laurel and peaches and Jarrod and burros. And Fowler. Yes, Fowler was definitely in the mix since I was hoping against hope that he'd develop some information that would help us figure out how to help Laurel. I had some recipes in mind once, but my mind was currently preoccupied.

"Salad dressing," I mumbled finally. "Mix it with olive oil and balsamic vinegar, and maybe some salt and pepper. Should taste okay."

Bridget narrowed her eyes. "I didn't think 'okay' was what we wanted on this one." She looked a little like my high school math teacher when I hadn't completed my homework assignment.

And she was right. "I'll try it out this evening. I promise. It shouldn't be that hard to put a good vinaigrette together. And tomorrow I'll come up with some more things we can post. The meatloaf I tried it on was good. That should work, too. And maybe crostini."

I must have appeared more harried than usual because Bridget backed off and let me get by with being scatterbrained. I really had let the tomato jam slide, and I really did need to get my ass in gear, but I also really wasn't up to it at that particular moment.

****

Nate didn't have a gig that night, but he was going to be working three in a row that weekend. Since it was a bigger than usual party for the Merchants Association, I'd promised to help with the Saturday event if he needed it. Right then, I felt like that was the last thing I wanted to do, promise or no promise. I also had no ideas for dinner and was just about to order out for pizza when he walked in with a couple of bags.

At that point I didn't care what it was. I'd definitely eat it. "Tell me that's dinner."

"Chicken soup with lemon and couscous. It's Coco's recipe. The people who like it *really* like it, but it's still a slow mover. I grabbed the leftovers and some dinner rolls."

"Praise the Lord. And you, of course." I leaned over to give him a quick kiss. There hadn't been enough kissing lately—both of us were just too tired. "I'm making a salad so I can try out some dressing. It'll be ready in ten minutes or so."

"Okay, let me warm this up."

The tomato jam dressing recipe worked out, as I'd

figured it would. It was sort of like Catalina dressing, but not quite so sweet, and the balsamic gave it a nice kick. "Tastes good," Nate said. "Are you going with the tomato jam for your special?"

I nodded. "I don't have time to come up with anything else, and I think it's decent. We probably won't sell much because it's not what people think of when they think jam, but I'll make up for it on the next one." I'd already decided I'd do amaretto peach for the next special, which would probably get us a ton of orders.

"You look tired," Nate said. "What's up?"

I launched into an explanation of what Fowler had told me about Kennedy. Nate's expression darkened as he listened. "So there's nothing we can do?" he said finally. "Not even call CBI?"

"Not really. Fowler thought the county attorney might call them in when he sees what a mess Kennedy has made of the case. But if Kennedy doesn't bother to bring the case to the county attorney, even that may not happen. And if nobody gets charged for Kell's murder, chances are everybody in Coalton will go on thinking Laurel killed him."

"At least she wouldn't have to go to trial," Nate said. "But yeah, I know that's not a great solution."

I closed my eyes, rubbing my fingers across my forehead. "I just wish I could do something."

Nate began massaging the back of my neck. "It's not your problem, Rox. I know you want to help. I do, too. But we've done pretty much all we can at this point. We go on supporting Laurel publicly so the people in Coalton can see not everybody thinks Kennedy has it right. You're burning yourself out, sweetheart. You need to ease off and let Magdalena do her thing. If the case goes to trial, we step in and do a fundraiser to help with the legal expenses. Otherwise, we wait and see."

I leaned against his hand. "I know. I'll concentrate on my jam for a while, just make sure Laurel's doing okay at the farmers market. Maybe Silas can keep an eye on her in Coalton."

Which reminded me of what Fowler had said. Silas was as viable a suspect as Laurel. But nobody thought of him that way, maybe because he was a long-time resident of Coalton. And maybe because he was Silas Goodman, Triple Crown winner.

The question was, did I want to think of him that way? Silas Goodman, my honorary godfather, whom I'd known from the time my dad first took me to see the burros when I was seven or eight years old? It was almost as tough to think of him as a killer than to think of Laurel the same way.

Right then I didn't want to think of anybody as a potential killer. Not Laurel, not Silas, not anyone else who'd happened to be wandering around the mountain that day. I wondered if they were absolutely sure Kell had been murdered. Couldn't it have been accidental death? Maybe a heart attack or something.

It was a measure of my distrust of Kennedy that I was even entertaining that possibility. If it had been Fowler, I wouldn't have any questions about his assessment of the victim or the verdict from the medical examiner. Probably.

"Let's eat," I said. "We can deal with all of this some other time."

The soup was delicious, which wasn't surprising. Coco was an amazing cook. I sopped up the last of it with the end of my dinner roll, leaning back in my chair to savor it. And to savor sitting down without thinking about a lot of things that I needed to do immediately.

Nate gathered the dishes together and started loading the dishwasher while I basked. "You want anything more?" he asked. "There's still some strawberry ice cream."

I shook my head. "Actually, all I want to do right now is go to bed. Maybe read a chapter or two and then go to sleep."

"Sounds good. I might join you." He voice was faintly wistful, and I remembered once again that we hadn't had much time together lately. We needed to do something about that. I wasn't going to let my relationship with Nate go on hold like the tomato jam.

I reached out and took his hand. "Please do," I said. "There's plenty of room for two."

Nate finished loading the dishwasher while I wiped down the table. He seemed to be moving with a little more purpose than he had a few moments before. So was I.

All for a very good cause.

****

The next morning, I set to work on the peach jam as soon as I'd cleared breakfast away. I was bound and determined that I'd have five cases of both peach and pepper peach by the end of the week so that I could cart them to the farmers market. Bridget reported that we were also selling peach jam at a good clip on the web site. Like I said, it was peach season, and everybody was already dreaming of peach cobbler and peach mojitos. Jam just got their juices going with a little more determination.

Dolce came in around ten after she'd helped her

mom with the honey they'd bring to the farmers market for their own booth. "Heard anything from Jarrod?" she asked.

"Nope. The last I heard, Laurel said he was doing great, and I don't feel like I can bring him here when she needs him." Plus there was always the possibility that Jarrod wouldn't want to come back quite yet. Making jam couldn't compete with making cheese and taking care of burros.

"But you need him, too," Dolce said, logically enough. "I mean, I'm heading to Ft. Collins the third week of August. You need to have somebody trained and ready to go by then."

My heart dropped a little at that. Realistically, I knew Dolce was leaving. But I'd been pushing that fact to the back of my mind. Now here it was at the front, where it probably should have been all along.

And she was absolutely right. I needed somebody. And I needed enough time with them to be sure they'd work out. "I'll put the word out among the local foodies, see if anybody knows of someone who wants to pick up some part-time hours." Even if Jarrod returned, I could use another person. When I'd had both Dolce and Jarrod working, we'd gotten a lot more done.

"I'll ask around, too," Bridget said. "Might be other high school kids who'd like to pick up some extra money and learn a trade."

"Thanks. That's a good idea. I'll check with Dolores Cantu at the high school." The last few high school kids I'd worked with in the mentoring program had zero interest in making jam, but maybe somebody new had joined. With money involved, one of my previous students might discover a new interest in the jam-making experience.

The bottom line was that I needed an assistant now. And given that I was losing Dolce and possibly losing Jarrod, until Laurel made other arrangements, I needed to get off my behind and start doing some canvasing.

Susa called a little before noon. "I've got some info on that company Kell was involved with, Pristine Refuse." Judging from her tone of voice, she considered the term *Pristine* ironic. "Want to grab some lunch?"

I would have liked to have grabbed lunch with Susa, but I'd already spent too much time away from my business. Dolce and I were almost caught up, and I didn't want to do anything to slow things down. "I can't today. Maybe this weekend?"

"Tell you what. Are you helping Nate with that Merchants Association party Saturday night?"

"Most likely." Since it was such a large party, Nate had decided he needed both Dex and me in the kitchen.

"Okay, I'm going to be there. Probably with Ethan. Maybe we'll have a chance to talk."

"Maybe. If not, there's always Sunday and Monday." My guess was I'd be working my tail off in the kitchen Saturday night. Not necessarily something to look forward to.

"Right. See you then."

****

I kept an eye out for Laurel at the farmers market on Saturday. Among other things, I thought Jarrod might come with her, which would give me a chance to discuss his future plans. I needed to know when he was returning. I wasn't ready to consider that the question might be *if* rather than *when.* She got there around twenty minutes before opening, cutting it close considering how many customers jumped the gun on the opening time in hopes of getting the best tomatoes before anyone else reached them.

Unfortunately, because Laurel was so late getting there, neither of us had much time to talk. Beck and I had to get the jam ready to go and to make sure the extra cases were conveniently located. The market was a madhouse, as anticipated. The two or three booths that actually had fresh peaches were swamped. And the people who didn't get a chance to take care of their fresh peach needs went searching for something—anything—to make up for their disappointment. We sold peach jam and pepper peach jam almost as fast as we could put it on the counter. I had six cases of each, which was a lot more than I usually stocked. But by noon, I was beginning to feel a little desperate. Then again, feeling desperate because I would probably sell out of all my peach jam variations was a good kind of desperation.

By one thirty, the rush of customers had died to a respectable flow. The pepper peach was gone, but I still had a few jars of the plain peach jam. Although realistically none of my jams are *plain*. I checked to see if Laurel was at her booth, then left Beck to take care of things for a few minutes.

Laurel was still doing a brisk business, although she'd taped up a *Sold Out* sign on the card advertising peach flavored cheese. I wasn't the only one who'd anticipated a peach frenzy this weekend. "Hey, Rox," she called when she saw me. "How'd you do?"

"Great," I said. "Best crowd so far."

"It was that." She finished giving change to her customer before turning back to me. "I'm a little ragged running all this myself."

I frowned. "Where's your assistant?"

Laurel's smile disappeared. "Suddenly unavailable. I get that a lot."

"What about Jarrod?"

"The kid's been working eight hours a day, every day. He's great. But I absolutely didn't want him to give up his Saturday, too. I thought I could handle it. And I did. Pretty much."

I was fighting off a ton of mixed emotions. Sympathy for Laurel, who was getting jerked around by a town that didn't deserve her. Envy for her having the hard-working Jarrod, whom I'd sent along without thinking about what I was giving up. And a certain amount of panic when I considered that I had only around a month to find someone to replace Dolce. "About Jarrod," I said.

Laurel bit her lip. "Okay, I feel bad about taking your assistant away, but he's an absolute natural, both with the cheese making and the burros. And he seems to be enjoying himself. I mean, he was probably enjoying his time with you, too. He's an easy-going kid. Even the goats love him, and he gets through the milking faster than anyone I've ever had working for me before."

I tried to remember if Jarrod had a good time working for me. He'd spent most of his time chopping fruit, but he'd been happy enough. Or anyway, I'd thought he was. He was never *unhappy* anyway.

"And Rox, to tell you the truth, I don't know how I could replace him right now." Laurel took a deep breath, and I had the feeling she was just holding herself together. "People in town seem to have decided I'm guilty, no matter what I say. And they don't want to do anything that might be seen as helping me out. Teri quit, and then Amy, my assistant at the market and my part-time shop manager, left. It's like they don't want to be seen with me."

Her voice quavered, and she was definitely fighting tears. I felt a mixture of rage at the jerks in Coalton and embarrassment about having made things even slightly worse by bringing up Jarrod and wanting him back.

"It's okay, don't worry about it," I said quickly. "If it's working out for Jarrod, I've got no problem with his staying on to work for you. We can figure this out after they find out who killed Kell and all this stuff dies down."

That assumed that the "stuff" would die down. That Kennedy would realize Laurel wasn't a viable suspect and find someone else. Who might be Silas. But I figured Silas could handle Kennedy better than Laurel could, given that Silas was a Favorite Son in Coalton.

"Thanks, Rox, I really appreciate it. And if you need Jarrod for a couple of hours to take care of something for you, just let me know. Maybe we can share his time."

"Maybe." I managed a smile that wasn't sincere. I needed an assistant for more than a couple of hours if I was going to keep up with the demand for Luscious Delights, both on-line and in the stores around Shavano where I'd gotten a toehold.

More and more it was looking like I needed to find another assistant. One who preferred jam to burros, no matter how cute.

Chapter 13

The Merchants Association party came as a major score for Robicheaux Catering. Given the number of restaurant owners and caterers who were part of the Merchants Association, the fact that they'd given the job to Nate was a win, an indication that the movers and shakers in town thought the Robicheaux catering business was big time.

Or it would have been if the association hadn't decided they needed more than heavy hors d'oeuvres for this party. Since they had a cash bar that would be open for the entire evening, they started feeling nervous about people getting soused and possibly driving drunk. Which, admittedly, wouldn't have made the association look great. More food was called for. And that also gave them a chance to hire a couple of other caterers and avoid any hard feelings about being passed over for Robicheaux Catering.

It wasn't entirely clear what the other caterers would be doing. Georgia Cummings was supposed to supply desserts, which meant cheesecake since that was what Georgia, a real old-school caterer, always did for desserts. And Blanchette's Barbecue was supplying barbecue since that was what they always did for everything.

That left Nate doing apps for people who might or might not be hungry, depending on whether they'd chowed down on ribs and potato salad from Blanchette's. Still, the association gave him a thirty-minute head start, which would probably stretch to forty-five since it might take that long for Blanchette's to get their serving line set up.

Robicheaux's Catering is a class outfit, so we were serving a suitable array of treats and hoping for the best. Nate had included a selection of Robicheaux's perennials that always got snapped up early: Asian meatballs, crudités with Coco's special cold spinach dip, and vegan filo packets. But he was also throwing in some special summer produce apps as well: caprese skewers with vine-ripened tomatoes, hummus with feta and dill, bruschetta with loads of fresh basil, and some eggplant spread based on baba ghanoush.

And because by now Nate knew what he was doing, most of these apps could be made ahead, getting reheated, if necessary, at the event center kitchen. Nate and Dex had done all the advance prep, which was good since I was up to my hips in peach jam that week and couldn't have done much to help. My assistance was strictly on the serving end of things.

Dex and I planned to stay in the kitchen getting things plated while Nate came and went, checking to make sure the supply of food didn't run low. We had some veteran servers, including, inevitably, Donnell. After discussing it with Madge and Bobby, Nate promoted her to head of the wait staff. She still did lunch and the occasional breakfast at the café, but her primary business now was making sure Nate had enough servers—and the right servers—for all the catering events. From all accounts, she was delighted and exactly the kind of no-nonsense server field marshal that Nate needed.

The party was taking place in an event center inside a downtown building. I thought of it as "the cursed center" because when we'd catered a wedding rehearsal dinner there, the host had been murdered. But despite my lingering sense of bad karma about that building, it was a nice place to work. There was a large kitchen on the same level as the event room so we wouldn't have to worry about getting dishes and trays up and down the stairs. The kitchen had ample counter space where we could set up the platters for Nate and the servers to carry out. And the dishwasher was big enough to take care of a lot of dirties at once. Plus, from the Merchants Association's point of view, it was great for their purposes since the owners were still struggling to turn a profit; therefore, the rent was very reasonable.

Nate was dressed in his catering finery: black chef's coat and trousers. I didn't bother to wear my chef's coat for this one because I was going to be in the kitchen all night. Instead, I stuck with jeans and a Robicheaux's Catering T-shirt and apron. Dex seemed to feel the same way since he was wearing pretty much the same outfit. The three of us toted the hotel pans of food from the catering van to the event center kitchen, storing a lot of it in the refrigerator until it needed to be warmed or arranged on the platters for refills. It was possible that Georgia and the Blanchettes might also need some refrigerator space. If so, they'd have to work around us, possession being nine-tenths of the law.

Dex put the meatballs into the oven while I started arranging the crudités on their platter. It was the last platter to be placed on the table, and the first few guests would be around to appreciate my artistry. "Showtime, y'all," Nate murmured as he hoisted the final tray onto his shoulder.

Given my choice I'd always prefer to be in the kitchen at an event rather than out on the floor. I've done floor duty, and it's always a little nerve-wracking. You have to be on the lookout for food that's running low and trays of dirty dishes that need to be toted to the kitchen. In his early days as a caterer, Nate had sometimes bussed the trays himself to save money. Now he employed a busser, having decided his time was better spent keeping track of the dining room than toting trays full of dirty dishes. The busser was the son of somebody at the café and had been hired by Madge. His first name was Lyle, and he was built like a football player. He seemed quite happy to spend his evening collecting dirty dishes and taking care of trays since he was getting paid a decent salary to do it.

After fifteen minutes or so, Dex and I had our routine going. He heated up the stuff that needed to be heated and got it out on the trays with accompaniments like the soy dipping sauce for the filo packets. I worked on the cold stuff, stacking caprese skewers like Lincoln logs and arranging triangles of pita chips around the hummus and the baba ghanoush. We split duty on the bruschetta, with Dex getting the bread slices into the oven to crisp up and me mounding on the chopped tomato and basil, with a brief spritz of olive oil.

Everything ran like clockwork, which was, let's face it, a little dull. Not that I enjoy kitchen disasters, but climbing out of the weeds can give you a real blast of adrenaline. Clockwork is just, well, work. After an hour and a half or so, Nate came down and surveyed the trays we had set up for him. "It's slowing down some," he said a little glumly. "Blanchette's got trays of ribs and sides, and Georgia's got at least five kinds of cheesecake."

We were down to the latter half of the food Dex and Nate had made for the evening, which meant we'd probably finish it all off by the time everybody went home. And Nate wouldn't lose any money either way, since he'd been paid for the number of apps he'd actually put together. But he wasn't happy. When he'd gotten this gig, it had started out as a big win for Robicheaux Catering. But now it seemed they were sharing the limelight with their competitors.

"You want some cheesecake?" he asked.

I shook my head. Georgia's cheesecake was so rich it stayed with you for hours after you ate it.

"Maybe," Dex said. "Any cherry?"

"Oh, hell yes. She's got every damn thing." Nate started toward the door.

Before he got there, the door swung open. I half-expected Donnell to have come down to tell us about some dining room disaster, which would have spiced things up. But it was Susa, looking unusually spiffy in a scarlet pants suit and four-inch heels. "Hey," she said. "Can you take a minute to hear about Pristine Refuse Removals?"

I glanced at Nate, who shrugged. "Go ahead. We're on the downhill slope from here on in." He picked up a platter of refills, then set a plate with the tail end of the hummus and pita chips between us. "Enjoy." He headed out to the dining room again, and Dex returned to the Asian meatballs.

"What's up?" I asked.

Susa reached into her purse and pulled out some folded sheets of paper. "Okay, you wanted to know about these guys. It took me a little digging to find them—they're a subsidiary of a subsidiary, like that. Which already sounds a little sketchy. Anyway, despite their name, they basically run landfills. *Bad* landfills. They've been involved in several lawsuits over water pollution and other assorted nastiness." She handed me a printout of a magazine article headlined, *The Dirt Merchants.* "That's a good summary of who they are and what they do. And don't do." She dipped one of the pita chips in hummus.

I dipped a chip of my own. "And Kell had some kind of deal going with them? To do what?"

"I don't know exactly, but these guys have a bad track record. In some cases, they buy up land outside a small town without letting the people know what's coming. They've been accused of bribing town officials to get the permits and then setting up a landfill or an incinerator before anybody can stop them."

"You think that's what they're going to do in Coalton?"

Susa shrugged. "Maybe. It would be the kind of thing they've done before. If that's it, Kell was probably their Coalton contact. And maybe he was getting them the permits they needed."

Dex had stopped arranging meatballs to listen to us. "Wait. You mean they're going to open a dump in Coalton?"

"We don't know that for sure," I said. "It's possible."

More than possible as I thought about it. Kell had been the Coalton City Manager. If anybody could expedite permits and do it quietly, maybe even greasing a few palms along the way, it would be him. The real question was whether he'd actually finalized the deal before he'd been killed. I grabbed another chip.

"Holy shit," Dex murmured. "We've been considering land over near Coalton, thinking about building. It's cheaper than Shavano."

Dex's wife, Rita, was a real estate agent, one of those people who knows everything that's happening everywhere and how to make the best deals. I figured she'd be a millionaire before she hit thirty, which was good since her husband enjoyed being a sous chef and a substitute middle school teacher.

It was undoubtedly true that land was cheaper in Coalton. It was a smaller town, and it probably didn't have the kind of property taxes we paid in Shavano. Of course, Coalton also had lousy streets and questionable city services. And now it might also have a brand-new environmental hazard setting up someplace in town. Pristine wouldn't have dared try that in Shavano. Too many people could have found out and anyone who tried to make the deal without letting the citizens know would have been eviscerated.

I paused to think. Had that been what had happened to Kell? Had someone found out what he was planning and with whom? All of a sudden, a lot of new possibilities were opening up.

"I guess we'll put the land on hold," Dex said slowly. He picked up a pita chip, munching disconsolately.

"Probably a good idea. If this was Kell's deal, it may not go through now that he's dead." I paused. We needed to know what Kell's deal had been, assuming we could find people who could tell us. "Do you think Rita could find out what kind of deal Kell might have had with these people?"

Dex gave me a dry smile as he plunged a chip into the hummus. He knew Rita's reputation as well as I did. "If anyone can find out, Rita can find out. Write down the name of the company. I'll tell her about it—she'll want to know anyway."

I handed him the printout Susa had given me. "Here, take this. I can get another copy. Rita needs the information more than I do."

Dex tucked the folded pages into his pocket. "Maybe the whole thing fell apart when Morehead died. That would be the best outcome for everybody."

Except for Kell. "Yeah, it would." On the other hand, if someone else had been involved in the deal along with Kell, that person or persons might still be pushing ahead with the project. Whatever that project might be.

"I wonder if Kell was the only one working on this," I mused. "Could there have been someone else, somebody who might still be doing some planning?"

Susa munched on a pita chip. "Not many people would have been involved, I'd guess. I mean, the more people who were in on the deal, the more chance people in town would find out about it. The whole idea with this kind of stuff is to keep it very quiet until it's far enough along that no one can stop it."

But surely Kell's death would put a crimp in their plans. Unless he'd been killed by somebody else who knew what was going on in order to make sure the plan went forward. I rubbed a hand across my forehead. The information about Pristine Refuse Removal should have been helpful, but instead it opened up a new series of questions for which I had no answers.

Susa put her hand on my arm. "Hey, at the very least this opens up a different line of questioning about Kell's death. It isn't just the ex-wife who had a reason not to like him. Half the citizens of Coalton would have wanted to string him up if they'd known what he was up to."

"But did they? That's the question. Did anybody know what he was up to? And was that the reason he was killed? And will Kennedy understand that this constitutes a motive for somebody other than Laurel?"

Susa grimaced. "Okay, that's the other thing I was supposed to tell you. From Ethan. He's done a little asking around, and apparently Kennedy's stuck on Laurel as a suspect. He doesn't have anybody else in his sights, and he isn't doing any further investigating. The fact that she's got a lawyer just makes him more certain that she's guilty."

"That's ridiculous," I snapped.

"I agree. But Kennedy isn't known for his brain power." Susa scraped the bottom of the hummus bowl. "Still, if we can nail down more information about this deal, we should pass it on to Laurel's lawyer. Even if Kennedy won't listen, she could get the details out so that other people know about it. That would relieve some of the pressure on Laurel. And it might make people in Coalton go after Kennedy to do more investigating."

I nodded. "True." If nothing else, I could tell Madge what we'd dug up. She'd make certain the news got around to the people who needed to know.

Nate swung into the kitchen again. "Okay, we probably need to do one more refill on everything that's left. We've still got people wandering by and grabbing whatever's still on the platters."

Dex put out the last clean platters, and we began

laying out the end of the apps. Susa pushed herself to her feet. "I'll get out of your way. Let me know if you find out anything more." She glanced toward Dex, waggling her eyebrows.

"Will do." I wondered fleetingly if anyone else would know the details about Kell's deal with Pristine. Possibly, but Rita was our best chance at finding that information.

We got everything out on the tables and loaded the dishwasher again. Dex seemed glum, probably because of the news we'd passed along about Coalton. Nate was also glum because the evening hadn't gone as he'd originally planned, although we did end up serving everything we'd brought. And, as usual, we got lots of compliments on the food and the service. I was glum because I'd begun to believe that nothing we came up with would make Kennedy remove Laurel from the top of his suspect list. Even though Kell was obviously someone who could have made a lot of enemies if people had found out about his plans for a Coalton dump site. If Kennedy closed out the investigation without any suspects besides Laurel, a lot of the people in Coalton would assume she was guilty even though Kennedy hadn't been able to prove it.

We cleaned up the kitchen, which was the only part of the event center we were responsible for. Nate paid Donnell and her crew. Dex left, having packed up a bag of leftovers to take home to Rita and their four-year-old son. Nate and I packed up the rest, which wasn't much. The presence of Georgia and the Blanchettes had been an annoyance, but in the end, we'd still made out fine. And for once we had no pots and pans to return to the catering kitchen since we'd just been rewarming the apps

Nate and Dex had made in advance.

Nate dropped the catering van off at Robicheaux's, then we drove my pickup to the farm. "It went well, didn't it?" I said. "In spite of…well, you know." He still seemed a little glum, but my cheerleading abilities were limited.

He sighed. "It was fine. And everything got eaten. Even Georgia's cheesecake."

The combination of ribs, potato salad, and cheesecake didn't strike me as all that appetizing, but whatever. "Any feedback from the Merchants Association?"

"They were happy, so far as I could tell. They liked the food." He turned onto the county road then glanced at me. "So what's making you unhappy?"

I thought about denying it, but why? "I'm okay mostly. Susa had some information about Kell Moorhead, or sort of about him anyway." I gave him a quick rundown of what Susa had said about Pristine Refuse Removal. It hadn't gotten any better since the last time I'd talked about it.

"Well, damn. So Kell was getting ready to screw Coalton. Sounds like a good motive for murder to me." Nate turned into our drive.

"It's a great motive for someone who's willing to consider alternative suspects. Unfortunately, Kennedy isn't that guy. Fowler told Susa that he's still zeroed in on Laurel. If Rita can actually get some details about what Kell was planning, it might help. Otherwise, he's not going to pay any attention."

Nate pulled up in front of the cabin. "The problem is getting the details nailed down so that it's more than just a rumor. The more specific you can be about what

Kell was trying to do, the more impact you'll have."

"Somebody had to know what he was doing. Somebody had to have heard."

Nate shrugged. "Somebody did. Remember, this all started because you heard a couple of people talking about this at the Blavatskys' place. So far as I know, nobody from the Coalton City Council was there, so the news must have spread beyond Kell's inner circle."

"That's right." I stared at him. Weirdly enough, I'd forgotten where I'd first heard about Kell and Pristine Refuse Removal. "What does Art Blavatsky do for a living anyway?"

"Something financial. I think he works with Tom Everett's bank."

"So the people who were at his party were probably movers and shakers."

Nate reached into the back to grab the few leftovers we had. "Probably."

"Damn. I wish I could remember who was talking about it." I rubbed my fingers over my forehead, pretending that I didn't feel a headache forming.

Nate looked at me. "Did you know any of the other people at that party?"

"No. Just the Blavatskys and their kids. And it was a big party."

"It was. But the fact that people there had heard about Kell's deal meant that it wasn't as secret as he might have thought." Nate opened his door and climbed out. "Other people knew he was up to something. Kennedy may hear about it through the grapevine."

I followed him. "But Kennedy probably won't know what to do about it. He's so focused on Laurel, other possibilities may go right over his head."

Nate opened the front door and stepped inside the cabin. "They won't go over Magdalena's head. If nothing else, maybe she can use Pristine Refuse Removal as a reason to get the county attorney involved. If Kennedy is blowing the case, maybe the attorney can call in CBI to take over the investigation."

I liked that idea a lot. Somebody needed to call Kennedy off, and he wasn't listening to counter arguments from people like me. I followed Nate into the kitchen. "Okay, if Rita digs something up, I'll pass it on to Magdalena. She'll probably know what to do with it better than I would."

"That's my girl." Nate opened the bag of apps. "You hungry?"

"Maybe," I said. "What have we got?"

Nate peeped into the bag again. "Caprese skewers, baba ghanoush, pita, and filo packets."

We always had filo packets left over, although they were delicious. The *vegan* label put some people off. "Sounds good. Let's eat. And before I forget it…" I leaned over and kissed him, putting a little more into it than I'd planned.

Nate's arms slid around my waist, pulling me closer. "We could have a snack in bed."

"We could. Let's do that." I picked up the sack of apps while he snagged a couple of beers from the refrigerator. "And by the way, you may have had to share the limelight with Georgia and the barbecue brothers, but your food was miles better than theirs."

"Damn right," Nate said. "Several thousand miles at least."

He began to nibble on my earlobe, and I decided to stop worrying about catering, Laurel, and Pristine Refuse Removal for the rest of the night.

Chapter 14

I had a few jars of jam left from the farmers market, but not many. Clearly, we were going to have to make a whole lot of jam to keep up with next week's market as well as my other customers. I decided I'd get a jump on things by making jam on Sunday afternoon after we returned from working brunch at the café.

Normally, Nate didn't work brunch anymore, but Marigold was still on a reduced schedule after giving birth to Astrid. Not that Marigold stayed home during brunch while the rest of us worked. She brought Astrid along and found a spot where she could observe the proceedings. Marigold was obviously dying to get back behind the flattop again. But Bobby wasn't nearly as excited by that prospect as she was.

I resumed my original brunch role, mixing mimosas and Bloody Marys. It kept me out of everybody's way as Bobby and Nate worked the grill and Coco took care of pastries and fruit.

After a while Marigold pulled up a chair beside me, sighing.

"Where's Astrid?" I asked since Marigold's arms were empty.

"Madge has her. All the grannies who come in for breakfast are passing her around the dining room. Fortunately, I just changed her a few minutes ago."

"You want a mimosa?" I wasn't sure what the rules

were with nursing mothers. I could probably have whipped up something with minimal champagne.

Marigold shook her head, sighing harder. "I'm at the point where I can have a glass of wine or a beer in the evening after she goes down for the night, but anything more might cause problems. Of course, she'll have to go on partial formula when I come back to work." She brightened at that prospect.

"Still going to try it next month?" The last I'd heard, that was the compromise she and Bobby had worked out. Marigold would be working lunch, but Bobby would still handle breakfast on his own.

She nodded vehemently. "Absolutely. Astrid's a trooper. I've already lined up someone to stay with her, although Madge wanted to bring her to the restaurant. We can do that in a pinch, but not every day."

I could see how having her infant daughter in the dining room might make it tougher for Marigold to concentrate on cheeseburgers. To say nothing of Bobby, who seemed to stand at attention every time his daughter gurgled. "Sounds like you've got it in hand."

"I do," Marigold agreed. "How about you?"

"What about me?" As far as I knew, I had everything in hand. Of course, there was no guaranteeing things would stay that way.

"You find a replacement for Dolce McCray yet?"

"Oh." Now it was my turn to sigh. "Not exactly. Did you hear about Jarrod Perrone?"

"Madge told me the gist. He was working for you, but then you loaned him to Laurel Beacham after her assistant quit. So what happens now? Does he come to work for you, or does he like cheese and burros better?"

"He probably likes cheese and burros better," I said.

"Although nobody's said anything definite yet." But by now I figured I was kidding myself if I thought Jarrod would return to the jam kitchen. Even if he did, he'd probably be miserable.

"So you've got nobody lined up to take Dolce's place permanently?"

"Not yet. I thought I'd get the word out at the high school. And maybe let people know around Second Street, just in case somebody needs a part-time gig." Second Street was restaurant row in Shavano.

Marigold gave me a long look. "Do you want another young assistant, like Dolce and Jarrod?"

I paused. I hadn't thought about age. I was so used to Dolce that I'd been thinking her replacement should be just like her. Now that I considered it, that wasn't necessarily true. "I don't know. I guess I thought of a high schooler because of Dolce and Beck, my market assistant. Teenagers usually need jobs. And they don't mind part time hours after school."

"Yeah, but they're also more likely to leave. How long are you going to be able to hold onto Beck?"

My stomach clenched. I was just getting used to losing Dolce. I didn't want to think about losing Beck yet. "Another year or so."

"Right. Well, here's the thing, if you're willing to consider someone who isn't a teenager, I know someone who might be interested." Marigold folded her arms across her chest, as if she'd just made her opening move.

"I'm willing to consider anyone at this point. Who did you have in mind?"

Marigold took a breath. "Ava McNeil."

I blinked at her. The name was familiar, but I wasn't sure why. "I've heard that name. Why have I heard that name?"

"She used to work for the city. She was in charge of the office where you went to pay parking fines and fees for permits—stuff like that."

A mental image of Ava McNeil popped into my head as soon as Marigold described her former job. A fierce woman with steel-colored curls and a collection of pastel cardigans. She was the terror of that office, able to reduce adult men to something close to tears. You simply did not mess with Ms. Ava. You paid your money, and you kept your receipt with you, exchanging the minimal words necessary to get your business done. And God help you if you decided to complain about the amount of your fine.

I tried to picture her in my kitchen, but it wouldn't come into focus. "Why would Ms. Ava want to make jam?"

"Because she retired last year, and she's going nuts doing nothing. Something I can relate to these days." Marigold gave me a dry smile. "Ava's a kind of relative of mine, the third cousin once removed type. I swing by her place every couple of weeks."

"But kitchen work?" I raised an eyebrow. "It wouldn't be like what she used to do for the city. Does she have any food prep experience?"

"She's a great cook," Marigold said. "Always has been. And she's got commercial kitchen experience, too. She cooked at my granddad's place when she was going to school. Short order stuff, but you know how that is."

I did indeed know how that was. Short order cooks could handle just about anything, as long as it was fried or toasted. "Does she make jam?" It could be a problem if she did. Whoever worked with me had to use my recipes and my methods, no matter how much they might prefer their own. Homemade jam wasn't like jam from a factory, but I still wanted Luscious Delights jams to be as standardized as possible.

Marigold shook her head. "I've never seen her make any. My grandma and my mom both canned up a storm, but I never saw Ava do anything like that. Right now, she's baking a lot—bread and pies mostly. Her husband, Bret, is complaining about how much weight he's put on since she's retired to their place. He'd love to get her doing something somewhere other than their kitchen."

I tried to think of any other reasons Ava might not be a great fit for Luscious Delights, besides the fact that she wasn't a junior in high school. I couldn't think of anything, which probably meant there wasn't anything standing in her way except my lack of imagination.

"Have you talked to her about this?" I asked.

"Nope. I wanted to make sure you'd be willing to hire her first. If you were set on a teenager, I didn't want to get Ava's hopes up."

"Two Bloodies," Coco called from her side of the kitchen.

"I'm not set on a teenager." I poured Bloody Mary mix into a couple of glasses then measured out the vodka. I wasn't set on anybody. It just required me to reprogram my thinking about my assistant. "If she's interested, tell her to give me a call. Then she can come by the kitchen and see what she thinks." I gave the Bloodies a stir, then inserted a couple of celery stalks.

Marigold grinned. "Thanks, Rox. I'll talk it over with her and see how she feels. If she's up for it, I'll have her call you."

The idea that I might have a candidate for kitchen

assistant took one source of stress out of my life. The more I thought about having a non-high-school student as my assistant, the better it sounded. It meant I wouldn't have to work around 4-H trips for once. My finding an assistant still didn't make things better for Laurel, which was my main stressor at the moment. But if she wanted to hang onto Jarrod, it wouldn't ruin my life.

****

I spent the afternoon making peach jam, raspberry jam, and strawberry jam—my foundation flavors. The house smelled of sugar and fruit, which meant it smelled delicious. The thing is, though, you can't double a jam recipe. If you try to do twice as much jam in the same pot, you don't have enough surface area on the mixture to evaporate the water in the fruit and thicken the jam. If I did that, I'd end up with rubbery jam, something I couldn't even sell to my friend Bianca for use in her kolaches.

When you want twice as much jam, which I definitely did, you have to make two pots. Fortunately, I had a commercial stove with six burners. But there was still only one of me, and I still only had two hands.

I also had a pot of tomato jam going on a back burner since it calls for a longer cooking time than the other jams. One of its few advantages was that it could simmer away undisturbed, unlike the other pots that require more regular stirring.

I had five jam pots going: two peach, one raspberry, one strawberry, and that slow-cooking tomato. I figured I'd get around nine jars from each pot. That would take care of my peach quota for the day since that would amount to over a case, but I'd still need another six jars each from the raspberry and strawberry. Which meant once I'd scraped one of those jam pots clean when I filled the jars, I'd put it to soak while I got the processing kettle going. Once the jars were being processed, I'd wash out the kettles and get a couple more batches on to cook while I got the tomato jam into jars.

The kettle held a dozen jars, which meant I could take care of the peach jam in one go. I had to let the jam process for twenty minutes or so because we're at around seven thousand feet and you have to account for altitude in the timing—water boils at a lower temperature above a thousand feet, and that's about as far as I want to go with that explanation. So once the peach was done, the raspberry and strawberry would be ready to scrap into jars and process. I figured I'd get a second processing kettle going once I had a free burner, and I'd take care of the tomato jam, too.

Once upon a time, I'd spend all my days doing this. These days, I'd figured out ways to get more done without my having to do it all. And if I hired Ava and she worked out and she wanted to go full time, maybe I could up my production that much more.

A lot of ifs there, Roxanne. And right then I needed to concentrate on all the things that I needed to get done by the end of the day.

After I got all the next jam run done and processing, I'd wash out the jam kettles and see how I felt. I wanted to finish a case of each flavor, and a case and half would be better. Then tomorrow I'd let Dolce loose on strawberry jam while I picked up the slack on pepper peach.

I was going full steam ahead when someone knocked on my door. "Come on in," I yelled. "It's open."

Yes, I know. That's a dangerous thing to do when

you live far out in the country like we do. But when you live far out in the country, you usually know the people who come calling. And I couldn't leave my jam kettles, regardless.

"Hey, Roxy," someone called, and I leaned around the kitchen entrance to see who was in my living room.

Rita Gleason. Dex's wife. "I'm in the kitchen doing jam," I called. "Come on back."

Rita always looks like a million bucks, even when she's dressed casually as she was when she walked into the kitchen. She wasn't wearing the Italian leather four-inch heels she favored on the job, but her running shoes were very high end, as were her jeans and T-shirt. And her makeup was perfection. All of a sudden, I was only too aware that I'd been working in high humidity all afternoon and probably had hair like Medusa.

Rita pulled out a chair at the kitchen table and dropped into it. "God, it smells wonderful in here. Like fruit and sugar and everything tasty."

"Thanks," I said. "Trying to get a little ahead on things. What's up?"

She sighed. "It's this thing with Pristine Refuse Removal that Dex got from you. I've been working my tail off digging into the details." She looked a little disgruntled, and I wondered if I should apologize for getting her into the mess that was Kell Morehead and his murder.

"You're working fast," I said. "I only told Dex a couple of days ago."

"I know. The thing is…" She paused, then lowered her voice. "This is strictly confidential. My agency was getting ready to do a major push on Coalton. The land prices are great right now, a lot lower than they are around here, and we figure the town's on the verge of getting gentrified. We've already got a developer who's interested in doing something outside the city limits. If we could buy up the land and then work with the developer on something upscale, I think we'd come out ahead. Way ahead." She blew out a breath. "Or anyway, I thought that until I heard about Pristine and Kell Moorhead. If there's a landfill going in somewhere near town, we need to know about it. And we need to know when it's going in and where. I appreciate the heads-up."

I picked up the pot of strawberry and began ladling it into the jars. "So is there a landfill going into Coalton?"

She shrugged. "Hard to say. People who knew Moorhead say he was working with Pristine—that's a fact. But whether he'd actually closed a deal with them is privileged information. I haven't been able to pry anything loose about the current status of the project. They were working with the mine owners, and those guys are as silent as death."

"The coal mine?" That was the only mine I knew of in Coalton, but the mountains around here are full of them, mostly old and mostly abandoned.

"The coal mine," Rita confirmed. "It's played out—they'll never open it again. And the owners would like to get rid of it. We already knew that at the agency. But I don't think it ever occurred to anybody that they could turn the mine into a landfill."

I paused in my jam tasks, staring at her. "You mean they were going to dump trash into the mine? Surely that's illegal. It would affect the ground water." A few years ago, an abandoned mine near Durango had had a catastrophic failure that sent tons of contaminated water gushing into the Animas River. It had taken years to get everything cleaned up and straightened out. Like most former mining towns, Coalton had problems with industrial waste. Dumping a lot of trash on top of that waste didn't strike me as a great idea.

"I'm trying to get more information," Rita said. "I mean, I don't even know who gives permits for something like a coal mine being used as a dump. If it's a city permit, we'll probably have a fight on our hands. The guys who run Coalton aren't known for being particularly responsible stewards."

"No," I said. "But surely a real estate development outside town would be better for Coalton than a garbage dump. Even the Coalton City Council would have to understand that."

"You'd think." Rita gave me a dark look. "Anyway, this whole thing with Kell Moorhead has sort of thrown a monkey wrench into everything. Kell was the front man for the deal, and now that he's dead, nobody's sure who's in charge. Do you think his partners could have killed him?"

I closed my eyes for a moment. "I've got no idea. All I know for sure is that his ex-wife didn't kill him. But the Coalton police chief is determined to prove that she did."

"Maybe somebody in town found out what he was up to and decided to go after him before he could complete the deal," Rita mused. "Maybe there's an environmental group with an axe to grind. So to speak."

"I don't know what environmental groups there are in Coalton. It's not an upscale place right now." And I didn't like the idea of assuming environmentalists would kill somebody, even if he was getting ready to do something nasty to the environment. "I'll make sure

Laurel's lawyer knows all about this deal of Kell's so she can show there were a lot of other people who might have wanted Kell dead. That's my main focus right now."

Rita pushed herself to her feet. "If you could keep the news about the development out of this, I'd appreciate it. We'd like to keep this quiet, so the land prices don't go through the roof."

"I'll try," I said. But if push came to shove, Laurel's freedom was more important than future development in Coalton. "Thanks, Rita. This puts a new focus on Kell's murder. I think even Chief Kennedy will have to consider this as an alternative motive."

"No problem." Rita inhaled. "It must be heaven to be around these smells all the time. Maybe I should learn to make jam."

I didn't know Rita cooked. But maybe she had her specialties just like Dex did. I grabbed a jar of peach from the cooling rack. Fortunately, it was pretty much room temperature. "Here you go. I just made it, so it probably needs to sit for a bit."

"Wow, thanks." Rita grinned. "Dex and Colin were making bread when I left. Now we'll have something luscious to put on it."

Colin was Rita's four-year-old. It sounded like he was taking after his dad. Well, there were certainly worse things he could do.

Like selling out his hometown to a trash company.

Chapter 15

I worked on tomato jam after Rita left so I could build up my stock in case we had a rush of orders when people saw the featured jam. That was probably wishful thinking on my part, but I was trying to be positive about the fate of my veggie jam.

When I told Nate what Rita had found out about Kell, he grimaced. "Jesus. Everything you dig up about that guy makes him sound worse. Who the hell would sell a closed-down mine for a garbage dump?"

"Somebody who wanted fast money?" I shrugged. "Rita hasn't yet found out if the deal is still going forward or if Kell's death shuts things down. If it does, it gives a lot of new people a reason to kill him."

"No shit," Nate muttered. "Including most people who live in the Shavano Valley."

I had no idea how to get in touch with Magdalena Ramos so that I could pass on the information about Kell and Pristine Refuse Removal, but I figured Madge would be a good start. She'd gotten Magdalena involved on Laurel's side to begin with, so she had to have her phone number.

The café was closed on Mondays, and I figured Madge might be up at the main house having coffee. I'd already seen Uncle Mike heading off to the arugula fields, since crops pay no attention to days off, so I probably wouldn't interrupt anything personal. I still had to remind myself occasionally that my uncle was married, and that, like most newlyweds, he and Madge needed their privacy.

Madge opened the door almost immediately after I knocked. "Roxy, for heaven's sake you don't need to knock. Just come in." She headed toward the kitchen. "Would you like some coffee? I was just getting set up to make some snickerdoodles."

Snickerdoodles rank up there as one of my all-time favorite cookies, but I had work of my own to get to. "Just coffee, thanks. I need to get in touch with Magdalena Ramos. I've got some news about Kell Moorhead she might be able to use. I figured you probably knew how to contact her."

"That sounds intriguing." Madge grabbed her French press and poured me a cup. "Can you share?"

"Sure." *Most of it, anyway.* I outlined what Kell was up to with Pristine Refuse Removal. Madge's expression became increasingly irate the more I filled her in.

"That man was the absolute pits," she snapped when I'd finished. "I'm not surprised someone killed him." She paused, a little shocked at herself. "I mean, not that it was right to kill him. It absolutely wasn't. But what he did, or tried to do, was awful. Once people in Coalton found out what he was up to, they'd have been furious. But by then it would probably have been too late to stop him."

That raised an interesting point. Obviously, most of the people in Coalton didn't know what Kell was doing since they hadn't raised a stink about it. So who had known? Assuming Kell was killed because of the deal with Pristine, who'd known enough about what was happening to decide to do something about it?

"I'll call Magdalena and have her get in touch with you so you can pass on the details. She can most likely find out more about everything than either of us. If this doesn't make that fool of a police chief go beyond Laurel for suspects, he's even more of a blockhead than I thought."

"Here's hoping." I rapped my knuckles on Madge's wooden table. I figured we needed all the luck we could get.

****

As I got the day's jam production set up, I tried to remember if I needed to contact anyone else about Kell and the coal mine landfill. I needed to call Susa and give her the details I'd gotten from Rita. After all, she'd been the one who'd started this whole ball rolling.

You need to call Laurel and let her know what's going on.

I closed my eyes. Of course, I did. In fact, I should have called her before I told Madge and Magdalena. I grabbed my phone and stepped outside on the front porch for a little privacy.

Laurel picked up on the third ring. "Hi, Roxy. I've been meaning to call you, but I'm just snowed under right now. I've got all these orders to fill. I swear Jarrod and I are working non-stop. Oh, geez, that's not why you're calling, is it? Tell me you're not taking Jarrod away. I can't spare him right now."

I suppressed a sigh. "No, no, that's okay. Jarrod can stay with you as long as you need him." Which well might be permanently, given that I hadn't heard from him in over a week and Laurel had made no moves toward sending him back. "Actually, I need to talk to you about some stuff I found out about Kell. Stuff that might make a difference in figuring out who killed him."

Laurel paused. "Oh. Okay. Look, I need to make a delivery in Shavano later this afternoon. Could we talk while I'm there? I don't think I want to do this over the phone."

"Sure," I said. "Can you come to the farm? I can give you lunch."

"Probably," she said slowly. "I'll most likely be too late for lunch, though. Maybe around three?"

"I can do that." And Dolce and Bridget would probably both be gone by then, which would cut down on inconvenient questions.

"All right. I'll see you then."

With both Dolce and me in the groove, by noon we'd each gotten a couple of cases done. Bridget worked on the mail orders and, as I'd anticipated, found a ton of orders for peach and pepper peach that we needed to fill. I delegated Dolce to making raspberry and strawberry jam, while I concentrated on the peach variations. "Any orders for tomato jam?" I asked Bridget.

She shook her head. "It's early, though. I just posted it as the special a couple of days ago."

What she didn't say was that we usually had at least a handful of orders for the special a day or so after it was posted. In truth, though, I was just as glad I didn't have to break my concentration on peaches to do more with tomatoes. I already had around a dozen jars of tomato jam ready to go. If we had a low volume of orders, it might be for the best.

And that *is why you'll never be a jam billionaire, Roxanne.* True enough, but not something I was likely to change. I figured I'd start checking for flats of local tomatoes at the farmers market that week. Then I could say the jam was made with fresh-picked summer fruit.

At lunch time, I ducked outside to call Susa. She was just as busy as I was, but I figured she might be taking a quick break to snarf down a sandwich.

"Hey, Rox," she said when she picked up. "What's up?"

"I wanted to fill you in about what Dex's wife found out about Kell Moorhead. Have you got a minute to listen?"

"Sure. I'll just go ahead and chow down on my bologna sandwich." She sounded like she was already doing that, which was fine with me.

I outlined Rita's information about Kell and Pristine and the landfill. Susa made an outraged sound halfway through. "That shit! That absolute shit!"

"Pretty much," I agreed.

"How many people knew about it?"

"Hard to say. Rita didn't know anything about it until she started digging. But I heard about it at the Blavatskys' party, so some local power types must have known. I don't know if it ever leaked out to the general public, though."

"Always the last to know," Susa muttered. "Is it okay if I tell Ethan about this?"

"Sure. Maybe he'll hear something he can pass on."

"Maybe. I'll call you if he does."

Dolce went home to grab some lunch a little after twelve-thirty. Bridget worked through her break because she wanted to leave a little early. One of her daughters needed to go to the dentist, and the other had to get a ride from band camp.

"Do you know Ava McNeil?" I asked her. I hadn't heard anything from Marigold, but I hadn't expected to this soon.

"Ava?" Bridget raised her eyebrows. "Sure. We're in strength training together. Why?"

I managed not to get sidetracked into asking Bridget when she'd started strength training and how many senior citizens were part of her class. "Marigold said she might be interested in taking over for Dolce when she heads to Ft. Collins. I guess she's kind of bored with retirement and trying to find something else to do." I didn't bother giving Bridget Marigold's last name because, after all, there was only one Marigold in Shavano.

"Yeah, I think she is, now that you mention it. Ava's always been a livewire—likes to keep busy. Don't know how she'd feel about cooking jam, though."

"Me, neither. But Marigold's going to ask her. You think she'd be okay working with us?"

Bridget grinned. "Oh, hell yeah. If she wants to cook jam, she'd be great in the kitchen. She's got much better gossip than I do."

That wasn't necessarily an asset since Bridget was already the most gossip-aware person I knew, with the possible exception of Bianca Jordan. But I was still willing to give Ava a try.

****

It was actually closer to three-thirty when Laurel finally made it to the cabin. She looked tired and harried and not at all like the cool cheese master I was used to. "Come in," I said. "Sit down. Would you like something to drink? I've got iced tea or root beer. Or real beer, if you'd rather."

She gave me a wan smile. "Iced tea, please. Could we sit out here on your porch? It's so lovely and cool."

"Absolutely." I ducked inside and grabbed a pitcher of tea that I'd made that morning. Fortunately, I'd dropped in a couple of sprigs of mint so it wasn't just generic.

Laurel settled heavily into one of the Adirondack chairs on my front porch. The porch is wide and comfortable, perfect for watching the stars come out, which Nate and I do whenever we're both around in the evening. I poured a couple of glasses of tea and handed one to Laurel. "How are you?"

"I've been better." She gave me another thin smile. "At least Kennedy left me alone this week. But I'm still getting weird looks on the street, and a couple of women gave me the cut direct at the grocery. I guess I'll try shopping over here at City Market until things calm down."

I wished I had something more substantial to tell her. "I don't know if what I've found out will make any difference, but it might shake things up a little. Did you ever hear Kell mention a company called Pristine Refuse Removal?"

Laurel shook her head. "No. Sounds sketchy."

"You have no idea." I took a deep breath and launched in. "They own landfills all around the country. They were interested in buying the old coal mine in Coalton."

"The coal mine?" Laurel frowned. "It's mined out. The coal that's left would cost more to dig out than it would bring when they sold it."

"Right, well, they weren't interested in the coal," I began.

Laurel stared at me, eyes widening. "Oh, Lord, you don't mean…They were going to turn the mine into a garbage dump?"

I nodded. "Apparently. Most of this is second and third hand, but from what I've heard they were negotiating with the company that owns the mine. According to a real estate friend of mine, the idea was it would become a dump site. And they were keeping it hush-hush because they knew a lot of people in Coalton would be upset if they found out."

"Damn straight," Laurel snapped. "The town's not a hotbed of environmental activism, but nobody wants a garbage dump on the mountain above town where it can affect the water. To say nothing of being an eyesore for anyone coming into Coalton" She paused. "Well, almost nobody would want that. There are people on the city council who'd be open to anything that would make money, no matter how bad it was for the quality of life. Particularly if some of that money made it into their pockets."

"They may have been the ones involved with Kell in setting this up. I don't know for sure."

"What did Kell have to do with it?" She seemed to be steeling herself for whatever was to come.

"As I understand it, he was the guy who was doing the negotiating between the mine owners and Pristine. He might have been the one who came up with the idea in the first place, although I don't know that for sure. Anyway, he's the one who brought Pristine to Coalton and the one who got them together with the mine owners."

Laurel closed her eyes, rubbing her fingers across her forehead. "Of course, he was. He wouldn't think twice about the cost to everyone else in town. He'd just think about how much money he could make himself. He and his buddies on the council."

She looked thoroughly miserable, and I felt sort of guilty for telling her what Kell was up to and ruining her day still further. "I don't know how far along the plans were on this. And I don't know if Kell's death will make any difference. It should, but it's hard to say. I did tell Madge about it so she could pass the information on to Magdalena Ramos."

Laurel sighed. "You think it will help my case?"

"I think it might get Kennedy off his obsession with you as the only suspect. If this is true, and I'm pretty sure it is, there would have been a lot of people in town who had reason to be angry with Kell."

Laurel rubbed her forehead again. "Such as who? Like I said, Coalton isn't a hotbed of activism. People would have been pissed if they'd found out, but I don't know if they'd have been pissed enough to kill him over it."

"There must be some environmentalists in town."

Because every town in the state had environmentalists, just like most everybody in the state felt a little environmentalist spark. You can't live in a place like the Colorado mountains without becoming deeply invested in keeping the landscape beautiful.

Laurel gave me a dry smile. "You'd think. I don't know if the local people are that well organized. Silas might know more about that aspect of things."

I felt a quick drip of ice down my backbone. "You mean Silas Goodman?"

Laurel nodded. "He's as close to an environmentalist as anyone I know. And he's lived on that ranch outside town all his life. If there's anyone in town who qualifies as an activist, he'd most likely know of them."

I thought of Fowler's warning. Silas was a viable suspect in terms of being on the scene when Kell died. And now he might have a motive. "I guess I'll go talk to him," I said slowly.

"Couldn't hurt. Besides, if he doesn't know about this already, he needs to be told. He's probably the best one to organize people to fight against it. And somebody needs to step up. Somebody other than me, obviously."

Talking to Silas would be one way to find what Kell was up to—not that I was entirely sure I wanted to know if he knew about Kell's activities. If anybody asked me, I wanted to be able to say I had no idea what Silas knew or didn't know.

Laurel pushed herself to her feet. "I've got to get back. I left Jarrod on his own to get the goats milked."

I blinked. "Jarrod milks the goats?"

"Oh, yeah. He's good at it. The animals all love him. I'm not worried about him getting the milking done, I just don't want to give him too much to do. He's so conscientious." She gave me an apologetic look. "I'm depending on him, Rox. And I think he enjoys what he's doing. He's a great kid."

"Yeah," I said. "He is."

Laurel smiled, patting me on the shoulder. "Thanks again for letting him come to work for me. I don't know what I'd have done without him."

"Sure," I said. "I'm glad he's working out." And I really was glad.

Still, as I watched Laurel roll up the drive to the county highway, I found myself hoping mightily that Ava McNeil wanted to get into jam making. Because it more and more it seemed like I wasn't going to reclaim my last assistant any time soon.

Chapter 16

I kept putting off my promise to talk to Silas about Kell Moorhead and his coal mine landfill. I finally asked Uncle Mike if he was planning on talking to Silas in the next couple of weeks. I figured I could have him pass on the details about Kell rather than having to do it myself.

Yes, it was cowardly. But the truth was, I figured there was no way I'd be able to deduce whether or not Silas killed Kell from a simple conversation. The most that could happen would be I'd end up feeling even more suspicious than I already did. And I really didn't want to feel that way. Not about Silas, my "honorary uncle," who'd been around most of my life.

My dad and Uncle Mike were both friends with Silas. I remembered visiting his burros when I was a kid and having Silas boost me onto his shoulders so I could watch the rodeo parade in Shavano when I was six or so. He was close to a family member, and I didn't want to suspect him of anything.

Uncle Mike shook his head. "Haven't seen him lately. He used to come into Bolger's for coffee once a week or so, but he hasn't been there for a while. 'Course, that fool burro race is coming up. Most of the people planning on doing the race are spending all their free time training."

I'd managed to forget all about the burro race, although it was what had gotten me involved in this

181

situation in the first place. "It's in a couple of weeks, isn't it?"

Uncle Mike nodded. "A week from Sunday. Guess that means Laurel won't be doing her stand at the market that week if she's going up that mountain with her donkey. Wouldn't want to be standing around the day before. Or anyway, I wouldn't want that if I was her."

"Maybe not." I wondered if I could possibly make it over to Coalton to see the start of the race since that was always the most fun. Well, the start and the finish. They were both worth watching. On the other hand, I wasn't sure I could drag myself out of bed at the crack of dawn on a Sunday morning, which was when the race was supposed to start.

"Anyway," Uncle Mike said, "if you're going over to Silas's place, you can take some hay for me. He ordered a few bales, and I haven't gotten them delivered yet."

"We're selling hay this year?" We didn't grow much hay, and we didn't always sell it, depending on whether we needed it ourselves or whether we'd promised it to someone in trade. Apparently, this year we could do what we wanted.

"We're not selling much, and it's mostly to Silas and a couple of other people. But he claims that burro of his is finicky. Likes the taste of our hay. Who am I to argue with a finicky burro?"

"Okay, I can take it to him if it's a small enough load for me to lift. Maybe tomorrow afternoon after we knock off for the day."

"No problem. Donnie and I can load you up, and Silas can help at the other end."

Dolce and I were doing a good job of building up

my jam supplies. I'd already taken care of what we needed for the next farmers market, and now we were getting ahead of the demand for mail orders. I'd even added a few more jars to my meager stock of tomato jam, hoping I'd have a rush of orders at some point.

I always felt a little better when the storage shed had several full cases waiting. I figured I could take a couple of hours off and head up to Silas's ranch.

Uncle Mike and Donnie loaded five bales of hay into my truck when I was ready to go. It didn't seem like enough for a burro like Oliver, but maybe he was both finicky and picky. Anyway, he wasn't my problem—Silas knew what his burro needed.

****

Silas Goodman lived on his family's ranch in the foothills outside Coalton. It was a stunning location, with a wonderful view of the Collegiate Peaks and spreading grasslands that bordered both sides of the road leading toward the house. The ranch itself was a Centennial Ranch, meaning it had been in the family for a hundred years or more. The ranch and Coalton had grown up together. I only wished Coalton had taken as good care of itself as Silas took of the Goodman Ranch.

A few of Silas's burros were in the field nearest the house, probably the ones he couldn't lease out for some reason. I knew he leased a lot of his burros to the tourists, just like Dusty Vance. I also knew, or I'd heard, that Silas was much more conscientious about training the tourists on burro racing basics than Vance and some of the other burro ranchers were. You can't let somebody loose on a trail with a burro unless they've had some basic instruction on what to expect, like Laurel telling me to keep ahead of the burro as we went downhill to avoid being jerked off my feet. Every year tourists got hurt when their burros got away from them. Fortunately, if you let go of your burro's lead rope, you were automatically disqualified from the race, which meant tourists who didn't know what they were doing got out of everybody's way pretty quickly.

Silas required the people who leased his burros to take some extended sessions with him so they could get used to the burros, and vice versa. Those tourists might still lose their hold on the burros' lead rope, but they were a lot less likely to slide down a mountainside in the process.

I parked near the ranch house and went looking for Silas since I didn't know where he wanted the hay unloaded. I found him in the barn, cleaning some bridles which could have been for the burros or for the two or three horses cropping grass in the field behind the house. "Hey, Roxanne," he said. "How are you? Haven't seen you in a while."

Not since we'd found Kell's body, in fact, although I didn't feel like bringing that up just then. "I'm doing well. I brought you some hay from Uncle Mike. Where would you like it?"

He put the bridles in the tack room and headed toward the house. "I'll come get it."

Both of us unloaded the hay bales into a shed near the corral, which reminded me that Silas wasn't a youngster anymore. If I had to guess, I'd put his age in the mid-sixties. But he was one of those older men who gave you more than a few hints of the impact he must have had on any woman who crossed his path back in the day. He wore his silver hair brushed away from his face, a little longer than his shirt collar, with a short beard and moustache to match. His eyebrows were still dark, however, like his eyes.

In his youth he was probably a Kris Kristofferson type, a real lady killer. So to speak.

We stacked the bales in the shed, and Silas wiped his forehead with his sleeve. "Oliver thanks you," he said. "Dang burro just loves that clover hay Mike grows. And it's got more nutritional value than the stuff I grow here. I want to build him up for racing season."

"How's he doing?" I asked.

Silas grinned. "I don't know whether to tell you he's not performing up to snuff and hope you'll up the odds against him or tell you he's a champ and do the opposite." Betting on the burros isn't an official part of the race, but nobody around here makes rules about what people can and can't do on their own time.

I grinned back. "I'm not betting, so you could just tell me the truth."

Silas shrugged. "He's not as good as his father, Stanley. But he's a game little guy. He's finding his stride now. He could take the Coalton race. Probably not Fairplay or Leadville, though. He's not up to the big endurance tests yet."

"Laurel will fight you for Coalton," I said. "I don't know what her plans are for the other races."

Silas leaned against the fence, watching one of his horses canter across the pasture. "How's she doing? I haven't seen her since that idiot Kennedy decided she was his top suspect for Kell Moorhead's murder."

"She's okay, I think." I took a breath, ready to dive in. "Things are a little better now that they've got some ideas about what Kell might have been doing that got people upset with him."

Brow arched, Silas glanced at me. "And what would that be?"

I matched his posture, leaning against the fence to watch the horses do their thing. "Have you ever heard of a company called Pristine Refuse Removal?"

Silas groaned. "Already I don't like this. No, I've never heard of them, and I'm guessing I should probably be happy that I haven't."

"I'm not sure ignorance is bliss in this situation." I turned to look at him. "They own landfills around the country. They want to open one in Coalton. In the old coal mine."

Silas stared at me, his eyes widening. "Jesus H. Christ."

I nodded. "Yeah, that's been the same reaction I've gotten from almost everyone I've told about this. Kell Moorhead was their local contact. He was the one doing the negotiations with the mine owners."

Silas's jaw had tightened noticeably. "They can't open a landfill at the mine. That violates more environmental regulations than I can count. The state would be on them like white on rice."

"I don't know how they planned on meeting the state regulations—or, more likely, get around them. They probably had a plan. I also don't know if the plan is still in place or if they've backed off now that Kell is dead."

"That's something I can find out." Silas pushed himself upright. "And I will find out, trust me. We can mobilize about this. They may think they've got us blocked with some kind of *fait accompli*, but they don't. We'll fight back, and we'll keep them in court longer than they're willing to stay there."

My heart rate promptly sped up. "Who is the 'we'

here?"

Silas frowned at me. "What?"

"Who are the ones who will fight this? Is there an organization that can take Pristine on?" And one that might have been angry enough about the landfill to take Kell out if they'd found out what he was trying to do.

Silas rubbed a hand across the back of his neck. "No organization. Just people. Locals. Ones who give a crap about the future of the town—enough to fight against some get-rich-quick scheme like this."

"Are there enough people in Coalton to fight against a company that has some power?" And enough people who weren't eager to make money from the deal themselves?

"Of course there are." Silas paused. "Or, anyway, there should be. We've got a bunch of fools on the city council right now, but I can pretty much guarantee that anyone who backs a plan like this is going to get voted out of office right quick."

"But Kell was the city manager," I reminded him. "He was working for the city council." Which meant he should have known what the city council's views on the deal would be. That could be why the deal was kept so secret.

Silas's mouth folded into a thin line. "Kell Moorhead was a crappy city manager. He did whatever the big money interests in the region wanted him to do. I'm not surprised he was involved in this."

"Do you think this was enough to have gotten him killed?"

Silas narrowed his eyes. "Gotten him killed by who?"

I shrugged. "People who didn't like the project.

People who thought he messed up the project. People who wanted to make money and didn't want to cut him in." All were viable possibilities, although I thought the first one was the most likely, as motives went.

Silas paused for a long moment, staring out at the playful horses again. "I'd like to think no one who was angry about the landfill would kill Moorhead over it. I'm betting he's just one of the people involved, and maybe not the most important one. He didn't have much money to invest, so far as I know. Killing him wouldn't necessarily stop the project going forward. It would just…confuse things."

"I hope that's true. But it just seems likely that Kell's death is involved with this deal. I mean, I figure it's probably the biggest thing Kell had going. Although I could be wrong about that."

"Probably true." Silas rubbed his eyes. "Coalton's basically a wide spot in the road for most people. Not much going on, not much opportunity, not much future. Moorhead probably saw it as someplace to get out of. And the fastest way to get out would be to sell out. To find a way to monetize your time here. God knows, he wasn't the only one who wanted to do that. Hard to find people who believe the town actually has much to look forward to."

"Laurel believes it," I said. "She's always coming up with ways to get Coalton some attention from the tourist trade."

"She has at that." Silas grinned. "One of the many reasons I like that girl. I'm always searching for people who believe in the town, who want it to have a future. Who else would think to get us a burro race, by God?"

"And a farmers market," I added. I actually needed

to check with Laurel about that. The second Coalton farmers market was supposed to take place next Wednesday afternoon. I had to make sure the suspicions about Laurel hadn't destroyed her projects.

"Damn straight. Everybody else has one. Why not Coalton? You just need someone willing to put in the work. We haven't had anybody like that until now. She's already made a difference. A big difference."

We were both quiet for a moment, probably both thinking the same thing. The difference Laurel was making would stop if she was charged with murder. In fact, it would probably stop even if she wasn't charged. If people went on suspecting she was involved in Kell's death, that suspicion might well be enough to drive her out of town. I wondered if that could be a motive for Kell's murder, but I decided that was a little too wildly paranoid even for me. Killing Kell to get rid of Laurel was too baroque to be real.

"Kennedy can't go on harassing her indefinitely," Silas said slowly. "He's not the brightest bulb on the tree, but even he has to realize he's got no evidence to speak of. And she's got a good lawyer, who could probably drive a truck through all the holes in his case. Plus, even though the county attorney is a politician, he isn't an idiot. If he takes a good look at Kennedy's case, he'll tell him to take a hike. Kennedy's got nothing on Laurel, and he's not likely to find anything."

"But will the town welcome her? Will they be interested in her ideas?" I bit my lip as I watched the horses again. "Or will they assume she got away with murder and that they don't want to work with her anymore?"

Silas sighed. "I wish I could tell you they'll take her

back with open arms, but I can't promise that. It's a small town, and Laurel hasn't lived here that long. And part of the time she lived here, she was married to Kell Moorhead. In an argument with Brendan Kennedy, they may go with the guy who's lived here longer, even though that guy's a real idiot."

I shook my head. Clearly it was time to end this conversation. I was tired of being depressed about Laurel and suspicious of everybody in Coalton. "Well, I wish you luck getting that landfill project stopped. It sounded like a disaster in the making."

"Another disaster in the making." Silas grimaced. "For a picturesque small town with a hard luck past, Coalton's gone through a lot of them."

"But they've got you," I said. "And they've got Laurel. And like you said, a lot of people may get motivated if they think the town's in danger."

"True enough." Silas paused and gave me a long look that made me feel like fidgeting. "And not one of those people would have killed Kell Moorhead," he said slowly. "God knows I didn't have anything to do with his death, in case you were wondering."

"I know you didn't," I said and hoped I sounded convincing.

"I wouldn't blame you. All I can do is tell you it wasn't me. And it wasn't Laurel. And I hope to God that asshole Kennedy gets himself together enough to ask just who it could have been. Because the town needs to know the truth before we move on."

I wanted to believe Silas, and I mostly did. But I also wanted to know who'd killed Kell Moorhead. Because in one area he was absolutely correct: Judging by the way things were going, the town of Coalton wouldn't be able to move on until this whole question was settled.

Chapter 17

I called Laurel after I got home to confirm that the Coalton Farmers Market was going to take place as advertised.

"So far as I know," she said. "It's been a tough week, but most of the vendors have checked in, and the city finally confirmed that the space was ours. I don't think they're happy about it, mind you, but they're giving us the space anyway. Which is only fair since I set it up weeks ago."

"They should be delighted. Last time you filled up the downtown and most of us vendors sold out. It was a big success." All of which Laurel knew, but I figured it wouldn't hurt to remind her that she'd been a hit. Particularly when people in town were ganging up on her without proof.

I packed a few cases of raspberry, strawberry, peach, and pepper peach—the flavors I knew would sell. And then I threw in a half case of strawberry basil and a little amaretto peach. They sold like hotcakes at the Shavano farmers market, but the Coalton farmers market was still an unknown quantity. I wasn't sure whether they'd take to my "exotics."

And speaking of exotics, I added a couple of jars of tomato jam. It hadn't been moving online. I'd sold no more than a dozen jars all told when my specials usually sold a lot more briskly. People were a little cautious about it at the Shavano market, too, although there they could taste it and swap recipe possibilities. I figured I'd keep bringing it and hope that the people who took some home would talk it up to their friends. And meanwhile, I'd try to make up for the slow online sales by stepping up the sales at the markets.

At the last minute, Nate came home early and said he'd go over to Coalton with me to help out. That was great on a whole lot of levels. Once again, we hadn't had much time together for the past week or so—he was working on a big party next weekend, and I was trying to keep ahead of demand by making jam hand over fist. It was great that we were both successful, but sometimes I missed the days when we had a few hours off now and then to sit around together.

Laurel's market was scheduled for the afternoon again, starting at three and running until six, great for attracting people as they were heading home from work. She wasn't doing a thank-you party afterward this time, but I figured no one expected her to under the circumstances. The city had closed off the same stretch of street, and Laurel had picked up a few more vendors than she'd had last time. The booths were casually packed together, which gave the sense of abundance and selectivity at the same time. You don't want so many vendors that people get lost in the crush. But at the same time, you don't want just a handful of people, which can give the impression nobody wanted to be part of your farmers market.

Right now, Laurel was hitting just the right level for a small market. It wasn't as big as Shavano's, but Coalton was a lot smaller town. It was cozy and friendly and smelled delicious.

Nate helped me set up my booth and then took off to see who else was around. I was next to Kathy Vargas's salsas and molés. Kathy was a former coder who'd decided she liked cooking better than coding. Everything she did was wonderful, and I was sort of amazed that she was at the Coalton market. She usually sold only at the big Front Range markets like Boulder, with the occasional drop-in at Shavano.

"Hey, Kath," I said. "Long time no see."

She gave me a dreamy smile as she arranged her half-pint jars by type. "This time slot just worked out for me. I couldn't take on another weekend market, but Wednesday suits my schedule fine. How are you doing?"

"Good," I said. "Last time we did this, it was surprisingly busy. I sold out pretty quickly."

Kathy set up a three-jar pyramid of her adobo. "You should come across the mountains. You'd sell out everything at Boulder."

"Maybe sometime." I managed a sort of sincere smile. The idea of doing one of the big markets like Boulder made my stomach clench. It would require a whole lot more product, and once I did it, I'd be committed to making the drive every summer weekend. I'd have to turn my Shavano booth over to someone else to run since I'd need to be on the Front Range.

Uncle Mike reminded me regularly that I needed to branch out if I wanted to go bigtime. The problem was, I wasn't at all sure I wanted to be any bigger than I was at the moment. *Not a problem to be solved right now, Roxanne.*

Someone started setting up on my other side, and I glanced over to see Bianca Jordan and her son Marcus unfolding a smaller version of her bake stand. Another new vendor for Coalton and another surprise. Bianca was the queen of the Shavano farmers market, a baker so talented she had lines out the door of her downtown bakeshop. But so far as I knew, she only sold in Shavano. She was so successful she didn't need to sell anywhere else, and she'd told me more than once that she didn't want to traipse around the state carrying loaves of bread that wouldn't taste nearly as good as they did fresh out of the oven.

As I watched the two of them set up, though, I could sort of see what they were up to. Marcus, Bianca's son, was a terrific butcher who made his own sausage and deli meats. Nate bought Marcus's stuff whenever he did a charcuterie board for an event, and it was always a hit. But Marcus wasn't as well-known as Bianca. He wasn't struggling, but he hadn't gotten the attention he deserved, given the quality of his stuff. The booth he and his mom were setting up actually featured Marcus's goods more than Bianca's. Marcus was laying out a display of his sausages on one side, while Bianca had added a few loaves of sour dough and rye, just to make her presence felt. The Coalton booth was clearly Marcus's show, which he emphasized by laying out a variety of his specialty meats for tasting. Bianca wandered off like Nate, probably also looking for familiar faces.

Giving tastes at farmers markets is sort of controversial. It's true you get a lot of people who just want free food and don't want to buy anything. And you get lots of kids who taste anything and everything just because they can. But you also get people who may be sort of on the fence about buying, and who can be tipped over into a purchase if they like what they taste. I always put out samples of my jams, but I also ride herd on repeat samplers under twelve. They can absolutely clean you out if you aren't careful.

"Hey, Marcus," I said. "I didn't know you were going the farmers market route."

He nodded. "I'm doing a dry run over here. If it works out, I'll try Shavano, but I may start out selling from Mom's booth first."

"Makes sense." Bianca's booth was one of the busiest in the Shavano market. If Marcus sold there, he'd have her built-in customer base. "Is Bianca selling with you tonight?"

"She's around somewhere." Marcus shrugged. "She said she was going to check out the other vendors and see if there was anything she wanted to buy. This set-up is small enough for me to handle on my own. That's what Laurel said, anyway."

"It probably will be." Although the number of customers might increase just like the number of vendors. Always assuming the citizens of Coalton didn't decide to shun Laurel as a possible murderer.

"Have you seen Laurel tonight?" Marcus asked.

I shook my head. "I talked to her this morning, and she said she was selling her cheese. She should be around here somewhere."

Although it was a little out of character for her not to be walking around talking to everybody. Maybe she'd decided that staying out of sight would be better for business.

"She's here. Or she will be. That's what she said." Kathy Vargas picked up a sample of Marcus's soppressata. "This is terrific."

"Thanks," said Marcus. "Did you bring any of that

molé poblano you had at the expo in Grand Junction last year? The stuff that was so good on pork shoulder?"

Kathy grinned. "I might be able to dig out a jar for you. Particularly if you're willing to trade for some of your garlic sausage."

"Sold," Marcus said quickly.

I thought about offering him some tomato jam, but that seemed a little desperate. Besides, it wasn't like I couldn't sell it at all. Or anyway, I hoped it wasn't like that.

Nate wandered back a few moments later, carrying one of our shopping bags. He raised it in my direction. "Fresh pasta from Eddie Romero. He says it doesn't need to be refrigerated, but I have my doubts."

"There's a cooler in the truck," I said. "And you can probably get some ice from somebody around here."

"Right. I'll see what I can find."

We were moving closer to the three o'clock start time, and I still hadn't seen Laurel. Not that I needed to see her necessarily. I'd been doing my booth at various farmers markets for a long time now, and I knew how they worked. But I wanted to check in with her, just to make sure she was doing okay.

Laurel's problems aren't your problems, Roxanne. You don't need to do a welfare check on her.

That was true, but I still felt antsy about things. When Nate returned with his ice-filled cooler, I asked him to take over the booth for a couple of minutes so I could check things out.

I walked the center aisle between the rows of booths, waving at a couple of friends and searching for Laurel's goat cheese. I finally found her booth almost at the end of the row. She'd given herself one of the less desirable spots, maybe so that the visiting vendors would feel more welcome.

I stepped up to the booth, but I didn't see Laurel behind the counter. Instead, Jarrod was standing in front of the cooler filled with goat cheese looking equal parts terrified and hopeful. "Hey," I said. "How are you? How are things with Laurel?"

Jarrod gave me a panicked gaze. "She just texted me. She said she's running late, and I should take over the booth. Only I've never done it before."

At least that was something I could help with. "You'll be fine. You know each of the types of goat cheese you've got for sale, right?"

"Yeah. Pretty much."

"And you know how much they cost."

He looked anxious again. "Sort of."

I took a quick survey of the counter. "There's the price list if you need it."

Jarrod glanced at the price list taped to the counter, then smiled a little more confidently.

"When they pay you, you open the cash box over there and put the money away. Then put the cheese in one of those bags and give it to the customer." I gestured toward the stack of paper bags next to the cooler.

Jarrod bit his lip. "What about if they need change?"

"You mean how do you figure out how much change to give?"

He nodded, nervous all over again.

I stepped behind the counter and opened Laurel's cash box, which was a lot like mine. And like mine, along with the twenty bucks or so in small bills, she also had an ancient calculator tucked at the back. "Just use this to figure it out."

Jarrod squinted at the calculator as if it was a visitor from Alpha Centauri. "I don't know how that works."

I took a deep breath. *Twenty-first century kid here.* "Do you have a calculator app on your phone?"

"Yes, ma'am."

"Then use it instead. They work the same way."

"They do?" Jarrod seemed doubtful.

"They do. Trust me."

"Okay. Thanks." Jarrod gave me a tentative smile. "Sorry I haven't been around to make jam. I guess Laurel talked to you about it."

"She did. It's okay. Are you enjoying the goats?"

His smile this time was a lot more definite. "Oh, yeah. They're great. And the burros. And I'm learning all about making cheese, which is super cool."

"Well, that's all right then. I'll check later to see if Laurel's s gotten here."

"Right. I'll tell her you were looking for her."

I worked my way to my booth, more and more convinced that Jarrod wouldn't be back with me again. I needed Ava McNeil or someone like her to make jam. In fact, I probably needed her more than she needed me. I figured I'd call Marigold this weekend and see if she had any news. If Ava decided she wasn't interested in the job, I might fall to my knees and beg.

Customers had begun to arrive, and the crowds built up slowly but steadily. Some farmers markets don't allow dogs, but Laurel had decided Coalton would be a "the more the merrier" kind of place. Now people walked the rows with dogs in sizes from Pomeranians to Newfoundlands. Since some people also came with strollers and babies, we had an instant crush as the various groups tried to sidle by each other and the dogs worked on either tolerating or intimidating the other dogs.

I put Nate in charge of the tasting bowls since his killer stare kept the under-ten set from emptying the samples. I got to work answering questions and taking money. After the first thirty minutes or so, things settled down a bit. I fielded a few questions about the tomato jam and how to use it, and I actually sold a jar to an adventurous senior who decided it would work in her mac and cheese.

Nate filled all the sample bowls, then walked off to see what was happening elsewhere. Marcus was doing a brisk business, maybe among those customers who were still trying to find something for dinner that night. Kathy's booth was surrounded by tasters and aficionados of her molé. It looked like Laurel had another hit on her hands.

Which made it all the stranger that she wasn't on hand herself. I was beginning to get a very bad feeling about all of this.

I was counting out change for a small boy who'd actually bought his own jar of strawberry jam when a shadow fell across the counter. I glanced up to see the very solid presence of Chief Brendan Kennedy looming over me. The boy with the strawberry jam beat a hasty retreat after a scowl from the Chief of Police.

I took a breath, resolving not to be intimidated. "Good afternoon, Chief. Could I interest you in some jam?"

The scowl intensified into something closer to a sneer. "You've been messing with my investigation. You need to stop it. Now."

I've gotten that same complaint before from Fowler,

but he and I have a decent working relationship. Of course, I had no relationship of any kind with Kennedy and Fowler never tried to frighten me. "What is it you think I've done?" I set about rearranging the jam jars, which didn't actually need rearranging.

"Moorehead's deal with the trash guys is none of your business," he snapped. "It's got nothing to do with his death. You're just getting people upset when they've got no cause to be."

I leaned back to look at him. He was a very big man in the sense that he probably weighed upward of two hundred pounds. I doubted that he was in great shape, though. Right now his broad face was suspiciously red, either from anger at me or the exertion of walking down the rows of market vendors to find my booth. "You don't consider the fact that Kell Moorhead wanted to bring a secret landfill to Coalton constitutes a pretty good motive for murder as far as some people are concerned?"

Kennedy's face got even pinker. "It wasn't a secret. All the people who needed to know about it already knew about it. And all the people who matter in this town were on Moorhead's side. Nobody killed him over it."

There were a lot of holes in that statement. "Funny," I said. "Nobody I've talked to had any idea what Kell was up to. And they were all pretty pissed about it when they heard. So maybe your definition of the people in town *who needed to know about the dump* is sort of limited."

Kennedy leaned close, eyes bright with malice. It's hard to loom over someone as tall as me, but he was giving it his best shot. "You don't get it, do you? This is none of your business. You don't even live here. And you sure as hell don't have any right to be sticking your nose into a police investigation. If I find out you're stirring things up around here, I'll throw you in a cell so fast your head will be spinning when you hit the floor."

I was pretty sure he couldn't do that legally. On the other hand, if he threw me into one of his cells, it might take me quite a while to get out of it. Logic argued for caution. Still, I hate being pushed around by guys who don't have any right to push me around.

"All I've done is pass along information I've heard to people who might be interested. So far as I know, that doesn't break any laws. Seems to me the people who live here need to know what's going on with their city. Maybe they're not as okay with a landfill above town as you are."

"You. Don't. Live. Here." Kennedy snarled. "Like I said, this is none of your business. Keep out of it and keep your mouth shut."

I gritted my teeth as I stared at him, trying to think of something to say that wouldn't get me into deeper trouble while conveying the point that he had no right to push me around.

Kennedy straightened, his gaze still burning, then swept one arm across the surface of the counter, sending jars of jam flying in all directions. I glared at him, furious and horrified.

The corners of his mouth edged up ever so slightly. "Oops."

Two jars of strawberry jam had smashed down against the concrete pavement, oozing bright red jam. Others rolled under the edge of my booth and into the booths on either side. One caromed off the side of Marcus's booth, cracking open as it fell.

Marcus jumped up, frowning. "What the hell?"

"What the hell do you think you're doing?" someone shouted, and I saw Nate striding down the aisle toward my booth. "Who the fuck are you?"

Kennedy's nasty smile broadened, and he pulled his two-way radio off his belt. "We got ourselves a situation here at this farmers market. Dangerous individuals causing a potential disturbance. May need to close it all down."

The other vendors around us stared at him. Marcus stepped out of his booth beside Nate, although Lord only knows what they could have done with the chief without ending up in jail themselves.

"Don't be an idiot, Kennedy. Let it go. Your buddies at the city council won't be happy if you bring down a lot of bad publicity on the town." Silas Goodman strolled easily down the center aisle, but his jaw looked tense. I didn't blame him. The tension in my own jaw was almost painful.

Kennedy's expression didn't change. "You got business here, Goodman?"

"I'm a customer," Silas said. "Lots of good food available. You should stroll around while I help Roxy clean up after your little 'accident.'"

The two men stared at each other for another long moment. Then Kennedy grimaced. "Place is supposed to close down at six. I'll be back then with some of my men to make sure everybody clears out."

He turned on his heel and stalked toward the street. I had not the slightest doubt that he'd do exactly what he said.

I knelt and started cleaning up the smashed jam jars. If I wanted to sell any more jam before six, I figured I needed to take care of the mess. Besides, scraping up the spilled jam kept people from seeing the way my hands were trembling.

Chapter 18

Nate was furious, and I didn't blame him. I was pretty furious myself. Also frustrated and annoyed at being helpless. And, to be honest, shaken up and still a little frightened. But cleaning up was about all I could do. After all, where was I going to go to lodge a complaint about Kennedy? The police station was obviously out.

The other vendors all milled around, looking concerned. I wished Laurel were there. The fact that a vendor had been vandalized—by the Coalton Police Chief no less—was, well, upsetting. If the cops went after me, might they go after other people, too? What kind of farmers market was this, anyway?

Gradually, people went back to their booths. Customers still wandered the aisles, most of them oblivious to my drama. The vendors might be unsettled by Kennedy's actions, but they still had products to sell. I didn't blame them. Fortunately, Nate helped me clean up the mess and retrieved the jam jars that had rolled under the counter. In between the tasks involved in getting my booth in shape, I had people who wanted to buy jam. In the end, I'd only lost a few jars, so I still had product to sell. And I was determined I'd sell out, just to show Kennedy he couldn't drive me out of business.

Around five forty-five, though, I started putting a few of the remaining jars into a box, leaving the bare minimum out on the counter. I might say I wanted to sell out, but I figured if Kennedy made good on his threat and showed up on the dot at six, mine would be the first booth where he'd stop.

Still, at five before six, it wasn't Kennedy who walked up the aisle but Laurel. She looked like she was holding herself together by her fingernails. Her jeans weren't the kind you'd wear out in public normally, and her faded T-shirt was more worn than vintage.

"Roxy," she said. "I'm so, so sorry. That thing with Kennedy should never have happened. You should lodge a complaint with the county attorney. I'll help. He shouldn't get away with this."

"Not your fault," I said as I closed up the carton of jam. "And my sales were better than last time, so I can absorb a couple of broken jars." That was my way of sounding like a tough girl. Inside, I was still trembling.

Laurel rubbed a hand across her forehead as if she was fighting a headache. "I know, but I really want you to lodge a complaint. Kennedy's moving way outside his lane, and somebody needs to stop him."

I wasn't anxious for that *somebody* to be me. "Where were you earlier? A lot of people were trying to find you."

Laurel gazed around at the vendors who were still in place. "I was at the police station. Kennedy said he had a few more questions, and he said it would be quick. He lied. It was a long session. I think he hoped he could screw with the market, but fortunately all of you were pros. You didn't need me to get things started."

So we had another reason to be mad at Kennedy. He'd tried to derail the farmers market for no purpose I could see beyond the fact that it was Laurel's project, and

Kennedy wanted her to be Kell's murderer. I wondered if he was following orders from the city council, or the members of the city council who'd known about, and possibly supported, Kell's project.

"This town is so screwed up right now." Laurel closed her eyes for a moment. "I only hope they leave the burro race alone. We've already got a lot of entries, counting the tourists who are just in it for fun. Figure in the money the hotel and restaurant people will make, and the town stands to clear a lot of profit off the race if they're willing to let me follow through."

That seemed like a prime example of cutting off your nose to spite your face. "Any sign that they won't?"

Laurel shrugged. "Who knows? Not many people on the city council are talking to me right now. I'm just keeping my head down and plowing ahead, hoping everything goes smoothly."

"How'd Jarrod do with the booth?" I asked.

"He was great." Laurel grinned. "We came close to selling out. I think we probably would have if I'd been able to get here in time."

I heard the sound of loud footsteps and glanced up. Chief Kennedy was stalking down the aisle, followed by the same two young cops who were his usual minions. His head turned right and left, checking to make sure the vendors were shutting down their booths.

"Oh, Lord," Laurel muttered. "The stormtroopers have arrived." She took a deep breath and started toward Kennedy.

Whatever happened between them, though, the market was clearly through for now. I got the last few jars of jam packed away and started loading the truck.

⁂⁂⁂⁂

Nate and I drove home mostly in silence. I didn't figure there was much to say. Kennedy was an asshole, and Laurel was probably right about lodging a complaint with the county attorney, but I thought maybe I'd talk to Fowler before I did anything drastic.

I wished I could file that complaint in Shavano, but that was clearly a non-starter. Unless Kennedy was dumb enough to carry his harassment beyond the city limits of Coalton.

Uncle Mike and Madge trotted down from the main house as we were unloading the couple of partial cases I had left. "Are you okay?" he asked. "Silas called and said some cop broke up your booth."

I squared my shoulders. "It wasn't that bad. He smashed up a couple of jars of jam and threatened to close down the market, but Silas talked him out of it."

"He was a bullying SOB, and Roxy's going to lodge a complaint with the county attorney," Nate snapped. He didn't seem to be nearly as doubtful as I was. But then I had to figure out the problem of just how to lodge that complaint without having to go through Brendan Kennedy.

"Oh, Roxy, how awful." Madge gave me a quick hug, which had the effect of making me feel like bursting into tears. Not what I wanted to do right then.

I closed my eyes and told myself to cool it. "I'm okay. Really. He scared me, but not as much as he'd hoped he would."

Nate stepped beside me, putting his arm around my shoulders and pulling me close. "You were a trooper. You didn't let him see how he'd shaken you up." He leaned down then and kissed my cheek.

I wished everybody would stop being so nice. Any

minute, I was going to start blubbering, and I was afraid I wouldn't be able to stop. I glanced up at Nate. "Do we have anything around for dinner?"

"Sure. Leftovers if nothing else." He gave my shoulder a quick squeeze, then picked up the cases of jam and started up the steps to the front door.

"You're sure you're okay?" Madge looked like she wasn't sure she should let me go inside without a physical exam.

"I'm okay. Like I said, a little shaken up but okay."

Uncle Mike gave me a thunderous look. "I'm going to find out who the hell this Brendan Kennedy is. The Shavano cops probably know all about him."

"They probably do," I agreed. But even if they knew about him, they couldn't do anything about his being a bullying jerk since they had no jurisdiction in his town.

Leftovers were never just leftovers when Nate was around. He did a quick stir-fry with some frozen rice and a couple of boneless chicken breasts. He's much better at tossing together sauces and seasoning than I am, so I let him do his thing. I set the table, then poured us both a glass of wine.

Nate raised an eyebrow. "Are you really okay?"

I was very tired of being asked that question, but Nate wasn't someone I felt like I needed to impress. At least not at the moment. "I'm getting myself together again. I'm not all the way there yet."

He stepped over from the stove, rubbing a hand across my shoulders. "Why was he at your booth anyway? More questions?"

"The opposite, more or less. He wants me to shut up and leave his investigations alone. He didn't like me telling people about Kell's deal with the trash vendors.

He said the people who mattered already knew about the set-up, and nobody else needed to hear about it from me."

Nate grimaced. "The 'people who mattered?' He said that?"

"He did. I think that landfill's a done deal. As far as the city council's concerned, anyway." Whether that ruled them out in the plot to kill Kell Moorhead was anybody's guess.

Nate stirred the fried rice again before adding the sauce. "People in Coalton won't be happy about that."

"Yeah, but they may not be able to do much about it if it's already set in stone." At least now people like Silas and Laurel would be fighting against it and making sure the people in Coalton knew what their city government was up to.

Nate picked up the skillet and spooned chicken fried rice onto our plates. Then he turned to me. "Do you think Kennedy could have been involved in Kell's death?"

I blinked. Normally, I'm the one doing the wild speculating while Nate herds me toward reality. "I don't know. I hadn't considered that. Why would he be part of a conspiracy, though?"

Nate shrugged. "Maybe Kell's deal with the landfill was causing trouble. Or maybe other people wanted to cut him out of the deal altogether. The Chief strikes me as the type who'd be glad to serve as somebody's muscle."

I nodded slowly. "He is at that. And he may be corrupt besides being incompetent. I mean, maybe that's why he's going after Laurel, even though most of us think that's insane. Maybe it's more about who he can shoehorn into being a suspect to distract from the people who might have wanted Kell dead."

Nate sighed. "If Kennedy's part of a plot that killed Kell, this whole thing may be way beyond anything you could investigate. That could mean powerful people are out to shut down any real investigation before it gets too close. I think I'd be happier if you took a step back here."

I was beginning to feel like I'd be happier if I stayed out of Coalton myself. "I can see your point."

"Are you going to lodge a complaint against Kennedy?"

"I don't know. Depends on whether there's anyone I could lodge a complaint with. Maybe I'll ask around."

"Do that." Nate gave me a long look. "Ask Fowler. If nothing else, it would be good to let other law enforcement people know just how bad Kennedy is. Maybe even how corrupt he seems to be. And you've got lots of witnesses: me and Marcus and probably Kathy, along with all the other vendors at that end of the market."

I let myself smile at that. "They might rule you out for being prejudiced in my favor."

He leaned forward, resting his palm against my cheek. "Some people call it prejudice, I guess. I call it love."

We've been together for a while now, but Nate still has the ability to make me weak in the knees. All of a sudden, I was eager for dinner to be over so we could go on to more enjoyable parts of the evening. After the afternoon we'd had, we deserved a night off.

****

I'd already decided to talk to Fowler about Kennedy before Nate had made his suggestion, and I figured I'd see if I could find him the following day. I had jam to deliver to my customers in town—Bianca's bakery and the Made In Colorado shop. I figured I'd head over to the police department afterward and see if Fowler was around.

Larraine Pearson, the ever-enthusiastic manager of the Made In Colorado store insisted on arranging most of the jars I'd brought on one of the display tables at the front, telling the customers that my jam was "just scrumptious."

That meant I was in a good mood when I got to Bianca's shop. Bianca herself was behind the counter, which was a surprise since she usually had counter help. "Hey," I said. "Where's your assistant?"

Bianca grimaced. "Sharon took a few days off to go see her mother in Gunnison. She's down with a stomach virus. Are you feeling okay?"

I wasn't sure whether we were still talking about the stomach flu or about the Coalton farmers market. "Sure. I'm fine."

"Guy's an asshole," Bianca muttered. "He needs to be replaced."

"He does," I agreed, although neither of us had any say in what happened in Coalton.

"Well, anyway, I'm doing double duty until Chantal gets out of her Pilates class and comes to work. What can I do for you?"

I raised the cases of jam for her to see. "Brought you some refills."

"Good. I'm out of peach." She gestured to the end of the counter. "Just put it there. I'll dig them out later."

Three women walked in the front door and made a beeline for the muffins. "I can put it out now if you want."

"That would be great. Thanks, kid. Give me an invoice." Bianca gave me a long-suffering smile and started toward the customers.

Fortunately, the jam display on the end of the counter wasn't all that elaborate. I put out some peach jam and then added a few jars of the other flavors just to make everything even. I'd just tucked the case with the remaining jars under the counter when the front door opened again and Chief Fowler stepped in.

Bianca was busy ringing up sales for the three women who'd come in earlier, but she nodded at him. "Hi, Chief, I'll be with you in a minute."

He nodded back, but he was looking at me. "Roxy Constantine," he said as he walked up to me. "Just the woman I wanted to see."

"Really?" I said. "Interesting. I want to talk to you, too."

"Grab some coffee," he said. "I'll get us a couple of cookies. My treat."

Bianca's coffee is as terrific as everything else in her shop. I poured a couple of cups and headed for one of the tables next to the front window. Fortunately, the coffee break crowd had already taken off and the lunch crowd hadn't yet arrived.

Fowler pulled out the chair opposite me and dropped a bag with a couple of chocolate chip cookies in the middle of the table. "So, you know people are talking about the farmers market at Coalton yesterday."

"I didn't know, but it figures." When it comes to gossip, Shavano is a small town, particularly the hospitality part of it, including restauranteurs and food producers.

"Tell me what happened," he said. "The versions

I've heard so far may not be accurate."

"Probably aren't," I agreed. "Chief Kennedy smashed up a few jars of my jam. He was pissed at me."

Fowler's eyes widened, then he gave me a half-smile. "Give me the whole story. From the beginning please."

"Okay. I was selling jam at the farmers market. Kennedy came to my booth and snarled at me because he said I was interfering with his investigation."

Fowler gave me another half-smile. He'd made the same accusation himself several times in past investigations. However, he'd stopped short of smashing things.

"In particular, he wanted me to stop telling people about a deal Kell Moorhead was trying to set up with a trash collection company. They were going to turn the old coal mine into a landfill. They may still be going to give it a try."

Fowler frowned. "What the hell? Can they do that? There's got to be a whole raft of regulations against it."

"That's the question everybody keeps asking, and the only answer I've gotten is, nobody knows." I grimaced, remembering Kennedy. "Kennedy claimed that the people who needed to know about the deal—the only ones who mattered, according to him—already know about it. And I was just stirring up trouble by telling other people. I argued with him over that, and he threatened to throw me in jail." I paused to sip my coffee and to loosen my suddenly tight shoulders.

"Throw you in jail for what?" Fowler asked.

"That wasn't clear. I think mostly for being nosy and getting into things Kennedy didn't want me getting into. Anyway, I told him I was pretty sure I had the right to talk to people, and he got pissed. He flung his arm across the counter at my booth and knocked off all the jam I had out. Some of it broke on the floor and some of it rolled away. Nate and Marcus Jordan saw it and told him to stop. Kennedy threatened to call in his men and arrest everybody for rioting, which was a crock since he was the only one getting violent." I paused. "I think that was everything that happened. Silas Goodman talked Kennedy out of closing down the market, but he came back a little after six and made it pretty clear we were all supposed to leave."

Fowler stared at me, his expression grim. Then he shook his head. "Okay, one thing you need to understand up front. There's nothing I can do about this. Even if I wanted to. Even if I felt like this was way out of line, I can't do a thing about it. It's completely out of my jurisdiction. I wouldn't let Kennedy come to Shavano and throw his weight around, and he sure as hell won't let me do anything like that in Coalton."

"I understand that."

"Okay. Having said that, what he did was really…" he paused, trying to think of the right word. "Inappropriate. Really, really inappropriate."

"I agree. Is there anything I can do about it? I mean, I obviously can't complain to the police in Coalton, although they're the ones who have jurisdiction."

"Right. You could file a complaint to go on the record, but my guess is it would end up in the trash."

Pretty much what I'd already figured out. "Right. So I repeat, is there anything I can do about it? I mean anything that will have any effect?"

"A couple of things." Fowler blew out a breath. "I can't believe I'm saying this, but go to your friend's lawyer, Magdalena Ramos. She needs to know what Kennedy's doing. She'll be the one to take statements and document how off the rails Kennedy is. She can also file a complaint with the county attorney about his behavior. Somebody ought to, and she's someone they'll listen to."

As opposed to me, whom no one was likely to pay any attention to. But he was probably right about that. "Thanks. I'll do that." Of course, I'd most likely have to go through Madge to do it since I didn't know Magdalena Ramos personally.

"I'd also recommend you stay out of this from now on." Fowler gave me the ghost of a grin. "But we both know how likely you are to pay attention to that advice."

"You never know," I said. "I may have gone just about as far as I can go with this." Truth be told, I would be happy to give all of this to Ramos, who probably could jab Kennedy a lot more effectively than I could.

Fowler pushed himself to his feet, wiping cookie crumbs from his fingers with a napkin. "And if Kennedy ever says anything to you in Shavano, let me know. This is my jurisdiction."

He gave me a smile as he replaced his Stetson. He'd most likely enjoy telling Brendan Kennedy what he could and couldn't do inside the Shavano city limits. I only wished Kennedy would be dumb enough to give him the opportunity.

Chapter 19

Nothing much happened for the rest of the week, or anyway nothing much happened that I heard about. That was fine with me. Madge told Magdalena Ramos what Kennedy had done at the farmers market, and she gave me a call. I wasn't sure if she could do much about it, but she said she'd bring it up with the county attorney, who already heard her complaints about his treatment of Laurel.

I filled all the orders we'd gotten for tomato jam, which weren't many. Bridget said it was a clear indication that savory jams weren't what our customer base wanted. I figured she was probably right, but I still wanted to try a few savory things now and then, just for the hell of it.

Dolce was full of questions about Coalton and Laurel and what I was going to do about the chief of police. I hated to tamp down her passion for justice, but the answer was *not much*. She was also full of details about her preparations for college. She had an orientation at Colorado State in August, then she'd be home for a couple of weeks before she moved into her dorm room in Ft. Collins. She said she wanted to work when orientation was over, just like she wanted to work over Christmas vacation. I was more than willing to let her, but the fact that she already had one foot out the door, more or less, reminded me that I needed to get a lot more serious about finding a replacement. Always assuming Jarrod didn't return, which seemed more and more likely by the day.

I called Marigold that afternoon. She was due to go back to work full-time at the café in another week, and she was counting the days.

"Hey, Rox," she said. "Heard about your run-in with the law. Are you okay?"

That was the question of the day that I was really tired of answering. "I'm fine. I was wondering if you'd had a chance to talk to Ava McNeil about working for me."

Marigold sighed. "Not yet. She's been up in Jackson Hole visiting her sister. She should be back soon, though, and I'll ask her as soon as she gets into town."

"Okay, great."

I fought down a moment of panic. What if Ava wasn't interested? How was I going to run the business on my own? I'd done it in the beginning, but that was when the business was a lot smaller. Without Dolce, I'd be working nonstop, and I still wouldn't be producing at the level I was now.

It would mean even less time with Nate than I was already spending. That thought started a hot coal of anxiety burning in my gut.

****

I decided I'd go to the burro races in Coalton as a form of stress relief. I wasn't going to watch the entire race since that would involve trotting up steep paths to the top of the pass while staying out of the way of the racers. But I could watch the start and the finish, both of which took place in downtown Coalton. They were both big events, or big events at the more established races. I figured there should be a few people around to watch the start and the finish.

I would probably be watching the start on my own since it happened around seven in the morning. While Nate was willing to cheer Laurel and Silas on, he wasn't willing to drag himself out of bed on a weekend to do it. Besides, he had to help with brunch at the café. Making it back from the seven o'clock start for the nine-thirty brunch prep would be a bit of a stretch.

I didn't mind. I sort of looked forward to being part of the small crowd of burro enthusiasts who'd get themselves down to the early morning starting line to cheer on the serious racers. The tourist—or "recreational"—racers had a different start time since few of them figured to go all the way to the top of the pass.

The separate start time was one of Laurel's innovations, and it was popular with the serious racers since it meant they wouldn't have to work their way around the tourists on the trail. It was also popular with the tourists since it meant they could take their time and have a little breakfast before they started running up the trail behind their burros.

I began the drive to Coalton around six-fifteen, and the road was relatively empty that early in the morning. The sun was sparkling on the dew, although the morning chill was still in the air. It was just me and the mountain birds and the beauty of the day beginning, all green grass and blue skies and distant looming mountains. I immediately began to feel more relaxed. Whatever problems might crop up with the race or with the people in Coalton, the mountain morning was beautiful, and I was glad to be out in it.

I pulled into the field near downtown that had been roped off for spectators. A lot more cars and trucks than I'd anticipated were already parked. I'd expected a small crowd of burro enthusiasts, but this was bigger than that.

By the time I got to the starting line, I was dodging groups of enthusiastic race goers, most carrying coffee cups since it was way too early for beer, no matter how traditional the beer and burros combination was. The spectators were mostly from Coalton or the other small towns around the area, including Shavano. Some of them were related to racers, but a lot of them were there just to show their support. And maybe because, like me, they enjoyed being out in the early morning air. There was a feeling of camaraderie, of being one of the people who knew what burro racing was all about. Go, Colorado!

A bright red line had been painted across the street and a lightweight rope had been pulled across above it. The race had a scramble start, which meant all the burros would be side-by-side and jockeying to get out in front. According to Laurel, lots of burros loved to run together since it reminded them of their days in the wild. But there were also burros who wanted desperately to be ahead of all the others, and those were the ones who'd be surging forward with the starter's pistol.

And, of course, there were always a few burros who just weren't feelin' it, and who'd refuse to go anywhere.

Usually somebody official welcomed the racers and wished everybody a good race. But Laurel would have been the logical choice to do that since the race was her idea, and she was busy lining up with Peggy Sue. That was probably a good thing, since I wasn't sure how a Coalton crowd would react to her.

A man I recognized as one of the oilier city council

members stepped up on a makeshift dais at the side of the road and waved a hand for silence. He didn't get it, but he used his microphone to talk over everybody anyway. He said something or other about the courage and perseverance of the racers and how glad everybody was to have the event in Coalton. I wasn't listening, and neither was anyone else. The city council guy was delighted to take credit for a race he'd had very little to do with.

Laurel was checking Peggy Sue's pack saddle, making sure everything was fastened tight so it wouldn't jiggle too much and distract her. Peggy Sue herself looked somewhere between blasé and annoyed. Like all the burros around her, she wanted to get out on the road where she could show her stuff. Standing around with a bunch of other burros wasn't doing much for her disposition.

As I watched, Jarrod broke through the crowd on the curb carrying a pack and a carrot. He handed the pack to Laurel and fed Peggy Sue her treat, which did make her perkier. Laurel pulled the pack onto her back and said something to Jarrod that made him nod sharply and head to the side of the street again. Apparently, he was Laurel's gofer and general assistant. He appeared absolutely delighted to be there.

Silas was at the other end of the line near the start. He was enough of a veteran to know that it could be better to be at the edge rather than the middle since it might give Oliver more room to get around the pack. Plus it minimized the risk of negative interactions with the other burros. Given Oliver's temperament, I wouldn't put it past him to do some kicking if he thought he could take out a rival.

Silas was checking Oliver's halter and lead rope while he adjusted the pack saddle, all the while muttering sweet nothings into Oliver's ear. At least I assumed they were sweet nothings. Knowing Oliver's attitude, Silas might have decided to go with vague threats and promises of retribution. Except that wouldn't be Silas's style. Sweet nothings, most likely.

The city council guy stepped up next to the starting line, brandishing a starter's pistol, and the racers all became a lot more focused. Some did a few warm-up stretches, although a couple of the burros would probably have yanked their partners off their feet if they tried anything fancy.

"On your mark," the council guy shouted.

The racers leaned forward, staring intently at the road ahead.

"Get set."

Some bent lower, getting into runners' stances.

"Go!"

The council guy fired his pistol, making some of the less experienced burros jump and bray. A man on the other side of the street yanked the rope away, and the burros rushed forward as the crowd yelled enthusiastically.

"Go, Laurel," someone shouted, and the crowd picked it up. "Lau-rel, Lau-rel, Lau-rel," they roared as more and more people joined in.

Laurel glanced up in surprise, which meant the guy next to her managed to slip by. Her expression was somewhere between shock and delight as she stared at the cheering crowd. A couple more burros pushed ahead, but then she was in the game again, urging Peggy Sue forward up the flat road toward the first switchback.

Silas was out in front with Oliver doing the burro version of a canter. It wasn't all that fast, but Silas was urging him on from behind as the larger pack of burros started nipping at his heels. The racers were calling to their animals, the crowd was cheering for the racers, and the burros were doing their thing. The rumble of their hooves on the packed dirt added to the general din besides kicking up some small clouds of dust.

I grabbed a tissue to wipe my eyes, pretending it was the dust that was getting to me. In fact, I was more touched than I could say at the way the crowd had cheered for Laurel. I didn't know if they represented the majority of the town's citizens, but I was glad there were some people in Coalton who had her back.

I started across the street after the last of the racing burros and their humans had headed off toward the upper trail. Jarrod appeared at my elbow, grinning. "Wasn't that cool? That was great. The way they all started off together and then kind of spaced out. And the crowd cheering Laurel. And Peggy Sue getting right up to the front. It was the best race start ever."

"Have you ever seen one before?" I asked.

Jarrod shook his head. "I didn't even know what burro racing was before this summer. And now I'm like a burro trainer. It's just…really, really cool."

Much cooler than making jam, no doubt. "Would you like a ride anywhere? I'll be heading to Shavano soon."

"That's okay. I'm going to stay all day. I want to see the recreational racers start, find out what that's like. And I've got to be here for the finish."

I paused, calculating. The recreational start would be in a little over an hour, and from what I'd heard, it was likely to be a hoot. A couple dozen experienced burros would be pulling a couple dozen mostly inexperienced amateur burro racers. My money was on the burros.

"I could stick around for the recreational start. Nate wants me to come pick him up so he can see the finish, but that'll be a while."

"Laurel said they might get down as early as two o'clock." Jarrod stared up the mountainside, as if he expected the fast burros to already be on the downward leg.

"They might be," I agreed. "I'll try to be here by then. Meanwhile, I need some coffee if I'm going to make it until the recreational start."

"They've got a coffee trailer over at the side." Jarrod gestured at a trailer with a sign for The Mountain Beanery, Coalton's only coffee shop. They also sold pastries, but I'd never gotten up enough courage to try one. "You want a latte?" I asked. I wasn't sure where Jarrod stood on the whole coffee question.

He shook his head. "I've got my water," he said, patting the industrial size water bottle he had on his belt.

****

Fifteen minutes later I had my coffee. The recreational racers were beginning to get themselves together as the burros arrived from the rental companies. I saw Dusty Vance—the guy who'd come to get Kell's burro, Buster—matching up burros with their temporary owners. Dave Ottawa, Silas's foreman, was doing the same thing with Silas's burro herd since Silas himself was already up on the mountain with Oliver.

It was probably just my prejudice, but Dave seemed to be taking a lot more care in making sure the right tourist was matched with the right burro and that they all had everything they needed. They were all supposed to train with their burros for two or three hours, and it made sense that he'd be concerned about making sure the amateur racers got the same burro they'd been with before. Vance didn't appear to be that interested, letting the tourists point out the burro they wanted instead of checking any kind of paperwork to make sure it was the same burro they'd spent time with before.

Jarrod and I wandered to the starting area. Someone had pulled the rope across the street again to try to keep the racers in some sort of organized group. Not that there was much organization to be found. The amateurs clearly weren't sure how they were supposed to line up, and some of them seemed more than slightly worried about the pack saddle. At the same time, others were tucking water bottles and jackets into the saddlebags, which some of the burros appeared to resent, given their tendency to sidle away from their humans.

In the midst of all this chaos, I caught a glimpse of a golden burro flank. I craned my neck to try to see over the rapidly growing scrum of burros and humans. "Isn't that Buster?" I asked.

Jarrod moved forward through the crowd, sorting through the constantly moving burro bodies. I followed him, figuring he'd be able to clear a path. He stepped between a couple of swaying animals, and we found ourselves next to a golden flank that was strangely familiar.

"Buster." Jarrod sounded delighted as he reached out to pet the burro's golden neck.

"He's not Buster. He's Prince Caspian the Great." The child's voice came from somewhere around Jarrod's knee. I looked down and saw a small, irate girl in a riding helmet and jodhpurs.

"Are you racing him today?" I asked a little doubtfully. I wasn't sure what the downward age limit was for racers, but I was guessing she didn't qualify.

A man stepped around Buster's—Caspian's—front legs holding his lead rope. "We're racing him. Kaitlyn and I." He smiled down at the still irate little girl.

"Oh," I said. "We know Buster. We took care of him for a while."

"He's not Buster, he's…," Kaitlyn began.

The man reached out and patted Buster's golden neck. "It's okay, Katie, they knew him before we did."

There was something sort of proprietary about that pat. "Are you renting him from Dusty Vance for the race?"

The man's smile broadened. "No, Ma'am. Prince Caspian is all ours. We bought him a couple of weeks ago."

"Really?" I said. "Congratulations. He's a sweetheart." And I was fairly sure Buster would be a lot happier with Kaitlyn and her father than he had been with Vance.

Kaitlyn's dad grinned. "He is, at that. I had to do some real negotiating, but he was worth every penny."

"How much did you pay, if you don't mind me asking?"

"I got Vance down to five thousand. Wasn't easy, believe me. He wanted ten."

I didn't gasp or blurt out my first response, which was *Five thousand? Are you kidding me?* I'd never heard of a burro going for more than five hundred, and one to two hundred was a lot more common. Of course, Buster was special, being gold and all. "Good for you," I managed.

Jarrod was staring at him, wide-eyed, and I willed him not to say anything about how much the guy had overpaid.

Kaitlyn's dad gave me a rueful smile. "Yeah, I know, it's a little high for a burro, but it's still less than the price of a purebred horse, believe me."

"That's true," I said. Although if he'd been willing to settle for a run-of-the-mill horse rather than purebred, he still could have been paying less than five thousand. "You got him a couple of weeks ago?"

"About that. Kaitlyn saw him in Vance's pasture at the beginning of the summer and fell in love. But then Vance rented him out to somebody. Once we settled on a price, he got him from whoever rented him, and we brought him home. Well, I mean, we brought him to the place we're renting here. When we head to LA, we'll have to find somebody to ship him for us."

"We can take him with us, Daddy," Kaitlyn piped up. "We can rent a trailer and pull him behind the car."

Her dad winced, probably at the thought of putting a trailer hitch on whatever expensive vehicle he was driving. "We'll see, honey. We'll see."

"Racers get ready," someone called from the sidelines, and Kaitlyn and her dad began moving into the line.

"Well, good luck," I said. I still wasn't sure how Kaitlyn was going to take part in the race since she only came up to Buster's shoulder and riding the burros was strictly forbidden.

"Oh we're not going all the way," Kaitlyn's dad said cheerfully. "Just up to the first switchback. I figure that'll give Katie a taste of racing, see how she feels about it."

"We're going to win. Prince Caspian the Great is the best of all the burros." Kaitlyn sounded like she had no intention of stopping at the switchback, but I figured that was her father's problem.

"Good luck, anyway," I said, and Jarrod and I returned to the sidewalk.

"Five thousand dollars," Jarrod murmured. "I mean, I like Buster. He's a great burro, sweet-natured. But five thousand?"

"Price is determined by what the customer is willing to pay," I said. "That guy was willing to pay five thousand because his daughter wanted a golden burro."

Jarrod rolled his eyes. "Golden is right."

The city council guy who'd spoken earlier had been replaced by someone less important, and no one tried to make any opening comments. Just as well, since I doubted anybody would have heard what he had to say in the chaos of the burros and their very uncertain handlers.

I noticed Kaitlyn and company had moved to the side where they'd be in less danger of being trampled. Probably a good idea, given the lack of organization in this crowd.

"Racers take your mark," the starter shouted.

The crowd did its best, but they seemed to have no idea where their mark was. I couldn't blame them.

"Get set."

A few of the racers did the runners' lean thing, but most of them just looked around, maybe trying to see where they were supposed to go next.

"Go!" the starter yelled as he fired his pistol.

The same man pulled the rope across, and the racers headed up the street in a much more confused group.

Most of them were going in the right direction, although a few lost their lead ropes right off the bat and earned a disqualification when their burros trotted off the marked course. A few of the racers did the smart thing and let their burros do the navigating. A few broke through at the front, with their human racers hanging on to the lead ropes for dear life.

I checked at the side and saw Kaitlyn and her dad following a gently trotting Buster up the road. They were well back from the crowd, but they were moving. I saw a few people snapping their picture as they brought up the rear.

"Go, Kaitlyn," I yelled. "Go, Caspian."

"Buster," Jarrod muttered. "Go, Buster."

I grinned at him. "Well, that was fun."

He seemed a little melancholy. "Hope they take care of him."

"I bet they will," I said. "Kaitlyn looks like she's got the burro bug."

We started walking up the street toward the coffee booth, although I'd already had enough coffee to cause heart palpitations.

"You heading to Shavano?" Jarrod asked.

I thought about it. "In a little bit," I said. "I'd sort of like to talk to Dusty Vance about Buster."

Jarrod nodded slowly. "Me, too."

Chapter 20

The guys from the rental places had come up to the starting area to retrieve the disqualified burros. Some of the tourist burro handlers wanted to do the trail anyway—or go up as far as they could without losing their animals again. They turned in their racing numbers and started off, probably holding on to the lead ropes a lot tighter. The tourists who stayed behind all seemed to be having a good time, but they didn't necessarily want to go up the mountain with a recalcitrant animal.

Vance had collected two donkeys and was heading toward the area where he had his truck parked when Jarrod and I caught up with him. "Those the ones that didn't make it?" I asked.

Vance shrugged. "I warned them, Not my fault if the tourists can't hold onto a rope."

He probably had warned them during that brief "training course" he provided. "Heard you sold Buster," I said.

Vance glanced at me, narrowing his eyes. "You the one who brought him down after Moorhead died?"

"That was me," I agreed. "You came to my place and picked him up. Jarrod took care of him for me." I gestured in Jarrod's direction.

Jarrod gave him a bland smile.

"Guy wanted to buy him for his daughter. He was willing to pay top dollar." Vance was suddenly cagey. "I took him up on it."

"So I heard. He said he paid five thousand."

Vance gave me a smug grin. "We bargained a bit."

"You started at ten thousand?" That still rocked me on my heels. Both that Vance would ask that much, and that Kaitlyn's dad hadn't walked away shaking his head.

"Like I said, he wanted the burro for his daughter. Figured I might as well see if he'd go high." Vance shrugged. "He wouldn't bite at ten, but he was willing to do five."

He tied the two runaway burros to a fence behind his truck, then started to remove their pack saddles and paraphernalia. Jarrod stepped up to help him, piling the shovels and picks into the truck bed.

"I thought you'd already leased Buster to Kell Moorhead for the summer," I said. "That's what he told Laurel and me."

Vance paused to give me a long look from under his bushy eyebrows. "He'd paid me the lease fee, but I refunded it. And I told him he could have the pick of the rest of the herd, for free. He was okay with it."

Vance returned to unloading the gear while the burros grabbed the opportunity to munch a little grass.

I frowned, remembering the first time I'd seen Kell and Buster, when Laurel had taken me out on her training run with Peggy Sue. He'd been pretty adamant about winning the race with his golden burro. And based on the little experience I'd had with him, Kell didn't strike me as the accommodating type.

"When did you sell Buster?" I asked.

This time Vance paused. "Why do you want to know?"

I shrugged. "Just curious."

231

"Curiosity killed the cat." He narrowed his eyes, then went back to unloading.

I took a breath. "I figure it couldn't have been more than two or three weeks ago. I met Kell on the mountain with Laurel about a month ago, and he didn't say anything about giving up Buster. In fact, he claimed he had Buster for the season and that he was going to win the race with him."

Vance grimaced. "Asswipe wouldn't have won the race with Buster or any other burro. He couldn't race for shit."

"But he still had Buster a month ago. In fact, he still had him the day he died. That's how I ended up with him." I was watching Vance carefully now. "Did you sell him after you got him from me? But you just said after you sold him, you got Kell's agreement to give you Buster and refunded his money. So how come Buster was still Kell's burro when somebody killed him?"

"He wasn't Moorhead's burro," Vance snarled. "He was never Moorhead's burro. Moorhead paid for a three-month lease. That's all. He was my burro until I sold him."

"Okay," I said. "I just want to get the timing worked out. When did you talk to Kell about switching burros?"

Vance was beginning to look as mulish as his animals. "Don't remember exactly. He maybe held onto Buster a few days after he'd agreed to give him back. Maybe it took him a while to make up his mind about which one he wanted in exchange, and he wanted to go on training while he decided. Can't remember for sure."

"So that's why he still had Buster when he died? You're saying he knew he wasn't going to have Buster for the race, but he was still up on the trail with him?"

Knowing Kell, I doubted he'd be up on a mountain trail just for the sheer joy of it. Particularly with a burro that wasn't his racing partner, even a sweet burro like Buster.

"I don't know. I'm tired of talking about it. You need to move on." Vance's expression had flattened. He shifted his hand to his hip, brushing his denim jacket aside to reveal the sidearm he had clipped to his belt. I don't know much about guns, but it looked sizeable.

I heard Jarrod's quick gasp behind me and remembered that I wasn't alone. Vance couldn't shoot either of us if he was surrounded by people. I could already see Dave Ottawa frowning in his direction. On the other hand, I was pretty sure Vance wasn't going to tell me anything else. At least not anything else that would be helpful.

I turned on my heel and headed toward the street. Jarrod fell into step behind me. "Was he threatening us?" His voice sounded somewhere between appalled and awestruck.

"He thought so," I said. I picked up my pace, but Jarrod kept up.

"Where are we going?" he asked.

"We need to tell somebody about this," I said. "About what Vance said. It's a different angle on what happened to Kell, and it makes more sense than any of the other theories that have been floated so far about what happened to him."

"It does?" Jarrod sounded confused.

I nodded. "It does. Vance has a chance to sell his burro for an ungodly amount of money—around ten times what they usually go for. But he'd already leased the burro for the season. He goes to Kell and offers him a deal where he gets a free burro for the summer. But if

Kell knows how much Vance is getting for Buster, he's not going to settle for that. My guess is he wanted money, probably a cut of the purchase price. Pay him or he keeps the burro for the summer—he's got a contract."

Jarrod frowned. "So Vance killed him to get Buster?"

"Maybe." It was a little thin, now that I thought about it. Surely five thousand wasn't enough for murdering somebody.

"But he didn't get Buster. He was still up on the mountain after Kell was dead."

"I don't know what happened at the end. But that sequence of events makes sense. Enough sense to warrant the police questioning Vance."

This time Jarrod looked more unhappy than confused. "You mean Kennedy?"

I blew out a breath. "He's the only law they've got here in town. We have to start with him." After that, I wasn't sure where we'd go. I could always talk to Magdalena Ramos. Or maybe the county attorney. Or even the county sheriff, although he didn't have any more jurisdiction in Coalton than Fowler did.

Jarrod bit his lip. "Okay. But what if Vance leaves before we can get the cops."

"He won't. He's still got burros up on the hillside. He won't leave until he collects them all again." I hoped that was true. If Vance was concerned about what we might discover and who we might talk to, he might take off even without his burros.

I approached the police station with some trepidation. I was under no illusions about how willing Kennedy would be to listen to this version of events. But we had to start somewhere.

As it turned out, though, we weren't going to start at the police station. The front door was locked tight, and I couldn't see any lights inside.

Jarrod frowned. "Now what?"

"There's got to be a cop around somewhere. They can't all have taken off on a day when they've got dozens of tourists prowling the streets." Or anyway that would have been true in any other mountain town I'd ever had dealings with.

We walked toward the street where the race had started, checking all the side streets we walked by. I finally saw one of Kennedy's minions directing traffic next to the event parking lot. Not that there was a lot of traffic to direct just then, but there probably would be later on.

He narrowed his eyes as we walked up to him. The name tag on his shirt front said Ryan. "Can I help you?"

"I hope so." I glanced around the lot, checking for any other police presence. "Is Chief Kennedy around?"

The minion looked suspicious. "He's fishing."

Right. It figured that Kennedy would take off on a day when one of Laurel's promotions was running. "I need to talk to someone about the Kell Moorhead case. I have some new information."

Now the minion seemed confused. "New information?"

"Very new. About a possible murder suspect."

Confusion transformed to something closer to panic. "A murder suspect?"

I took a deep breath. Clearly, this was going to be a long morning. "Could I outline this new information to you, Officer Ryan? Then maybe you'll want to do something about it."

Ryan looked like the only thing he wanted to do about new information was give it to someone else as quickly as possible. "Do something—" he began, then paused, closing his eyes for a moment. I had a feeling he was gathering his thoughts. "I guess I can do that."

I paused. "Do you want to record this? Take notes?"

"Notes." He shook his head. "I don't…"

"You can use your phone," Jarrod cut in. "It's easy." He showed which buttons to push on Ryan's cell phone, and we were in business.

By now I had the whole story pretty clearly in my mind, so it didn't take long to spell it out: the sale of Buster, the fact that Kell had leased Buster for the summer, the fact that Vance had probably lied about Kell having agreed to return Buster since he still had him on the day he'd died, and his boasts to Laurel and me that he and Buster would win the Coalton race.

Ryan was obviously a hometown boy. "Five thousand? For a burro?"

"Guy's from California."

Ryan looked as if that explained everything, which it sort of did. "So you think Dusty killed Kell to get the burro and sell it?"

"Maybe," I said. "That's certainly what happened in the end. Once Kell was dead, Vance could reclaim Buster and get him to the guy who wanted to buy him. He hadn't managed to do that while Kell was still around."

Ryan nodded slowly, and he seemed intrigued enough to maybe check into it. "What do you want me to do now?"

I took another of those deep breaths. "Bring Vance in for questioning. Maybe you can get him to tell you what Kell wanted in exchange for returning Buster. Maybe he'll let something slip about the day Kell died."

Ryan seemed horrified. "I can't leave my post. I'm the only one here. Chief's off fishing and Leary's up the mountain with his burro. Won't be back until mid-afternoon."

It figured that the Coalton police force wasn't up to dealing with an emergency.

"You can bring Vance to the station for questioning. That way you'll be around if there's an emergency." An emergency other than a possible escaped murderer.

"I guess I could do that," Ryan said hesitantly. "Is he over by the corral where they have the rental burros?"

"The last time I saw him, he was."

Ryan pushed himself to his feet. "Come on. You can show me where he is."

He could probably have found Vance on his own, but I didn't have a problem with helping him. Anything that would get the ball rolling and maybe exonerate Laurel before she got down the mountain.

The three of us started toward the rental burro area where I'd talked to Vance. It was always possible he'd had to track down missing burros, particularly if they'd gotten loose on the trail, but that was a problem for another time. I could see Dave Ottawa getting water for Silas's burros and another man I didn't recognize loading his burros into a trailer.

And then I saw Vance.

He'd collected a couple more burros, and he was removing the gear as he had before. He glanced up as we came closer, and then he froze. Maybe it was the fact that I'd come back again, but Officer Ryan was a lot more impressive standing in his khakis and Stetson than he'd been when directing traffic on the corner. He was, in fact, the very embodiment of The Law.

Vance took a final look at us—Jarrod, me, and Officer Ryan—and started running. Well, loping, but close to running. Probably top speed for him. Ryan was so shocked he didn't understand what was happening. "Hey, Dusty," he called. "Wait up." When this didn't produce the desired effect, Ryan finally realized his suspect was escaping, more or less, and went after him at a dead run. I figured Vance was probably in his fifties, maybe his sixties. Ryan, on the other hand, was in his mid-twenties at most.

There wasn't any contest. Ryan caught up to Vance within the first hundred yards. He grabbed his arm and spun him around. "What the everlasting hell…"

"It was an accident," Vance cried. "I didn't mean to hit him so hard."

There had been some noise around Ryan and Vance up until then, people shouting and running after them. But after Vance blurted out his confession, there was absolute silence.

"You're saying you hit Kell Moorhead," Ryan said carefully.

"Five thousand bucks," Vance muttered. "Five thousand freakin' bucks. For a burro. Son of a bitch."

Ryan stared at him before he seemed to recollect who and what he was. He pulled his cuffs from his belt. "Dusty Vance, I am arresting you for the murder of Kell Moorhead. You have the right to remain silent. Anything you say can be used against you in court. You have the right to talk to a lawyer for advice before I ask you any questions. You have the right to have a lawyer with you during questioning. If you cannot afford a lawyer, one will be appointed for you before any questioning if you wish. If you decide to answer questions now without a lawyer present, you have the right to stop answering at any time."

It was the longest speech I'd ever heard Ryan deliver and he did it word perfect. Maybe he'd been waiting a long time to say it. I almost felt like applauding.

Ryan started to hustle Vance toward the police station. "Hey, wait a minute," Dave Ottawa called. "What do you want us to do with his burros?"

Ryan glanced at him. "Put 'em in the corral for now. Chief will know what to do with them."

"Yeah, right," Dave muttered, but he gathered Vance's burros together and led them into the corral. Somebody would make sure they got food and water, since I had no doubt Silas would take care of it when he got back down.

I stared after Vance and Ryan, wondering if I should go along. There was no logical reason for me to be there, but I worried Kennedy would find a way to make Vance's confession disappear.

"Aren't you supposed to pick up Nate so he can be there at the finish?" Jarrod asked.

And he was absolutely right. I needed to go to Shavano and find Nate and spread the word. Although I was pretty sure the word would be spread around Coalton within the next hour. There had been a lot of people listening, after all.

Kennedy could try, but after this morning, he'd have a hard time convincing anyone that Laurel had killed Kell Moorhead.

Chapter 21

I drove to Shavano and picked up Nate. And as we drove back, I tried to explain what had happened, but it sounded off the rails, even to me.

"Wait," Nate said. "Hold up. This guy Vance killed Kell because he wouldn't give him his burro? That's nuts."

"I really think that's what happened, though. I mean it was a very valuable burro. And knowing Kell, he probably tried to force Vance to give him a cut of the five thousand he was getting for Buster."

"Five thousand." Nate shook his head. "For a burro. Hell, that animal probably cost Vance a couple hundred at most. That's also nuts."

"No kidding. My guess is Vance wanted Kell to give him Buster the day he was killed. The fact that Kell still had Buster, even though Vance wanted him, seems to mean Kell hadn't agreed to give him Buster, no matter what Vance said."

Nate blew out a breath. "Five thousand is a lot for a burro, but in the great scheme of things, five thousand isn't all that much. Certainly not enough to kill somebody over."

Just what I'd thought earlier. But I'd had some time to cogitate since then. "I guess it's all in the way you look at it. From Vance's point of view, it was a windfall, and Kell was making it impossible for him to collect." I

240

wasn't on Vance's side by any means, but Kell probably hadn't gone out of his way to be helpful. That wouldn't have been in character.

The parking lot had many more cars this time around. People who didn't want to drag themselves out of bed to see the start of the race were showing up for the finish. Nate took my hand, and we threaded our way through the crowd.

In the time since I'd left, food trucks and booths had been arranged up and down the street where the race was being run. I smelled hot fat, sizzling hamburgers and bratwurst, tacos, corndogs, kabobs, and all the other carnival foods that would produce waves of indigestion that night. A beer stand had appeared near the coffee trailer that had been set up earlier, with a knot of people standing in front talking animatedly.

A man I sort of remembered from the barbecue at Laurel's house turned when he saw me coming. "There's Roxy," he said. "She can tell us."

I assumed a sort of fixed smile. I had a pretty good idea what they were going to ask. "Tell you what?"

"Was it Vance? Did he kill Moorhead?" By now the entire group had come my way.

"I don't know," I said. "It's possible."

"Is he under arrest?"

"Again, I don't know. The last time I heard he was being questioned."

"By Kennedy?" The person who asked this appeared doubtful.

"Chief Kennedy is out fishing today. I think Officer Ryan is doing the questioning." At least I hoped he was. Although there was no guarantee that Ryan would be up to the task.

There were a few knowing smirks. It was reassuring to know other people also thought Kennedy was incompetent. What kind of police chief goes fishing on a day when several hundred people are due to show up in his town?

"They're coming down the trail," someone shouted from farther up the street.

Since we were all supposedly there to see the finish of the race, that cut off further conversation. Nate took my hand again and pulled me down the street toward the finish line, which was in the same place as the starting line had been, although now it had a bright red ribbon across with a paper sign that said "Finish" in the middle. I could see people and burros on the trail, coming down the mountainside at a good clip, although not as fast as they'd gone up that morning. They certainly had a lot more energy than I'd had when I'd come down that same trail several weeks ago.

On the day Kell Moorhead had died.

Everybody was leaning forward, trying to see who was in front. It appeared to be a man, but not Silas. That let out the two people I cared about most in the race, but it didn't dampen my enthusiasm.

Running burros are adorable. Also hilarious. There's just something inherently funny about these fierce little beasts galloping for all they're worth. Their human companions were out in front this time so they wouldn't get jerked off their feet by an over-eager donkey. The humans were a little ragged, their stride not quite as assured as it had been when the race started that morning. After all, they'd just climbed several miles up a steep and rocky trail while coordinating their run with a not always cooperative burro. But they were doing their best to keep up with their animals now. All the burros seemed to be doing just fine, thanks.

I recognized the guy out in front—Arnie Pell and his behemoth of a donkey, Prometheus. I guessed it figured that Arnie would take it. Prometheus was one of the biggest donkeys I'd ever seen and a real competitor. Arnie himself was a former endurance racer, so he was no slouch when it came to keeping up. The cheering started as soon as Arnie and his burro entered the end of the street and started jogging toward the finish.

Another racer was coming up fast behind him, but I couldn't immediately see who it was. It wasn't until I heard the "Lau-rel, Lau-rel, Lau-rel" chant start up again that I knew. Laurel and Peggy Sue were keeping up a dogged pursuit, even though both of them looked worn out.

Arnie glanced over his shoulder and lengthened his stride, pulling Prometheus along at a somewhat faster pace than the burro had been doing on his own. For a moment, I thought Prometheus would dig in his hooves and insist on running his own race—burros have been known to assert themselves at the least opportune moments. But Arnie knew his donkey, and he urged him on. When Prometheus heard the clattering of Peggy Sue's hooves on pavement coming up behind him, it was like the last bit of stimulus he needed. He increased his own pace, almost sweeping Arnie off his feet, and the two of them thundered across the finish line side-by-side. Laurel made it maybe three minutes later.

Several well-wishers surrounded Arnie, pounding him on the back and offering him celebratory beers. In reality, he gave the impression he'd prefer to collapse at the side of the road, but he stayed upright long enough to give his name to the race official at the finish line.

I headed toward Laurel, but she was engulfed by people hugging her and kissing her cheek. A couple of them even kissed Peggy Sue, who remained unimpressed. I wanted to tell Laurel about Vance, but I didn't want to intrude on her triumph to do that. She'd taken first place in the women's division, even though she hadn't been able to get around Arnie and Prometheus at the end.

Jarrod worked his way through the crowd and grabbed Peggy Sue's lead rope so he could get her out of the crowd. Laurel saw him and put a hand on his arm. They leaned together for a moment, muttering. Then Jarrod pulled Peggy Sue away, heading toward the corral.

Shouts down the street told us that more racers were coming, and Laurel moved off to the side, still surrounded by supporters. I saw Silas in the pack of three who were heading up the street now. He'd pulled off his shirt to deal with the heat, although he still wore his battered straw cowboy hat. And he'd tied Oliver's lead rope to his belt, so that the two of them were running together like a matched team.

They made it across the finish line in fourth place. Silas looked winded. Oliver looked like he was thinking of kicking somebody. Running fifteen-plus miles had not improved his disposition.

Nate stepped forward and gave Silas a pat on the back, and then the rest of the crowd enfolded them.

I finally managed to break through the crowd around Laurel. She seemed a little dazed, but she perked up when she saw me. "Roxy! Just the person I wanted to see." She smiled a little desperately and began to pull away from the crowd. We worked our way to the side of the street as more racers trotted across the finish line.

"What's all this about Vance and Kell?" she murmured. "Is it true?"

"Seems to be. Let's find a place to sit down and I can fill you in."

I saw Nate a little farther up the street with Silas and Oliver. Dave Ottawa was making his way through the crowd, probably so he could take Oliver to his holding pen. Given the donkey's generally bad attitude, I thought getting Oliver off the street and away from possible targets was a very good idea.

****

Ten minutes later we were all sitting at a café table near the creek. Nate had found us a pitcher of water and a bucket of beers, both very much appreciated by all of us. "All right," Silas said, placing his beer on the table, "I've been hearing wild tales ever since I got down off that damned mountain. What's happened?"

I gave them a sort of summary, including Vance threatening Jarrod and me and then taking off when Officer Ryan walked over.

Laurel bit her lip. "Jarrod said he had a gun."

"He had one, but it was in a holster on his belt, like half the ranchers around here. He never drew it. He just told us to go away and leave him alone."

Silas grimaced. "Dusty has never been the brightest bulb on the tree, but this stretches the limit. He killed Moorhead over a five-thousand-dollar burro?"

"Possibly," I said. "I don't know all the details. I know the guy who bought Buster for his daughter paid him five thousand. And I know he had to get Buster from Kell to sell him. But since Kell still had Buster on the

245

day he was killed, my guess is he wasn't cooperating with Vance."

Laurel held a cold bottle of beer against her cheek. "He probably wanted part of the money. That would be typical. If somebody was making money off Buster, Kell would have wanted a cut."

Silas nodded slowly. "That would make sense. They probably had a fight over it, and Dusty lost his temper. He may not have meant to kill him, but he's always had a short fuse."

"He said something about not meaning to hit Kell so hard. He may have just lost it and hit him without thinking." Although that could also have been Vance trying to come up with an excuse after the fact.

Laurel leaned back in her chair, closing her eyes. "Kennedy's not going to be happy."

"He'll have a solved crime," Nate said. "Maybe he didn't solve it himself, but he'll still get the credit most likely."

Silas narrowed his eyes. "Not from people in Coalton. They'll know who did what, and they'll remember Kennedy was dead set on charging an innocent woman." He glanced at Laurel then placed his hand over hers.

She opened her eyes and smiled at him.

Interesting. Silas was twenty years older than Laurel, and possibly thirty. But he still had that silver fox thing going with his flowing hair and beard. If they had something together, I was all for it.

"You should still let your lawyer know," I said. "Just in case Kennedy decides to be a real idiot."

"Oh, I will. Magdalena has already run rings around him, and if he doesn't back down on this, my guess is he'll wish he had."

We sat together a little longer as people wandered by, sometimes pausing to congratulate Laurel and commiserate with Silas. Racers were still finishing, and the tourists were turning their burros in to the rental places. I thought I saw Kaitlyn and her father strolling the street with Buster/Prince Caspian. The breeze began to pick up, and clouds started to build up over the mountains.

"Afternoon thunderstorm coming up," Nate said. "Better get under cover."

"You want to come to my house?" Laurel shrugged. "Don't know what else I have, but I've always got cheese."

"That's okay," I said. "You should go put your feet up. You ran a hell of a race today."

"I did, didn't I?" Laurel grinned. "Peggy Sue came through. I'm going to enter her in the Leadville race."

"I'll be there, too."

"With Oliver?"

Silas's smile dimmed a bit. "He's got a lot of heart, but he doesn't have the stamina yet. I may bring Poppy out of retirement."

"What about Prometheus?" I said. "Is he unbeatable?"

Silas and Laurel both gave me sour looks. "He's big, but he's got no finesse, no heart," Laurel said. "He's all about powering through. But power won't be enough when he hits the top of Mosquito Pass and can't catch his breath."

"Arnie's good, but he's a lot like Prometheus—all power and no guile. Guile's what wins races around here." Silas gave me his own man smile. If guile was needed, I figured he'd have a good supply. "Plus Laurel's right, he doesn't have a lot of heart. Not like my Stanley did, back in the day."

Silas's smile faded a bit, and Laurel reached over to pat his shoulder. "Stanley was special. Every once in a while, you get one that is."

Silas smiled at her. "Yeah. Every once in a while, you do." I was pretty sure they weren't just talking about donkeys.

An hour or so later, Nate and I ambled toward the parking lot, his arm draped over my shoulders. "Quite a race," he said, finally.

I glanced around the still-crowded streets. "Yeah, looks like it was a success, based on the number of people who showed up. Of course, they were lucky there were no problems, given they only had one cop around to take care of things."

"And he ended up being busy." Nate leaned down to unlock the truck, then turned to me again. "About the gun."

I shook my head. "He didn't threaten us with the gun. Not really."

Nate's eyebrows went up. "But?"

He knows me way too well. Which has its upsides and its downsides.

"But at one point, he put his hand on his hip and pushed back his jacket so we could see he had a gun. I guess that's close to a threat, but he didn't have the gun in his hand. And I don't know if he would have drawn it, or if he was just making idle threats. That's my vote, by the way."

"But you backed off?"

I nodded. "We did, actually. That's when we went

to the police station. I figured I'd tell Kennedy and hope maybe he'd be willing to check it out." I was unwilling to concede the point. "But honestly, we weren't in any danger. Dave Ottawa was a couple of feet away, and I saw him glowering at Vance. And there were other people around. It wasn't like we were in a dark alley with an armed man."

Nate blew out a breath. "Rox, I'm not happy about you being anywhere with an armed man, whether it's light or dark."

I started to repeat that we were okay, but I decided not to. He had a point. "When we first got there, I didn't realize he had a gun. And honestly, I didn't know what was going on. I was just…curious about Buster. I mean, we took care of him for almost a week. He's a sweetheart. And when Vance finally showed up to take him away, he didn't seem to care about him. I wanted to hear some details about the sale."

I trailed off, remembering that I'd felt uneasy about Vance when he'd taken Buster away. Afraid he might mistreat him. Little did I know. "He didn't mention he had a buyer. He just loaded Buster into the trailer and drove off. He didn't even thank me for taking care of him."

"Well, he'd already had some bad luck telling people about that sale. He probably didn't want to take a chance that you might want in on it, too." Nate paused. "And I'd guess he was in a hurry to collect his five thousand."

"Right." I sighed. "It's so weird to think this is all over. And that it was over something so basic. All that stuff with the landfill. And all the suspicions about Laurel. And it was just about Buster all along."

Nate shrugged. "Money, love, and vengeance. The three prime reasons to kill somebody from what I've heard. And this time it was just the first one."

I leaned against his shoulder, staring off at the thunder clouds building up over the mountains. "It's going to let loose soon. We should head home."

"We should."

"Plus Uncle Mike and your mom will want to know about all this."

"They will."

I suddenly felt more tired than I could say. Solving murders isn't as much fun as you might think. "Any chance we could put it all off until Monday?"

Nate pulled me closer, resting his forehead against mine. "A good chance. A very good chance. Let's go home and have nachos and beer. And pull up the drawbridge."

"Yeah." I snuggled closer. "Let's do that."

Chapter 22

Of course, the whole situation with Dusty Vance confessing to Kell's murder created a huge stink. That was to be expected. But the dimensions of that stink surprised even me.

First of all, Brendan Kennedy got nailed to the wall. Totally. He hadn't just been off fishing—which would have been bad enough, given that he was neglecting his duties as chief of police. Kennedy had been off fishing at an exclusive resort near Aspen with executives from Pristine Refuse Removal, who were rewarding him for his efforts on their behalf.

Exactly how much money Kennedy had invested in the landfill project was a subject of much discussion around Coalton. Some people said he'd sunk all of his retirement money into it, but that was unlikely, given that his wife, Mary Beth, oversaw their joint retirement money and wasn't likely to approve a project like the landfill. Kennedy might have been crooked as a dog's hind leg, but Mary Beth had a reputation for honesty and pragmatism.

The more likely scenario was that Kennedy had been given a stake in the project as an incentive to make sure the sale of the coal mine to Pristine went smoothly. That meant keeping a lid on any kind of information leak since the people involved knew only too well that the project wouldn't be popular with the citizens of Coalton.

Arresting Laurel for Kell's murder was meant to short-circuit any investigation that might reveal the deal Pristine and Kell had been putting together.

Apparently, Kennedy agreed with those of us who thought the murder might well be the result of Kell's involvement in the landfill plans. It hadn't occurred to him to investigate any other possibilities since he wanted to limit the scope of the investigation before it uncovered what was going on behind the scenes. Since Kennedy was convinced that Kell had been killed by someone who opposed the landfill, and since he was certain Laurel would very much oppose the landfill if she knew about it, he felt perfectly justified in pursuing her for the murder. Even when it became obvious that Laurel couldn't have done it, Kennedy kept his focus on her, trying to keep people from digging into what had actually happened.

People like me, for example.

Given how weird the real story was, it's quite possible Kennedy wouldn't have heard anything about Vance and Buster and Kell unless someone had explained everything to him. And even then, he'd probably have been skeptical, maybe for good reason. But the fact remained that he hadn't even tried to find other suspects. He'd kept his tunnel vision on Laurel while Vance literally got away with murder.

Almost got away with it, that is.

The real hero of the story was Officer Ryan, who took Dusty Vance into custody and got his confession, after very carefully reading him his rights a second time and making sure he understood them. Dusty was feeling talkative and filled Ryan in on his problems with Kell, who had, as most of us had speculated, demanded a sixty-forty split of the five thousand in exchange for relinquishing all rights to Buster. The sixty, needless to say, would have been Kell's cut.

Vance admitted hitting Kell with a rock, although he claimed it had been self-defense since Kell had threatened to beat him up if he tried to take Buster. That might or might not have been true. Given that Kell had been hit in the back of the head, it didn't seem to add up. But I figured that was something for the lawyers to work out.

Kennedy was under heavy pressure to resign, although the members of the city council who'd hired him were still in office so it was possible he might skate by. But that would only happen if the city council itself survived intact, which seemed more and more unlikely. The council members who'd been in cahoots with Pristine were up for recall if they didn't resign first. The people who were running to replace them included Laurel, who'd be the first female member of the Coalton City Council. And most people I spoke to agreed she had a very good chance of being elected. After all, she was the organizer of a very successful burro race and an equally successful farmers market. And many citizens of Coalton felt like she deserved some recompense for what Kennedy had put her through.

In the midst of all this general hubbub, Pristine Refuse Removal announced that they were no longer interested in building a landfill in Coalton, Colorado. Assuming that this wasn't just Pristine's way of waiting until the heat of outrage died down, Coalton had dodged a bullet.

All in all, the town was in for a major shakeup, finally moving beyond being a former coal mining town to being another Collegiate Peaks tourist mecca. That had its good and bad points, but at least they'd avoided having a landfill built on the mountain above town.

****

In the midst of all this activity, Marigold finally called me about Ava. "She's interested in the job, but she needs more information than I could give her. Could she come by to talk to you some afternoon?"

Yes, yes, Lord, yes. I was already dealing with the chaos created by Dolce's imminent departure. Conscientious girl that she was, she'd worked overtime to help me get enough jam on hand to see me through the summer. But once she went down for her orientation in Ft. Collins, I would be mostly on my own. I was already envisioning late nights in the kitchen, slaving over a boiling jam pot, only to start the whole thing again the next day.

I'd just cleaned up after a double run of raspberry—which tends to leave a sticky residue on a large part of the kitchen—and was working to make the place look like a comfortable work environment. I tried to see it through the eyes of a stranger: lots of light from the kitchen windows, large work area that I'd put in when I first moved to the cabin to start Luscious Delights, the oversize professional stove with six burners to keep the jam pots and the canners at a boil.

I wasn't sure I could even see the place clearly anymore. I'd worked here for so long, it was home. Plus I lived here, so it literally *was* home. I almost wished I'd asked Bridget to stick around so that I could get a second opinion on the kitchen as a professional environment.

You are behaving like a nut. She's not going to base her opinion on whether to work with you on the size of your kitchen.

Besides, Dolce and I had worked together fine. We'd even been okay for the short time Jarrod had been here. All three of us had had space to work. There was plenty of room. There absolutely was.

Just as I was on the verge of driving myself crazy, someone rang the doorbell. I checked my watch and confirmed that Ava McNeil was right on time. I wiped my suddenly sweaty palms on my thighs and went to answer the door.

Ava stood on my front porch admiring the view off toward Mt. Oxford. "Nice place," she said when I opened the door. Then she stuck out a sturdy hand. "I'm Ava McNeil. I guess you're Roxanne Constantine."

"Roxy," I said quickly as I shook her hand. "It's Roxy. Come on in."

I estimated Ava was in her mid-sixties. She had the kind of rounded body lots of women develop when they decide they're not going to trouble themselves over carbs anymore. Her silver hair was short and wavy, and she wore peach-colored knit slacks with a matching short-sleeved sweater. Her face was unlined for the most part, but she hadn't made any effort to seem younger than her age. In fact, she looked like somebody's granny, and she probably was.

"I guess Marigold told you what I do," I said as we walked toward the kitchen.

Ava shrugged. "Oh, Marigold didn't have to tell me much about your business. I've been buying jars of your jam from Bianca Jordan for a couple of years now. I like that pepper peach a lot. And the strawberry."

Since I'd probably need to put Ava to work on the strawberry first, I was glad she liked it. Strawberry had been Dolce's specialty, and I'd gotten out of practice on doing it. But I needed it in mass quantities. "Glad you like it. It's one of the first ones I made when I started the business. Strawberry and peach."

Ava gave me a kind of neutral look. "Takes a lot of stones to start a business on your own. But it's worked out for you."

"It has," I said. "It's gotten too big for me to do on my own, though. I've got somebody to take care of the mail order side of things."

Ava nodded. "Bridget Sullivan."

I paused. "That's right, Bridget said you knew each other."

Ava gave me a slow smile. "Oh, honey, I know everybody, more or less." I had to grin at that. Ava and Bridget probably had a lot in common.

Ava stepped into the kitchen, and I followed. "This is the workspace," I said. "I had it enlarged when I decided to work out of the cabin. It's the biggest room in the house." And it showed off well, I decided. Although now that I took a good look, I could see the curtains needed washing. Still, it wasn't too small. Definitely not.

Ava's expression was back to neutral. She raised an eyebrow as she studied the stove. "Big range."

"It is. When I'm cooking jam, I need a lot of burners. I've usually got a jam pot and a processing kettle going at the same time. And I try to do double and triple batches so I can get all of one flavor done at once. You have to do each batch in a separate pot."

Ava frowned, considering. "How many jars in the processing kettle at once?"

"Usually, nine to twelve. I do half-pints and pints. I can get two or three dozen done in a morning."

Ava nodded slowly. "Never made jam myself. I do pickles, though. Chutney. Chow-chow. That kind of stuff."

"That's similar," I said. "But I do bigger quantities."

Ava surveyed the kitchen, studying the layout. "So what would I be doing?"

I took a breath. "Basically, the process is chop the fruit and any other ingredients, mix it with sugar and lemon juice and sometimes pectin, and put it on to boil. Then after it's cooked down, we put it in the jars and process it in the canning kettle. So some days you'd be chopping fruit. Other days, you'd be mixing and boiling and pouring it into jars. It sort of depends on what we've got on hand and what needs doing."

Ava nodded again. She seemed a little bored, and I couldn't blame her. It wasn't a barrel of laughs making jam.

She stepped toward the counter where I had a few miscellaneous jars set out. "What's that?"

"Tomato jam." I sighed. "It was the special on the mail order site this time around, but it wasn't a big hit. Sort of experimental." I was ready to mark off the tomato jam as a respectable failure. People just weren't as keen on it as they were on fruit jam. And I had to admit to myself that I'd never gotten it entirely right.

Ava picked up the jar and studied it. "Can I taste?"

"Sure. That jar's already been opened."

She picked up a tasting spoon and scraped up a small sample. For once I wasn't concerned about what she thought. The tomato jam was a miss. Worth trying, but I probably wouldn't make any more. Ava narrowed her eyes as she tasted, her expression thoughtful. "Little bland."

I grimaced. On reflection, she was absolutely right. And that was probably what had doomed the jam. "Yeah. I tried using jalapeños and a few Serranoes, but it never worked out."

She tasted again. "Needs dried chili."

I blinked. "Dried chili."

"More intense flavor than fresh. Easier to work with, too. Maybe…" Her lips curved up in a wicked grin. "…cayenne."

"Cayenne." My jaw dropped a bit. We grow cayenne around here. Some people use it raw, but most dry it. It's one of the hottest chilies around—it'll take the top of your head off if you're not careful. I only use the powdered kind, although I'd considered it in passing when I was thinking of chilies for the tomato jam. "You use cayenne?"

"Use it in chow-chow. Gives it a kick."

"I bet," I said. "What else goes into it?"

Ava frowned as she thought. "Whatever you've got. Cabbage, usually; cucumber, peppers, onions, garlic. Whatever you've got in the garden that needs getting rid of. Or whatever you've got that's been sitting too long in the hydrator."

"In vinegar?"

"Right. Different kinds, though. Sometimes I put up some herb vinegar for pickling and eating. That makes an interesting chow-chow."

This was sounding more and more intriguing. "And you make it savory."

"Yeah. Southerners make it sweet. Never liked that much—that whole agrodolce, sweet and sour thing. Give me spice every time. Pickles, now, pickles I'll do sweet. Fruit pickles particularly. Peaches, watermelon, salted plums. All of it works."

I nodded, visions of relish and pickles dancing in my head. You could pick up the bruised produce at the farmers market that people can't sell. Chop it up, mix it with spices and vinegars, serve it with ham or pork or chicken. Fun to experiment with.

Ava's eyes were shining with excitement as she talked about her ferments. It's not often I run into someone who gets excited about fruits and vegetables. As excited as I do, anyway.

"I haven't made watermelon pickles in years," I said, remembering that piquant taste. Of course, I hadn't had the time to do any preserving to speak of. I was making jam.

Ava watched me, that same slightly wicked smile edging up the corners of her lips. "If you're thinking I'll be bored doing your jams, don't worry about it. Anything with vegetables and fruits gets my juices going. I'm going to like seeing what you do with your stuff. And maybe I can suggest some other things to do now and then."

I took a breath. "So you're interested?"

"I'm interested." She paused. "You got any kind of dress code?"

"Dress?" I stared down at my own jeans and T-shirt. At least they were clean. And the T-shirt didn't say anything rude. "No dress code. Well, as long as it's practical. Tutus are probably out."

Ava chuckled. "Tutus have been out of my life for a long time. But overalls make a lot of sense in a kitchen. Yes, I'm interested. I think we'd work well together."

I nodded. "So do I. Yeah, so do I."

We talked about the essentials—wages and hours. I

still wasn't able to offer medical insurance, but Ava didn't need any since she already had it from the city as part of her retirement package. She could work more hours than Dolce since she wasn't going to high school, but we decided to start small. Let her see how she liked it, then we could ramp up later.

I figured she was going to like it. I figured I was going to like it, too. As I watched Ava drive away, I felt as if a huge weight had been lifted from my shoulders. Not a moment too soon either.

****

For once, I had dinner well under way when Nate got home that evening. Not that dinner was all that exciting—chicken and couscous with a green salad. But on so many previous days I'd been making jam and feeling stressed all afternoon. So stressed I had no interest in cooking anything more. We'd been relying on leftovers from the café, which made me feel a little guilty since we weren't the only ones with claims on those.

Nate grinned as he sniffed the air. "Whatever it is, it smells terrific."

"Thanks. It's chicken and couscous with the chicken thighs from Sylvano's. I felt like cooking for a change."

"Okay. I brought dessert." He held up a paper sack. "Coco was experimenting with blueberry bars. She thinks it was a bust, but they're more than edible."

"Absolutely." Anything Coco did was more than edible in my book.

Nate raised an eyebrow as he put the sack on the counter. "Does the fact that you're cooking mean today was a success?"

I gave a cautious nod. "I think so. Ava seems like someone who'll do a good job and maybe enjoy doing it."

"Great. One more problem solved. And Kell Moorhead's killer is under arrest. And Laurel's out from under suspicion. Now you can relax." He wrapped his arms around my waist, pulling me against him. "You can relax about some things, that is."

I turned so that I could put my arms around him, too. "What can I not relax about?"

"Well, there's the Historical Society Gala you said you'd help me with next month."

I groaned. That was a major event, and all hands on deck. "Is it in the Blankenship House again?"

"Yeah, but outside in the yard. In tents."

Which could be good or bad. The weather in August was always iffy. Of course, if we had thunderstorms we could always go inside the house, which had lots of empty rooms. "Yeah, okay, I'll tense up about that in a few days, once you've got the menu figured out. What else?"

"Farmers market this weekend. Supposed to be the biggest of the year."

Something I was well aware of, but Dolce and I had made enough jam for the rest of the month. "I'm good. What else?"

He shifted slightly, leaning back so that he could look at me. "Well, you could marry me."

My heart gave a mighty thump. "You already know I will." We'd discussed it in a general way after Uncle Mike and Madge had gotten married. But we hadn't gone much further in the planning.

"I know you will, but I don't know when. Why don't we set a date?"

Not fair, not fair. I'd just gotten through a huge load

261

of stress and now he was handing me another bunch.

Only I'd discovered something over the summer. I absolutely wanted to marry Nate. I wanted to spend my life with him. I'd known it before in a general way. But now I knew it bone deep. We just needed to take that next step and get things moving. And that meant I needed to woman up and stop dithering.

I took a deep breath, countering the tension that returned to my shoulders with a vengeance. "Spring. We can do it next spring. That gives us enough time to plan but gets us through the big holiday catering and gift-giving season."

"Define spring. Around here that could be any time from May to July."

I took another deep breath, trying not to hyperventilate. "May. Or April. Do you have a preference?" I gave him a challenging look. Let him make some decisions here, too.

He took a deep breath of his own. "How about May? That's usually a slow time for catering. I can take time off for a honeymoon."

It was also a fairly slow time for the jam business, although I'd need to get started on farmers market jam toward the end of the month. "May." I swallowed hard. "May it is."

Nate pulled me close, giving me one of those kisses that made my toes curl. I resolved then and there not to think about all the things we'd need to decide before we got to our wedding day. Or not to start thinking about them until I was trying to fall asleep that night. I might not be able to avoid it then.

He stared down at me again, his smile fading. "Well, that takes care of relaxing."

"It does," I agreed.

"Are you okay with it?"

I took a moment to check for feelings of panic. And I didn't find any to speak of. In fact, I felt weirdly calm. That didn't mean I'd still feel that way tomorrow, but at the moment, I felt terrific. "I'm very okay with it. Honestly, I am. Very okay. I feel like things are falling into place." I grinned up at him. "We're getting married."

He grinned back. "We're getting married. Tomorrow, the rings."

My stomach did a flip-flop. "Oh, God."

"Don't chicken out now."

I paused. "Rings? As in plural?"

"If you wear a ring, I wear a ring." He pulled me in for another kiss that became a bear hug, his forehead resting against mine. "Unless you'd rather have a burro."

I paused again. It was, in fact, a real question. But the answer was clear. "No. I'll go with the ring."

"Good girl."

Still, as I dished up the chicken and couscous and Nate poured a couple of glasses of champagne, I found myself thinking of Buster. He was gold, after all. Sort of like a ring. And he had those beautiful big brown eyes. And eyelashes. He was a sweetheart of a burro.

Nate handed me my champagne, and I tucked all thoughts of Buster far away. There was only room for one sweetheart in my life.

Even if he'd never win the Leadville Boom Days Pack Burro Race.

"Here's to you," Nate said as he raised his glass.

"Back atcha," I said, raising my own.

Show time

A word about the author…

Meg Benjamin is an award-winning author of romance and cozy mysteries. Along with her Luscious Delights series for Wild Rose Press, she's also the author of the Konigsburg, Salt Box and Brewing Love series. Her other work includes the paranormal Ramos Family trilogy and the Folk series. Meg's books have won numerous awards, including an EPIC Award, a Romantic Times Reviewers' Choice Award, the Holt Medallion from Virginia Romance Writers, the Beanpot Award from the New England Romance Writers, the Carla Crown Jewel of Books award, and the Award of Excellence from Colorado Romance Writers.

Meg's Web site is http://www.MegBenjamin.com.
You can follow her on Facebook
(http://www.facebook.com/meg.benjamin1)
and Instagram (meg_benjamin).

Meg loves to hear from readers—contact her at meg@megbenjamin.com.
http://www.MegBenjamin.com

Thank you for purchasing
this publication of The Wild Rose Press, Inc.

For questions or more information
contact us at
info@thewildrosepress.com.

The Wild Rose Press, Inc.
www.thewildrosepress.com